THE CANARY GIRL'S SECRET

DEBORAH KLÉE

Copyright © 2025 Deborah Klée

The right of Deborah Klée to be identified as the Author of the Work has been

asserted by her in accordance with the Copyright, Designs and Patents Act 1988

All rights reserved. This book or any portion thereof may not be reproduced or used in any manner whatsoever without the express written permission of the publisher except for the use of brief quotations in a book review.

Characters in this book are entirely fictitious. Any resemblance to real persons, living or dead, is coincidental and is not intended by the Author.

Print book ISBN: 979-8-273-07064-6 First Printed 2025

Published by Sherman House

BOOKS BY THIS AUTHOR:

Secrets of a Sunken Village Series:
The Evacuee's Secret - Book one
The Canary Girl's secret - Book two

Other books:
The Borrowed Boy
Just Bea
The Forever Cruise
The Last Act

For Marian

1

SATURDAY 11TH JUNE 1966

'Six months ago, we would have been looking down at the church spire and the crumbling cottages of our childhood playground,' Louise said as she leaned against Richard.

He slung an arm across her shoulder. 'I'm sorry the valley was flooded; of course, I am. The grocery was our family business since great grandfather's day. But would it be dreadful if I said, I love this? The way the sun reflects off the water? The sweeping flocks of knots and formations of geese? The way the landscape changes with the season and weather? I could stand here all day just watching.'

Louise knew exactly what he meant. She had loved Yorkshire, Thorncrest specifically, since she was evacuated there as a twelve-year-old Londoner. Beck's farm where she lived with Ma and Pa Beck, and the valley of uninhabited cottages: a little church, Richard's family shop – Braithwaite's – and the old mill where they had played make-believe and shared secrets, had been wondrous to her. But there was something magical too about the reservoir that stretched out before them, the cottages, mill and shop hidden beneath its still surface.

'Unfortunately, watching the reservoir is not going to get our home built, and we've a meeting with the Corporation this afternoon.'

Richard squeezed her shoulder and pointed left of the reservoir where seven geese flew by, forming a perfect V. They gazed in silence as each one glided onto the water creating a ripple. Her heart ached with love and loss. Love for Richard and the aching loss of losing Ma and Pa Beck and all that might have been if… if her mother hadn't lied to her, if she had known she wasn't responsible for Pa's accident, if she had returned to Thorncrest sooner to claim her inheritance from her guardian Ma Beck, and find Richard, the love of her life.

'Okay. I'll finish cutting those timbers. Two-thirty, you said?'

Louise nodded. 'I did. I'll make us some lunch.'

She wandered over to their caravan, taking her time, as Richard returned to the task of sawing wood. He stripped off his shirt before lifting a timber beam onto his workbench, an improvised system for sawing wood outdoors, and triggered the chainsaw. Forget the wonder of flying geese, she was mesmerised by his body in motion. His strong shoulders, the way his back muscles tensed as he took the weight of the saw. The high-pitched whine of the saw died. A chunk of wood fell from the bench. Richard looked up and caught her staring. He grinned, his eyes dancing with light. They didn't need words. Friends since they were little more than children, she knew that he knew she'd been watching him; that she wanted him and would have claimed him there and then if circumstances allowed. Later, she told herself, and with a wave of her hand went inside to prepare a ham salad.

The Canary Girl's Secret

. . .

'Today's the day,' Louise said, as Richard pulled up in the car park of High House. 'How long do you think before the money's in my account?'

Richard grinned. This was the next big step in their exciting new venture. 'No more than a week. We should go out tonight and celebrate.'

'That little bistro in Harrogate Esther was talking about? Maybe ask Bill and Esther to join us?'

Richard leaned across and kissed her. 'Let's go sign the contract. It's taken long enough.'

Fliss was in reception and jumped up to greet them. 'Hi, you two. I don't see enough of you nowadays, Louise.' They had become good friends when Louise was working for the Corporation last year.

They exchanged kisses and hugs. 'I've got something to tell you,' Fliss said.

'Ah. Mrs Boyd and Mr Braithwaite.' Mr Formoy strode into reception.

Louise raised her eyebrows at Fliss. 'Later,' she whispered as they turned to follow Formoy into his office.

Richard squeezed Louise's hand, and she threw him a look of excited anticipation, her eyes wide, and mouth contorted as she tried to tame a joyous grin.

Formoy invited them to sit and made small talk, updating them on plans for the reservoir. The demolition of Thorncrest Church, because swimming out to climb the exposed spire had become a local sport and was a safety hazard.

Louise asked after her old boss, Fitzpatrick. He was working on another project in Wales. Then Fliss interrupted them with refreshments. Coffee and biscuits.

'So,' Formoy said, straightening his spine, his hands spread wide on the table.

At last. Louise took a sip of her coffee. They could drive into Harrogate or Leeds at the weekend and look at soft furnishings. A big, colourful rug. Cushions and curtains. The floor to ceiling windows overlooking the reservoir would need something to give them privacy, but they wouldn't want to lose the light or views. Ma and Pa's chairs could sit by that window. She imagined Richard and her watching the water in the evenings in the same way Ma and Pa had gazed at the fire in their hearth.

'I'm afraid I have bad news,' Formoy said.

'The contract's not ready for signing?' Louise said. She might have guessed. More bureaucracy.

'No and it won't be for some time. There's been a development that throws into question your ownership of the Beck's farm estate.'

Louise felt Richard tense beside her. She spoke quickly to stem the torrent of angry words that would inevitably flow from him. 'I thought we'd provided all the evidence requested: a valuation made before the flood, photographs of the interior, Elizabeth Beck's will.'

'Indeed. This has come as a surprise to me too.' Formoy drank his coffee. 'Yes. An unexpected turn of events.'

'What exactly is the problem?' Richard said.

'Our legal team have advised us that Louise Pearson, as named in the will of Elizabeth Beck, cannot be recognised as the beneficiary.'

'Why?' Louise exclaimed. She had almost drowned in her quest to retrieve Ma's will from beneath the floorboards of the farmhouse before the dam opened. 'I had a solicitor confirm it was legal. Just because it was handwritten doesn't make it less valid.'

'No. Of course not.' Formoy loosened his collar. 'But a will is only valid if um… the person is deceased.'

Louise laughed. Richard let out an exasperated breath. But Formoy wasn't joking; his face paled and he pursed his lips. Then he took a deep breath and said, 'Elizabeth Beck's grave was reported empty. There's no evidence that she's um…dead and therefore her bequeathing the farm to you is of no consequence. The Corporation must assume the owner is alive and as the compulsory purchase order cannot be delivered, the estate becomes the property of the Corporation.'

He waited as his words sank in. Louise sat open-mouthed.

'That's ridiculous. I saw her grave, before it was moved from Thorncrest church to the new cemetery,' Louise said. 'And how does your legal team know that her body wasn't in her grave. Did they open it?'

Formoy poured them each a glass of water. Louise realised her throat was dry. Her hands a little shaky. Richard squeezed her knee. She was grateful for his silence, at least until they had all the facts and she had time to process.

Formoy took a sip of water and continued, 'The relocation of the graveyard from Thorncrest Church to the burial site above the valley was a complex and sensitive operation. The space allocated was insufficient to accommodate all the coffins and so a decision was made to transport and bury the exhumed bodies in caskets created for that purpose.'

Louise had been working on the reservoir project team at that time. Her job had been liaising with Reverend Cummins and the church committee about the relocation of graves. A health official, Dorothy Lombard, had overseen the exhumation process. Surely someone would have said something at the time? A missing body was a significant event. And it wasn't *any* body. It was Ma's. Of course, nobody knew of Louise's relationship with her at that time, but surely, as the

Chief Engineer's personal assistant, this information would have been known to her. They had it wrong. This was typical of the Corporation. The thought of a stranger opening Ma's coffin, treating her precious remains as though they were junk to be disposed of, sickened Louise. The relatives had no idea their loved-ones' bodies were being manhandled – removed from caskets thoughtfully chosen – and repackaged in economy size. Her body was shaking. It was so cold.

Richard broke his silence, and the tirade Louise knew he'd been suppressing was released. 'This is unacceptable. Inhumane. Disrespectful. You're talking about my partner's beloved guardian. If a body's gone missing, the Corporation's responsible. Never mind the bloody will. We'll take legal action against you for negligence. The church relocation operation was a shambles from beginning to end. Moving a graveyard of bodies in little more than a week was ludicrously ambitious. The Corporation didn't want to lose money by missing the deadline for the reservoir. So, shortcuts were taken. I'd be surprised if this is the only corpse the Corporation lost in the process.'

A sob from Louise. She was angry, hurt, and confused. Richard put his arm around her, but Louise didn't want to be comforted; she wanted answers. 'What do you think happened to Elizabeth Beck's remains Mr. Formoy?'

Formoy cleared his throat. 'It's been suggested Elizabeth Beck was not buried in the grave marked with her name. And, if she didn't die, you understand …'

'No. I don't understand. Are you saying she might be alive?' Louise would give anything to see Ma again. To hug her tight. Take back the lost years. But it was impossible. Only death would have taken Ma from Thorncrest and her beloved farm.

A bead of perspiration settled in the furrow of Formoy's brow. 'I'm just communicating the directive from our legal team. You may appeal if you have evidence that contradicts this finding, for example, a death certificate.'

'I understand,' Louise said, standing up. She just wanted to get out of there.

Richard remained seated. He glared at Formoy, and for a moment Louise was afraid he might prolong the discussion. There was nothing else to say. She would get a copy of the death certificate, and this ridiculous pantomime would be over. 'Richard,' she said in a warning tone.

Richard sighed and got to his feet. 'You've not heard the end of this, Formoy. We'll go public if we have to. Tell that to your head office.'

2

SUNDAY 12TH JUNE 1966

Louise lay awake most of the night, haunted by images of Ma's body being exhumed from the grave. She knew the cemetery had been relocated, and the graves transported to a new resting place, but it was only now the reality hit home. And if Ma's body wasn't in her grave, where the hell was it? Dismembered by wild dogs? She tried hard to dispel this grisly image, but at three in the morning her mind would not comply. Louise tried another tact, imagining Ma alive, waiting for her with outstretched arms. But if she was alive, why had she allowed Louise to believe she was dead? It was cruel. Why? Why? Why?

She was sitting on the step of the caravan when Richard joined her, his hair tousled from sleep. 'You're up?'

'Sorry, did I wake you?' Louise stood up.

'No. Well yes. I reached out for you and the bed was cold. Stay there. I'll put the kettle on for a brew. And then, I'd better get to work.' He didn't need to say that without an injection of cash, the building of their new home would be seriously delayed. From the slump of his shoulders and the way he dragged a hand through his hair, Louise knew he was worried.

They had great hopes for this land. The building of a timber house overlooking the reservoir was just the start of their audacious plan. A holiday village of cute timber cabins would follow. Richard's ambition as a teenager was to build a village, an antidote to growing up in an abandoned village of dilapidated cottages. That she could make his dream come true, filled Louise with joy. But without the money from the sale of Beck's farm, they were scuppered. Discovering Ma Beck had left everything to Louise was a complete surprise. She had been Louise's guardian when she was evacuated to Yorkshire during the war. But she couldn't say 'easy come, easy go,' because there had been nothing easy about her mad dash to rescue Ma's will from beneath the floorboards of the farmhouse moments before the reservoir was flooded and a mudslide almost killed her.

'Here,' Richard said, handing Louise a steaming mug of tea.

'I was just thinking about what we went through to retrieve Ma's will. You could have drowned, Richard. Money isn't important. You are. Ma was. Is?' Louise cast her eyes to heaven, as if seeking an answer.

'Bill mentioned to me that Eddie Boyd's death is still being investigated,' Richard said.

'A post-mortem is standard practice. It was a tragedy he drowned in the flood. I didn't want to be married to him but I would never have wished him dead. He was a good man who did bad things. I should never have married him.'

'Why did you?' Richard said. It was a conversation they had returned to several times since they got back together last year.

'I was taken in by the glamour of his lifestyle. He was a philanthropist. On our first date he took me to Annabelle's nightclub in London. Eddie knew lots of celebrities. I guess I was a bit awestruck. Then, when we were on our honeymoon in Las Vegas, staying at The Desert Inn, I discovered I was living in a gilded cage and Eddie's boss, Big Jim, held the key. I was sipping champagne by the swimming pool, thinking I was Jackie Kennedy, when Eddie told me we had to work. Work? I said, we were on honeymoon. A honeymoon that I discovered had been paid for by Big Jim. We had to entertain some associates.' Louise sighed. She had been shallow, naïve. There were plenty more words of disgust she had thrown at herself. Somehow, she had freed herself from that lifestyle. Then, Eddie had come looking for her.

Richard squeezed her hand. 'I know. Sorry. It just makes me so angry that he mistreated you. That day, the day of the flood, when he tried to force you into his car, I lost it. Honest to God, Lou Lou, if the mudslide hadn't swept you away at that moment, I might just have killed him myself.' Richard paused as if considering his next words. 'This investigation into the cause of Eddie's death is more than a standard postmortem. Bill heard from someone in the hospital it's become a police investigation. They suspect foul play.'

A wave of dread swept over Louise. 'But you didn't. Did you?'

Richard stood up and stretched. He picked up their empty mugs. But he didn't look at Louise or answer her question.

'Richard?' She raised her voice, afraid now.

'Of course not. Okay. I'd better get on. Maybe I could put together some coffee tables to sell. There're some beautiful cuts of wood in the pile.'

Louise shook off her feeling of unease. This was Richard. Kind, sensitive Dicky, her childhood friend, not Eddie the Rick. She'd been around Big Jim and the Mob for too long.

'Good idea. I'll make some bacon butties. You can't start work on an empty stomach.'

Richard could lose himself in work – carpentry was his passion – but Louise could not settle to anything. It was Saturday, a day she usually relished to write, walk across the moors, or hang out with her friends, Esther and Fliss. Anxiety and dread immobilised her and yet made her restless. She paced between the caravan and house, loitered around Richard, who was too absorbed in his work to notice, and then around their new house, a notebook in her hand, but she couldn't remember what her intention had been. Eventually, she gave up.

'I'm going out,' she called to Richard.

He paused in his work and looked up. 'What do you think of this cut? Isn't she a beauty? Just look at those markings.'

Louise put her arms around him, reassured by his solidity. 'It would make a wonderful table. I might drop into the museum barn, and if I do, I could be awhile.'

Richard nodded, but she had already lost him to his art.

Driving helped to calm Louise. Her mind was still chugging through an endless loop of questions – was Ma alive? Where could she be? Why would she fake her death? And if she was dead, where was her body? Oh my God. Her poor broken body – but her focus on the road kept her steady and gradually her thoughts became less frantic.

Her car, Mini, had a mind of its own. If Louise wasn't fully aware of where she was headed, Mini was. Beck's farm. It was a bit like visiting an elderly relative. Louise knew its days were numbered, and so she treasured these glimpses despite its ramshackle appearance brought on by the mudslide. The farmhouse looked as though it had been picked up and reposi-

The Canary Girl's Secret

tioned by a child playing with a toy village. When Louise lived with the Becks, their farm had been at the end of a lane, surrounded by trees. The turnoff to the farm was little more than a dirt track; the farm high on the hill. Now, it was on the edge of the reservoir. A bit misshapen, but still the farmhouse she knew and loved. Louise parked Mini further up the road and strolled back down. There was red tape surrounding the farm.

She gazed at the site that had once been her whole world. A few cars went by, but nobody paid any attention to her. A need to feel close to Ma drew Louise onto the farm. She slid under the red tape, like a frightened child seeking comfort in her parents' bed. Louise knew it was dangerous, the foundations no longer anchoring the house, but she wanted to immerse herself in happy memories. Soon it would be gone. Its broken bones laid to rest.

The door to Pa's work barn hung open. Louise went over to close it. It was where Joan, the Land Army girl, had been working on the tractor the day of Pa's accident. A place where Pa went to think. He loved everything about farm work: his cows, his beloved Fordson tractor, tinkering with engines, mending fences. The door had come off its hinges and leant heavily to one side. A shovel lay in her path, and Louise bent down to tidy it away. Pa would never have left his tools out in the open. 'You need to respect your tools. Take good care of them and they will serve you well,' he had said, when Louise, a child of twelve, sat on a stool alongside him watching as he sharpened the blade of his saw.

'How did this get out here?' she said to herself, picking it up. The mudslide had moved trees and tilted the house, so a shovel thrown out of the barn was nothing.

Handling anything of Ma's or Pa's felt sacred, as though she was connecting with them. Her longing to have just a little more time with them was, at times, unbearable. 'I'll store it safely away,' she said, imagining Pa watching over her.

Louise squeezed through the wedged-open door into the barn, carrying the shovel. The scent of Pa's pipe had long gone, but traces of engine oil and wood shavings still haunted the air. She inspected the shovel as if saying goodbye. Dark red on the spade. She smiled. What was the last thing Pa had dug up? Maybe Ma was the last person to use it. Or Susan, who helped out on the farm. Louise had used the same shovel as a child tending her vegetable patch. Dig for Victory. She remembered holding it aloft, trying to shake thirteen-year-old Richard out of his glum mood.

She took a closer look at the spade. Put a finger on it. Sticky. Something was stuck to the dark red substance. Hair. Human hair. Louise threw the spade away from her. Her stomach lurched. No. No. No. What exactly had Richard said yesterday morning? Eddie's death was being investigated by the police. They suspected foul play. Richard was the last person to see Eddie alive, according to police records. They had interviewed both Louise and Richard.

Eddie was okay when Richard left him. At least that's what Richard said. The police told them Eddie was unconscious when he fell into the reservoir.

'He didn't. He couldn't have. Not Richard,' Louise said to herself. 'They were fighting on the road above the farm, not down here.' But her knees felt weak. If the police found this spade, they would jump to conclusions. Richard was innocent. He had to be, but she couldn't risk them finding it.

She held the shovel at arm's length and manoeuvred her way out of the barn, under the red tape. A quick scan of the surrounding area; a distant figure, maybe a dog walker. Louise strode to the water's edge. She swung the shovel high above her as though about to chop down a tree and used all her

The Canary Girl's Secret

strength to thrust it into the water. It made an awkward arc and then tumbled into the reservoir with a splash. Not as far out as she'd hoped, but at least it had disappeared from view.

Pa wouldn't be happy she had ruined one of his tools. If she had left it out overnight after digging her vegetable patch, he would have given a stern but kindly lecture on respecting all things that serve us, whether they be people or objects, because mistreating them would have consequences. And Louise realised with a shiver, her actions today could well have consequences. What have I done, Pa? Have I made things worse? Please, God, let this be an end to the nightmare. How could her world have changed so much in one day?

Louise fled the scene of her crime. She wouldn't tell Richard what she had done. He would be furious. Of course, he was innocent. But it was too late to tell the police what she had discovered. They would question why she had tried to destroy evidence. Stupid. Stupid. Stupid. How could she think straight when she was trying to process shocking news?

The adrenaline had fired her body into action, and now she drove with purpose to the museum barn. There must be something hidden within its treasures that would help her discover more about Ma's life.

The museum barn was originally used by Hardwicks, the house clearance company employed by the Corporation, to store furniture from the uninhabited cottages. Situated in a field off the main road, it was filled with furniture and other possessions from houses and businesses located in the valley before it was flooded. Louise had negotiated on behalf of the community for the barn and its unclaimed contents to be transformed into a museum. In their little free time, Louise and her friend Esther were volunteer curators. Louise had a vision for the museum. It would stage scenes from dwellings depicting different decades. The flax mill and Parish church would have dedicated space to display records from archives. A model village, a replica of Thorncrest, created by Richard when he was a teen, would greet visitors at the entrance. Sadly, the project was taking longer than she had anticipated, but assisting Richard with building their new home, and working with Esther, manning the mobile library, meant she had little free time.

'Hello, Ma and Pa,' Louise called as she pushed open the big barn doors. Immediately, the timeless comfort of timber warmed by the sun, and the energy of possessions once loved, wrapped Louise in a hug. There was still much to do before the barn resembled a museum. Until then, the only visitors were Louise and Esther. Sometimes she wondered if progress had been slow because they wanted to keep the treasures to themselves for a while longer. They both loved immersing themselves in history, wondering about the lives of the people who had left these things behind. So many stories to be told. But the only one she wanted to hear today was Ma's. Here, Ma felt more alive than at the empty farmhouse. If only she hadn't stopped there on route. There was nothing Louise could do about the shovel, so she tried to put it out of her mind.

Louise took her time wandering through the barn to the end, where she had created her first tableau; a recreation of the living room at Beck's farm as she remembered it in 1945. She collected a box of photographs and other memorabilia and settled in Ma's armchair. It was a favourite pastime, imagining herself visiting Ma and Pa, a time traveller.

A flyer for Halifax Zoo. A well-thumbed book about pioneering women pilots. A cloakroom ticket from The Crown Hotel fluttered out of the pages as if it had been used to mark the reader's place. Ma? Pa? The book fell open on a chapter about Harriet Quinby who flew across the English Channel in 1912. Ma had no interest in planes. Pa loved all things mechanical, although tractors were more his thing. Louise read a few paragraphs. It told her nothing about Ma. Halifax Zoo. The Crown Hotel. Had Ma kept these mementos for a reason?

A Mother's Day card she made for Ma, the faded daffodil crayoned on the paper now barely visible, but Louise remembered drawing it. Had she sent a similar card to her mum? She couldn't remember.

Sepia photographs of Ma and Pa on the farm. Several of her, with either Ma or Pa. There was one of Kurt, the German prisoner of war farmhand. He was a handsome man, no wonder she had a crush on him. But nothing here told her anything she didn't already know. Louise closed her eyes, absorbing the warmth of the sun as it penetrated the barn's timber, and tried to imagine Ma as a younger woman, before she became the Ma Louise knew and loved.

3

NOVEMBER 1915

Beth peered out of the misty teashop window. Outside, the smog of Leeds and inside, the fog of cooking steam, gave the illusion she had been conjured there in a puff of smoke. And it felt as though she had. When Beth left home that morning carrying all her worldly possessions in a small trunk, she had not known her final destination. She had left Harrogate, where she was no longer required as a lady's maid – her employer having moved to Devon to live with her sister for the duration of the war – to attend the recruitment centre at Wellesley Barracks. Rosie Barton, the daughter of a woman Beth met whilst queuing for sugar, had told her about the recruitment drive. Three pounds a week for a munitions worker. One pound and seventeen shillings for sweeping the factory floor. If she hadn't been successful, Beth would have gone on to Knaresborough to live with her parents. There would be more space in the tiny cottage with her two brothers at war, but the thought of living back home filled her with dread. She loved her parents, but Beth was twenty-five and was afraid there was nothing more to life than getting married – a fate she had thus far escaped. She needed adventure and excitement. And this was exciting. She would be making bombs –actual bombs – to blow up the enemy. It was akin to holding a rifle. Women could make a real difference in this war. She understood her brothers' excitement now, how they had been full of bravado and anticipation when they signed up. And now it was her turn.

Crockery chinked and conversation hummed. A waitress in a black dress and white pinafore stood at her table. Beth requested a pot of tea and a scone with, she was promised, a lick of jam.

'I'm celebrating,' Beth said, desperate to share her news with someone. 'I've been recruited as a munitions worker.'

'A Barnbow lass,' the waitress said as she scribbled down the order. 'Well, enjoy your leisure whilst you can. I hear it's hard work.'

'Six days a week, with only one Saturday off each month. I start training next week.'

The waitress's attention alighted on her next customer, and she was off, leaving Beth alone with her thoughts. She would need lodgings close to Barnbow. If only she had bought a local paper, she could have used this time to skim the advertisements. Outside the window, an indigo-blue hat caught her eye. It's cut understated; the style exquisite. Beth craned her neck to glimpse the face of its wearer. At that moment, the girl looked up and their eyes met. The girl grinned. Then waved. Beth was wondering if it was a case of mistaken identity when the hat wearer burst into the tearoom.

'Beth Hardy? I thought that was you. Have you moved down here? I'm guessing you got recruited?'

Beth's heart soared. 'Rosie. Rosie Barton. I'm so happy to see you. Yes! I've just come from Wellesley Barracks.' The waitress arrived with Beth's order. 'Please join me? My treat.' When Rosie agreed, she ordered more tea and another scone.

'I was admiring your gorgeous hat,' Beth said, pouring Rosie a cup of tea from her pot.

'Isn't it divine? Not mine, I'm sorry to say. It belongs to my landlady, Daisy St Clair. Her wardrobe is to die for and she doesn't give a hoot – honestly, her garments and accessories are strewn around the house with no care. I take far better care of them than she does.'

'Where do you live?' Beth's stomach fluttered with anticipation and possibility.

'Gainsborough Gardens. Just around the corner from here. It's my day off. I was going to catch a tram. Halifax Zoo. Want to join me? Please say you will. It's no fun going alone.'

Beth lifted the tablecloth to indicate a travelling trunk stowed away at her feet. 'I would love to, but I need to find someplace to live or I'll be carting my belongings around with me.'

'Perfect. You can move in with me and Daisy. I'll introduce you and then we can go to the zoo.'

Beth laughed at her suggestion. It was a wonderful idea. Preposterous, of course. This Daisy St. Clair knew nothing about Beth, and most likely didn't want another lodger, but Rosie's enthusiasm was infectious and this was already a day like no other – so nothing to lose by asking.

Rich, melodic notes Beth recognised as Chopin filled the wide entrance hall. Several hats as beautiful as the one Rosie wore adorned a hat and coat stand, along with discarded shoes at its base and an assortment of men's and women's cloaks and jackets. 'How many people live here?' Beth whispered.

'Just me and Daisy. But people are always dropping in,

mostly artists, and poets.' Rosie giggled. 'You have to watch out for Heydon. He'll try and take liberties, honest to God, it's like he has more hands than an octopus.'

Beth shrank back, afraid she had made a terrible mistake coming here. 'Who's Heydon?'

'An artist. Paints nudes. Which is no surprise. I swear he looks at you and imagines you naked. Oh, don't worry.' Rosie laughed. 'He doesn't live here. Just comes to some of the salons.'

Beth frowned. She didn't want to seem ignorant, but what was a salon? Rosie caught her expression. 'Daisy invites artists, musicians, and poets to her house for what she calls a salon. Best keep out of the way when they get started.'

Beth felt awkward standing in the hallway with her travelling trunk. Rosie's friend Daisy would think her presumptuous. The frantic piano playing stopped.

'Maybe I should just go,' Beth said.

'Why? There are loads of spare rooms. Daisy's always complaining it's a waste when people need somewhere to live. Just leave your trunk there. We'll find you a room when we get back from the zoo.'

'Is that you, darling?' a languid voice enquired.

'It's Rosie.' She took Beth's hand and led her into a room flooded with light from a wide bay window.

A beautiful woman with thick curly hair, worn unfashionably loose around her shoulders, sat at the piano. She held a cigarette in a long jade holder. Beth was aware of her intense scrutiny.

'Daisy St Clair, allow me to introduce my friend and colleague, Miss Beth Barton. I told Beth she could move in with us as she starts work at the munitions factory next week. That's okay, isn't it?'

Daisy lit her cigarette with a decorative brass lighter and took a long drag. 'Where are you from, Beth Barton?'

'Knaresborough originally. I was a maid to Mrs Maud Edgerton of Harrogate before leaving to work here in Leeds at the Barbow munitions factory. I'm sure she would be glad to give me a reference, if you would like one.'

'Have you any pets? That includes pythons – I don't like snakes. Or bears. Not in the house.'

'No. Absolutely not.'

'Husbands? Jilted lovers? An unpleasant father?'

'No. My two brothers are fighting in France. My parents live in Knaresborough and will have no cause to visit me here. That's if you are kind enough to allow me to lodge with you.'

'And you don't sleep walk? Or play the trombone at three in the morning?'

'No.' Beth didn't know if Daisy was joking or being serious. She had met no one like her. But Daisy St. Clair was from a different class. Since the start of the war, it felt as though some of the social divides were blurring.

Daisy set down her cigarette in an onyx ashtray and resumed playing. She half-closed her eyes as though lost in the music.

'Come on,' Rosie said. 'She likes you. You can stay.'

They caught a tram and settled into seats on opposite sides of the aisle.

'A bear escaped from this zoo a couple of years ago,' Rosie said. 'A big grizzly bear.'

'Aye. Took the lion tamer, and a strong-man from the carnival to track him down. Tore the shirt off his back.' A woman sitting behind Beth joined in their conversation.

'Set a trap they did,' the tram conductor said. 'Halifax Zoo?'

Beth nodded, and she printed off a ticket. 'Hear it's closing down next year. Not enough visitors, what with the war.'

'Good thing I say,' the woman behind Beth said. 'Awful cruel.'

Rosie grinned at Beth and rolled her eyes. Beth had been hoping to sit next to Rosie to ask the many questions that crammed her head, but it wasn't until they left the tram and set off arm in arm that the opportunity arose.

'How do we travel from Leeds to Barnbow?'

'There's a special train for Barnbow lasses. It'll take us from Leeds, right up to the factory gates. The railway's been extended to transport material in and out of the factory. We work eight-hour shifts, six days a week – which is why…' Rosie squeezed Beth's arm before letting it go to twirl and skip. 'I'm making the most of my day off.'

Beth laughed and ran with her to the zoo gates, where a peeling poster advertising The Zoo for Whitsuntide gave a nod to days before the war. There was no queue outside today. Beth wondered if they would be the only visitors. It felt a bit eerie – the big manor house with its deserted gardens.

Inside the gates, a nanny in uniform wheeled a perambulator, accompanied by a small boy. An elephant trumpeted somewhere hidden from sight, and Beth clung to Rosie's arm.

'So, what's it like living with Daisy St. Clair? Was she joking when she asked me those questions?'

Rosie laughed. 'Yes, she has an odd sense of humour. She pretends to be aloof but she's really caring. Not just kind to the artists and musicians who, to my mind, take advantage of her – asking for money, or an introduction to her rich friends – but kind to me, and Clara, the maid.'

'Does her family approve of her bohemian lifestyle?'

'Her mother died in childbirth so she was raised by her father and governess. And he's been gone for some time. He had her late in life. Daisy says her friends are her family. It must be liberating not having that pressure to conform.'

Beth wasn't so sure. Much as she wanted independence and freedom, she loved her family – Mum, Dad, and her brothers, Fred and Archie. She wondered if Daisy was perhaps lonely, despite the constant trail of visitors Rosie had described. 'We didn't discuss rent.'

'Ten shillings a week. Is that okay?'

Beth had expected it to be more and sent up a prayer of thanks for her good fortune. 'Perfect.'

The girls strolled arm in arm around the zoo, not paying a great deal of attention to the sad-looking elephant complaining in its pen, or the camel with a manky coat. They talked about the munitions factory, their families, past loves – several in Rosie's case, none in Beth's – their hopes and dreams.

'When this war's over, I'm going to learn to fly, become a pilot like Raymonde de Laroche,' Beth said. 'The war has shown the world what women are capable of. We don't have to become wives and have babies.'

'Then it doesn't concern you that you've not yet found a husband?' Rosie said delicately. She was some years younger than Beth, and possibly thought her new friend was already an old maid.

'Certainly not. Women should be able to vote and have the same opportunities as men. When the war's over, women will get more respect. I mean, look at us making bombs. Women are driving trucks, working as mechanics, and radio operators.'

They had circled the animal compounds a couple of times, and the air was turning cold and damp. Without voicing their intentions, they headed for the exit.

'You sound like Daisy. That's another thing she supports – the Suffragettes.'

Beth smiled, pleased to be likened to a strong, independent woman. 'What about you? Have you potential suitors?' She said this with a smile in her voice, mimicking the language of their parents.

'None that I would welcome. Not one of the past loves I mentioned had the slightest interest in me.' They both laughed.

'Ah, but you are not yet twenty. How old, may I enquire?'

'Nineteen. So, almost twenty-years. And now, there are no men to be found.'

'Then let us enjoy our freedom. I don't mind hard work and I'm glad to have found a friend in you.'

When they arrived back at Gainsborough Gardens, Beth's trunk was still in the hall.

'I'll check which room you're to have,' Rosie said.

There was nobody in the front room where they had last seen Daisy playing the piano. Without Daisy's scrutiny, Beth cast her eyes around the room. It had a warm, cosy feel despite the grandeur. Silk shawls and peacock feathers had been artfully arranged as if strewn casually, pencil sketches – nudes and portraits, beautiful ceramic tiles surrounding the fireplace, abstract paintings. The room was crammed with artwork.

'Does Daisy paint?' Beth squatted to take a closer look at some canvases leaning together against the wall. 'These are good.'

Rosie looked over Beth's shoulder as she flipped through, studying each one. 'No. Those are Camille's. She often stays over. They seem close, Daisy and Camille.'

Beth stopped at a watercolour of a woman, her long, luxurious hair protecting her modesty as she sat naked on the edge of a bed, her face tilted as she gazed up at the artist. There was something in her eyes that moved Beth; an unguarded expression of love and hope. As though she knew her heart was about to be broken. 'It's beautiful,' she said.

'Don't you recognise the model?'

Beth looked closer. 'Daisy?'

'Yes,' Rosie said.

The front door closed, and the girls jumped as if caught behaving badly. Rosie went to the window. 'That's Camille Beaufort, the artist, leaving now.'

A petite woman wearing bloomers climbed onto her bicycle and with a couple of rings of her bell set off down the street.

'I'd love to own a bicycle,' Beth said wistfully.

'I'll ask Camille to look out for one for you,' Daisy said, making Beth jump.

'I didn't see you come in,' Beth said, feeling wrong-footed. She glanced at the canvases, embarrassed to see the one with Daisy posing nude still on display.

'Has Rosie shown you to your room, darling?' Daisy said.

'I was just about to,' Rosie replied. 'Did Mrs Kavanagh deliver the pie she promised?'

'I'm not sure. There've been a lot of comings and goings today. Would you mind taking a look in the kitchen, darling? I'll show Beth her room. We'll eat at seven. If there's no pie, I'm sure we'll rustle something up.'

Daisy climbed the sweeping staircase, followed by Beth. An embroidered silk wall-hanging fell the length of the stairwell; polished newel posts, each topped with an acorn, stood at the foot of the stairs.

'It's a beautiful house,' Beth said.

'Thank you. I think so. When the world is so bleak, it's important to surround ourselves with things pleasing to the senses. What creative delights will you enchant us with, Beth?'

Beth froze on the last stair. Had Daisy misunderstood, taken her for an artist? She didn't want to disappoint and, more than that, didn't want to lose her room before she had even set eyes on it. 'Oh. I'm not. I mean to say. Well, I'm not very creative. I can play the piano––badly and dance a little. But I can't paint or draw.'

'Then I'm sure you have other delightful attributes. Maybe some you have not yet discovered. Those, I believe, are always the best. Here we are.' Daisy opened the door at the end of the passageway. Beth had counted five other rooms.

It was a bright and airy room. Bigger than the ground floor of her childhood home in Knaresborough, where her little cot bed had taken up most of the bedroom, her belongings stored beneath.

'As you may have gathered, we do not have any live-in staff. I let them all go when war broke out. Mrs Kavanagh delivers daily supplies to the kitchen. An excellent cook, but with food shortages as they are, we're grateful for her inventiveness––we've had some odd meals. Pigeon pie tonight if we're lucky. Don't ask where she found the pigeon.

'Clara comes twice a day. She'll light the fire in your room and carry up a jug of hot water. You'll have to let her know your work shifts. Other than that, we all muck in.'

Beth could not have imagined such comfort, not in her wildest dreams. There had to be some catch. Would she be asked to model nude for Daisy's artist friends? Or entertain her male friends? The weekly rent seemed too low for this luxury.

'Are you sure ten-shillings a week is enough to cover my rent? If you need more for food or towards the cost of employing Clara and Mrs Kavanagh…'

Daisy seemed to consider this for three heartbeats – Beth knew because she could feel them.

'No. That should be adequate. Let's just say I'm doing my bit for the war effort. I admire your spirit working in the munitions factory. Us women have to stick together. I hope you don't regret becoming a Canary Girl.'

Daisy's words hung in the air. What did she mean by a Canary Girl? As Beth transferred her few belongings from trunk to wardrobe – her two day-dresses and one for best looking a bit pathetic within its spacious grandeur – she felt uneasy. What had Rosie got her into? Was Daisy expecting her to sing in a club, or perform in some way? Why had she said she could dance? They used canaries to detect gas in the coal mines. Beth shivered as the image of being sent into a dark cellar or tunnel taunted her. There was a reason the rent was so low. She was going to find out before she got in any deeper, even if it meant losing her bed for that night.

4

MONDAY 13TH JUNE 1966

'A person can't be buried without a death certificate,' Esther said, looking up from the counter of the mobile library, where she was updating index cards. 'I did some research after you told me. You'll get Elizabeth Beck's death certificate from Somerset House, and then the Corporation will be falling over themselves to be seen in a good light. It's bad publicity for the reservoir project, losing a body like that.'

'Yes. I know you're right. But in a way that's worse – losing her body. They would have moved the remains from the original coffins into smaller caskets––boxes. Urgh. It's horrible. What if a fox got hold of Ma's body?'

'More likely her body was buried with another person's remains. Your Ma will be snuggled up next to one of her friends, in their new suburban home,' Esther said.

'I hope so.' Louise slung a book into the return pile with a little more force than she intended. 'Sorry.' She straightened up and sighed. 'It's not just Ma's missing body. Although that's worry enough; it's just everything's taking too long. We should've finished the house by now and be ready to move in. But we were depending on my inheritance and without that, Richard's had to do most of the work himself. We were hoping the money would come through soon to pay for plumbing, electricity, a kitchen, and bathroom.'

'And there's no way you can lay claim to your husband Eddie's estate? You should have inherited everything from him.'

Louise felt a wave of guilt, as though she had done away with Eddie. It was that wretched shovel. She'd almost told Richard last night but stopped herself before he realised that for a fleeting moment, she thought he might have used it on Eddie. She sighed, 'I inherited his debts. Ill will. The curse of Big Jim.'

Esther laughed. 'I'd love to meet this Big Jim. Is that really his name?'

'Believe me, you would not. He's the head honcho of a notorious London gang. Friend of the Kray twins. When Eddie died, he owed Big Jim a lot of money. There was bad blood between them. We came to an agreement. I would hand over everything in Eddie's estate to him. The flat we lived in belonged to Big Jim, anyway. In return, he would leave me alone. He knew about my inheritance but was willing to let me keep that. I was just glad to be free of him and the Mob.'

'Bloody hell. You really live on the wild side, Louise Boyd.'

'Pearson. I don't want any association with Eddie Boyd. He wasn't a bad man. Not really. Just misguided. But I don't want to carry the legacy of his criminal life. I won't go to Big Jim cap in hand. In fact, I don't want anything more to do with him. But if I don't inherit from Ma, I'm pretty much destitute. A burden on Richard. He might regret giving everything up to be with me.'

'Let's take a break before heading for the next village. Did you bring a flask and sandwiches?' Esther put aside the index cards and turned her back on Louise to retrieve wrapped sandwiches from her satchel.

'Richard packed my lunch.' Louise smiled to herself. He always added a little note and treat. She peeked inside the brown paper bag: sandwiches wrapped in waxed paper from a loaf of bread, and a Wagon Wheel biscuit – her favourite treat. But it was a luxury, and if they were to make ends meet…she would have to talk to him without sounding mean or ungrateful. The little note, wrapped in on itself as many times as was humanly possible, was the treasure she sought. Louise unfolded it whilst Esther busied herself clearing a space on the bench to sit down.

Sorry, I've been a bit moody. Just angry on your behalf. A quote for you from Jane Eyre, sent with my love and a Wagon Wheel.

'I have a strange feeling with regard to you. As if I had a string somewhere under my left ribs, tightly knotted to a similar string in you. And if you were to leave, I'm afraid that cord of communion would snap. And I have a notion that I'd take to bleeding inwardly.' Charlotte Bronte, Jane Eyre

Louise read and reread the words and smiled. When she was an evacuee recovering from measles, Richard had given her a copy of Jane Eyre. That book was her most cherished possession because in the years they were apart it kept him close. She smoothed out his note, the multitude of folds creating diamonds across Richard's slanting scroll.

'Another love-note?' Esther grinned. 'And you say, Richard might regret giving everything up for you? Hmm. I don't think so. Honestly, even if you were living in a garden shed, or a cave, you would still be the happiest couple I know. Anyone can see how much he adores you.'

'And I him. When we were apart, I felt as though part of my soul was missing. But I want him to have the life he dreamed of. When we were kids, he said he wanted to build houses, create villages. Maybe it was growing up in the valley, living with the knowledge that one day it would be flooded. We played in the deserted cottages and climbed over the old mill ruins. I thought he would move away, maybe become an architect. He's an amazing carpenter. Did you know?'

Esther nodded her head slowly, her eyes dancing with amusement. She had received this news many times. Richard's attributes were Louise's favourite topic.

'Anyway. I persuaded him to give up his family's grocery business rather than go into partnership with Ferocious Fiona. And now, instead of living in Simms Manor with her ladyship, building an empire of department stores, he's living in a tiny caravan, which leaks water every time it rains and just about enough funds to finish building our home––if nothing else goes wrong. And what then? My income isn't enough to live on. My inheritance was going to fund the building of a few cabins to rent to holiday makers. A holiday village. So, maybe he will regret giving everything up to follow an impossible dream. He thought he could rely on me and I've let him down.' Louise bit into her ham sandwich and listened to the rain pattering on the roof of the mobile library. Had she emptied the bucket in the caravan? If not, it might overflow.

'Fiona Simms has certainly risen to the challenge.' Esther said. 'I know she went into the grocery business believing she was going to marry Richard, but she loves having the responsibility of doing it alone. Fiona's always been her daddy's girl; living in her family home––Simms Manor as you call it – and the reputation of Simms Building Society. This new venture, Simms Emporium, has transformed her. She's so confident. A natural business woman.'

Louise clenched her teeth. Fiona bloody Simms. Richard

might well have married Fiona if Louise hadn't returned to Thorncrest. But he had been keeping the grocery business alive out of a misplaced loyalty to his deceased mother, trying to fulfil her dreams and those of his brother who died in the war. Richard was so good. And kind. He would do anything for anyone, but that sometimes meant overlooking his own wants and needs. Had she been selfish in reminding him of his childhood ambitions? Encouraging him to follow his heart? Yes. She had. Because she knew that following his heart would lead him back to her and look where they were now. Would he have been happier if she hadn't come back? Richer, that's for sure. And what about the family business – Braithwaite's Grocery, established in 1910? His family thought it would pass from generation to generation, and now Fiona had taken his brother's dream of creating a chain of department stores and branded it Simms.

'She could have kept the name. Or at least called it Braithwaite and Simms as she and Richard once planned.' Louise tried to keep her loathing of Fiona in check. Fiona was Esther's neighbour.

'You've got to allow a little retaliation from a woman scorned. I know you're not Fiona's greatest fan, but you did steal Richard's heart from her.'

Louise wanted to retort, Fiona had never held Richard's heart, but she didn't know this to be true. He hadn't asked Fiona to marry him, despite Fiona's obvious intentions that he would. But then, he hadn't asked Louise to marry him either. Not that she could. It was too soon after losing Eddie. And with no savings, she had nothing to contribute to their partnership.

'But you see my point. Richard sold the business planning to build a holiday village with me, but without my inheritance we're going to run out of money.'

'We can search the parish records when we're in the museum barn. We really ought to try and get on with that project. I've been researching flax mills to help curate that section. Why don't you write to the Corporation's head office? Kick-up a fuss about them losing a body. You might as well ruffle a few feathers and it might make you feel better,' Esther said.

'Anything's better than doing nothing. I feel so helpless.'

Louise concentrated on writing her letter, whilst Esther read from a local history book. They ate in silence, each of them absorbed in their task. The patter of raindrops on the metal roof slowed to an occasional ping.

Esther stood up and stretched. 'Better?' She put out a hand for Louise's rubbish.

'Strangely, yes. A good rant's exactly what I needed. I don't know what I'd do without you.' Louise sighed. Esther was an absolute treasure. The best friend she had, after Richard.

'Well, I'm grateful that you came to work with me. It was lonely and hard work doing this job single handed. But with you, it's fun. Have you thought any more about training as a librarian?'

'One day.' When she didn't need to earn a regular income and could afford the tuition fee. She noticed Esther's uneaten sandwich. 'You haven't finished your lunch. We can wait a while longer.'

Esther rubbed her chest. 'It's okay. I'm not very hungry. A bit of heartburn.'

'Indigestion, on account of my emotionally charged conversation. I'm sorry. I'll be calm.' Louise let out a long breath. 'See? As tranquil as the reservoir, I left Richard gazing at this morning.'

'Good.' Esther laughed. Let's get going. She climbed into the driver's seat and started the engine. It had stopped raining.

The Canary Girl's Secret

The sun stretched long fingers of light through the clouds painting puddles in the lane with iridescent rainbows.

Louise scrambled into the seat alongside her. 'Pewston next? I've saved a Beano Annual for Dylan, Susan Jeffrey's grandson. He hates reading books but that might just be the key.'

As the mobile library trundled into the village, figures stirred from the dry-stone wall of the post office and others crossed the road, ushering toddlers, one mother pushing a pram. It lifted Louise's heart to know the anticipation and joy they were bringing to the village with their library of books.

Susan Jeffreys and her two grandchildren, Dylan and Janine, arrived when the rush was over. Louise was tidying the shelves and Esther updating the loaning record when Janine careered in breathless. 'I told Nanna to hurry!'

Janine reminded Louise of herself as a child, she had read all the children's library and was now interested in adult books suitable for a child of eight. Janine's words. It made Louise smile. But, finding a book for Janine was a challenge she enjoyed.

'Dentist,' Susan explained, when she joined them with Dylan.

Janine was running her finger along the spines of books in the children's section. 'I've read most of these.'

'I've got one you haven't read,' Louise said, enjoying Janine's excitement at being around books. 'It only came in this week and I was a bit naughty because I put it aside for you. A Wrinkle in Time by Madeleine L'Engle. A science fiction book. It's about a girl like you solving a mystery.'

Janine jumped up and down clasping her hands together. 'Thank you. Thank you.'

Louise knelt down to unlock a cupboard beneath the shelves. Her life was spent living in confined spaces, the mobile library and the caravan. Thank goodness for the Yorkshire moors where she could stretch her legs, after living like a rabbit in a hutch. Susan was talking to Esther.

'I thought you would've had the news sooner than the likes of us mere mortals. John told me. Heard it at market. But you'll have to check the facts before repeating, in case he's got it wrong.'

'What's that? Louise clambered up, clutching Janine's book and the one she had put aside for Dylan.

'They've started draining the reservoir. Everything's got to come down. The church, the buildings. Then, it will be re-flooded. So, more disruption.'

They had all known this would happen – stage two of the reservoir project. The initial flooding was a trial. But Louise hadn't expected it to be so soon. The shovel. It would soon be exposed. Water would wash away any fingerprints. Would it cleanse away the blood and hair? She was being paranoid. Making problems that didn't exist. So, why did she have a sickening feeling that her misjudged action was going to catch up with her? It was too late to confess to Richard now, and if she went to the police, they would question her motive for trying to destroy evidence. Maybe she could retrieve it and then hide it where it couldn't be found.

5

WEDNESDAY 15TH JUNE 1966

What was worse? To admit to the police that she had thrown the shovel into the reservoir and subject herself to the inevitable questions, and Richard's hurt that she had doubted him? Or wait for them to discover it and hunt her down? There was no evidence that she was the culprit. But what if someone had seen her? Louise paced back and forth outside the police station. Confess. She couldn't live like this, always looking over her shoulder; she'd spent too much of her life running away.

As Louise turned to march into the police station, something caught her eye. It was a feeling rather than a sight. Her heart quickened as her senses went on high alert. She took a deep breath and swivelled around.

'Louise Boyd. Funny, I still think of you as Jane Cox.' Pete Murray was standing before her. She hadn't seen him since the day of the flood.

'What are you doing here?' she stuttered.

Pete grimaced. 'Oh, I thought Fliss told you.'

Louise sighed as she tried to gather her scattered thoughts.

Fliss. 'I haven't seen her since…' Louise cast her mind back to the day she found out Ma's body was missing from her grave. '…Oh, she said she had something to tell me. But I left before she could. I'm guessing you're about to enlighten me.' Louise tried to keep the loathing out of her voice. There had been a time when she considered Pete a friend and an ally, but that was before he did the dirty on her, informing Big Jim of her whereabouts.

Pete did at least look uncomfortable as he rocked from foot to foot. 'Thing is…Fliss and I are living together. Here. In Thorncrest.'

Louise's mouth fell open. 'How? When? I thought you were in Manchester. At Uni.'

'I am. Well, obviously not right now. I've got a reading week, well a few, so I'm spending the time with Fliss. She moved out of the High House dormitory into a one-bedroom flat.' He gave a dreamy smile. 'It's going well. I'm spending weekends with her and any free time from Uni,' Pete said.

'What about Dion?' Louise was still trying to process this news. How had Fliss not told her, she thought they were friends? Then, her cheeks warmed as she realised it was she who had been neglecting Fliss. Louise hadn't even followed up with Fliss when she said she had some news.

'We didn't get together until Dion was off the scene. I fell for her the day I saw her sitting in reception with the sun shining on her cascade of red hair, turning it to gold. I'd made a string of conkers, a throwback to my childhood, and when I saw her sitting there, like a princess, I hung them around her neck.'

'And you said it was National Red Heads Day,' Louise said, remembering.

'I did. And it was. I'd read it in the newspaper that day. So, we started writing when I moved to Manchester. Just friends at first. I didn't tell her how I felt. But then, she finished with Dion. So…' Pete shrugged as if it was nothing, but the huge grin gave him away. He was smitten.

'I'm pleased for you,' Louise conceded. 'But you'd better treat her right or I'll be on to you. I'm guessing Fliss knows nothing about your connection to the Mob or your past occupation?'

Pete frowned. 'There's no need for her to know. As you say, it's my past. I've moved on. I know you blamed me for Eddie finding you in Thorncrest, but Big Jim asked me to follow you as soon as you left London. I didn't know you when I started the job. He would have found you anyway. I'm truly sorry, Louise. Can we try and put it behind us?'

Louise wanted to, but she felt uneasy. It was the business of the bloodied shovel that unsettled her. She felt as though she would never be free of Big Jim and his cronies.'

'Are you still in contact with your uncle, Big Jim?'

'I'm trying to separate myself from that life. My mum's broken all links with Jim. He got too closely involved with Mum and me after Dad died working for him. He's my uncle, but there's no love lost as far as I'm concerned. He's an evil bastard. Thankfully, he's left us alone. Except…' Pete trailed off and looked over his shoulder.

'Except what?' Louise's skin prickled as a chill ran down her spine.

'He's here in Yorkshire.'

'He's what?' Louise exploded. 'What the hell is he doing here?' She wanted to run. Not again. Not now. She thought Big Jim was in her past.

'Mum told me. He doesn't know where Fliss and I live, she wouldn't tell him. It's something to do with a nightclub in Harrogate. Some unfinished business. Don't worry, he's not going to bother you.'

Louise wasn't so sure. Big Jim had entrusted Eddie to complete a job in Harrogate; it was the day before the flood. Eddie had left Louise in Thorncrest whilst he stayed in Harrogate and returned the next day intending to take her back to London. He had been forcing Louise into his car when Richard hit him.

'But he knows where to find me,' she said. The thought of Big Jim entering her orbit, tarnishing her life with Richard, made Louise want to retch. If Richard found out. If he came face to face with the man who had caused Louise so much distress, she could guess how he'd react, and Louise was terrified. Richard had no idea what Big Jim was capable of.

'Forget him,' Pete said. 'He's got bigger fish to fry. What are you doing here? It looked as though you were about to go into the police station.' Pete gave a quizzical frown.

'Oh, I was going to pick up some public information leaflets for the mobile library. Please tell Fliss, I'm sorry I've been such a lousy friend. If you're both happy, then I'm delighted for you.'

Pete opened his arms. 'Good. Do I get a hug now?'

Louise wanted to put the past behind her, but she was afraid. Big Jim was in Yorkshire, and she had committed a crime, it would be just as before. A life spent looking over her shoulder, afraid of her own shadow. She had to protect Richard.

6

LOUISE FRIDAY 17TH JUNE 1966

Louise and Esther finished work early on Friday, so they could spend some time on the museum curation. The fireside scene depicting life at Beck's farm in the 1940s, a display featuring the flax mill in the 1820s, and a library of parish record archives and old photographs – Esther's obsession – were the only areas of the barn that resembled a museum.

'There's a stack of old diaries here.' Esther called over from where she was comfortably settled in a huge leather chair, which would have looked at home in the library of a stately home. 'Somebody was meticulous about entering details of visitors, bookings, and social events for the church.'

'Is there a diary for 1951 the year Ma died?'

'Hold on.' Esther put aside one book after another as Louise made her way across the barn. If they couldn't find anything about Ma's funeral in the archives, Reverend Cummins might still have the information in his current records.

'Here it is.' Esther triumphantly held aloft a desk diary. '1951. Which month?'

'Until I get hold of the death certificate I don't know. Her gravestone had her date of birth but only the year she died. Is that weird?'

'Kind of. But there are gravestones with only the date of birth. A person might have bought their gravestone and plot before dying but if there was nobody to complete the process on their behalf – maybe no money to pay for the date to be engraved?' Esther shrugged. 'It can happen.'

'Not to Ma.' Louise couldn't bear to think Ma had died alone with nobody to arrange a proper burial. As soon as she was able, she would arrange for the date to be properly engraved on Ma's headstone.

'Okay, we'll just start at the beginning and work our way through. There's everything in here: flower rotas, correspondence received, bills paid, wedding banns to be read for Gloria Peters and Harold Jones. I know them!'

'Let me see.' Louise knew if she didn't take the diary away from Esther she would dwell on every entry until an hour or so had ticked by. I'll take this home and return it when I've had a good look. Is there anything else in the parish records about Elizabeth and John Beck?'

'Possibly, but without the benefit of data recorded on a microfiche it's like looking for a needle in a haystack. See how you get on with that diary. It might lead us in the right direction.' Esther yawned. She had been doing that a lot lately. Louise worried she was low in iron, as Esther had always been so full of energy.

'Maybe we should call it a day,' Louise said. She was eager to get home and immerse herself in the 1951 diary.

'It's good you passed your driving test, Lou. Are you a confident driver?'

The Canary Girl's Secret

Louise was surprised by her question. 'Yes. I guess. Considering I've only been driving for five months. Why?'

Esther frowned as if pondering whether to ask the next question. A few seconds passed, then she said, 'Do you think you could drive the mobile library if you had to?'

'Why? What's happened? Have you been diagnosed with a serious illness? I knew something was wrong. Are you at risk of having a heart attack? Or a seizure? Are you afraid I might need to jump in and take over if you became unwell at the wheel?'

Esther laughed. 'Calm down. Nothing like that. I know, come round to our house for supper tonight. You and Richard. About seven?'

'Why?' Louise wasn't convinced all was well. Esther had been acting out of character. Something was definitely on her friend's mind.

'Just say you'll come over. We'll tell you everything then.'

'Okay,' Louise said hesitantly. 'But in answer to your question, there's no way I would try driving Moby. She's a big girl, too big for me to handle. Sorry.'

Louise was impatient to get home. Richard was unlikely to finish work before six thirty and so, if she hurried, there would be one precious hour to check through the diary entries for 1951.

But as she was about to follow Esther out of the door and lockup the barn, a thought occurred to her. 'You go ahead. I'll see you at seven,' Louise shouted as she did an about-turn.

Ma kept a meticulous record of expenses. An account ledger that spanned the years of her marriage to John. If Ma and Pa had paid for their gravestones to be prepared in advance of their demise, it would be in those ledgers.

So, with her arms full of books: the diary and ledgers, Louise clambered into her red mini. The glorious feeling of independence when she sat behind the wheel of her car had not left her. Living in London, she had no need for a car, and when she first moved back to Thorncrest, she had enjoyed cycling the hills and valleys of her childhood home, falling in love again with the rugged Yorkshire moors. It would be good exercise to cycle to and from work, but a car gave her the gift of more time. More time to read and to write. The bounty of local history stored in the museum barn had stimulated her imagination. She had been jotting down story ideas, hoping one day to write a novel. It was a closely guarded secret as she doubted her ability and didn't want to be exposed as a fraud. One day.

'Come on Mini-Mouse,' she coaxed as her little car climbed the hill. 'Nearly home.' They reached the top and Louise saw before her a herd of cows blocking the road. A young man in a hat guided them across, but they weren't going anywhere fast. She switched off the engine, resigned to the inevitable wait. But there was something calming about cows. Ma and Pa were dairy farmers. Ma made butter and cheese to sell at market, a luxury during the war years, and Louise had learnt how to milk a cow. The smell of hay and beast, the warm feel of hide, Kurt, the prisoner of war farmhand, singing a German lullaby to relax the cows. It felt like yesterday, and yet Ma had been dead fifteen years. There would be no time now to examine the diary and ledgers before they headed over to Esther and Bill's.

'Shepherd's pie. Hope that's okay,' Bill said, when Louise and Richard stepped through the back door into a steamed-up kitchen. 'Esther's in the living room. Go through. This won't take long.' Bill was a nurse at the General hospital. He often prepared the evening meal when he had worked an early shift. 'I'll join you in a minute. Just need to pop this into the oven.'

Richard and Louise exchanged a look. They had been discussing the reason for this invitation on the way over.

'Moving house,' Richard had said.

'No. She wouldn't! We're working on the museum barn. Esther's my closest friend as well as work mate. They can't move out of the area. What if she's seriously ill? Oh, please God, don't let it be that. I've lost Ma to cancer. Not Esther too.'

'Or Bill? Maybe it's not Esther but Bill.' Richard had said, as they pulled into the driveway of Esther and Bill's pretty cottage.

Bill looked well enough, but in the living room, Esther was fast asleep in an armchair. She jolted awake with a gasp when Richard greeted her. 'Esther. Thanks for asking us over. It meant I didn't have to cook this evening.'

Louise thumped him lightly. 'Beans on toast? Again.' But it's what she would have prepared had they not received this invitation. Money was tight.

Bill joined them. 'Right. Supper's in the oven. What would you like to drink, Richard? Louise?' He rubbed his hands together.

Louise frowned. 'That depends. Is this a celebratory drink? Or is it a help us recover from the shock of hearing your news drink?'

Bill laughed. 'Celebratory. Sparkling wine? And for my beautiful wife--lemonade?'

Esther laughed. 'Perfect.'

Louise grinned as Bill prepared their drinks. Esther's loss of appetite, fatigue and avoidance of alcohol now made sense. Richard caught her eye and winked. He reached for her hand

and squeezed it, only letting go when Bill handed them each a glass.

'We're pregnant,' he announced. 'Four months.'

'I'm sorry I didn't tell you sooner,' Esther said to Louise. 'We wanted to wait until after the first trimester in case anything went wrong. But all is well. The midwife says baby is cooking nicely in there.' She rubbed her belly, and Louise noticed for the first time her bump. A baby.

'Congratulations, mate.' Richard raised his glass. 'To both of you. Wow. That's incredible news. So happy for you.' And he looked happy. His face infused with a soft light as though he had just glimpsed heaven; the miraculous wonder of a new babe.

Louise's heart contracted – with love? Or fear? They hadn't discussed having a family. Spending the rest of their lives together was as far as they had got in discussing a future. Marriage. Babies. They hadn't come up. Louise hadn't thought them important. She had been married to Eddie, and it hadn't come anywhere near the closeness she shared with Richard. In her view, a marriage certificate wasn't needed. They knew what they meant to one another. If Richard wanted to get married one day, she was open to persuasion, but babies? A family? No.

Richard was bubbling with questions and suggestions. Had they decided on names? Which room for the nursery? And then, the one question Louise wanted to ask, was Esther giving up work?

'Only when I have to. I hope to return to work after the baby's born but maybe not for the first year or two.'

Bill put his arm around Esther and kissed the top of her head. 'My amazing wife. So, after that bombshell – who's ready to eat?'

Bill and Esther had asked Louise and Richard to be godparents. Richard was overjoyed. Louise terrified. How could she be a godmother when she had messed up her own life? There was no way she could take responsibility for a child, even as a godmother, but she heard herself thank Esther and promise she would do her best, even though she prayed there would be nothing required of her apart from being present at the christening and remembering birthdays.

Managing the mobile library in Esther's absence was the more pressing worry. They had established Louise wouldn't be confident driving Moby. Qualified librarians were scarce, and whilst Esther's boss hoped to fill her position, it might take some time.

'We'll make sure you have someone to work with who's happy to drive Moby,' Esther had said. 'If you train as a librarian, you could take over from me.'

'You make it sound as though you're not coming back to work,' Louise said.

'Being a mother's a full-time job,' Esther said, and Bill nodded his agreement.

'Quite an evening for revelations,' Richard said as they drove home. He seemed happier and more relaxed than he had in days, but Louise was unsettled by Esther's news. The headlights of the land rover illuminated a rabbit, who stopped to stare before hopping to safety.

'I should have noticed,' Louise said. 'First Fliss, and then Esther. I'm not a good friend.'

'Is Fliss pregnant?'

'No. I mean, I neglected her.'

'What have you done to upset Fliss?' Richard said.

Damn, she hadn't told Richard about meeting Pete outside

the police station. He knew what Pete had done, how he had led Eddie to Thorncrest, putting Louise in danger. 'Well, um. Remember how Fliss said she had something to tell us, just before we met with Formoy?'

'Ye-es,' Richard said. For once she had his full attention, why couldn't he be distracted as he often was? Where was an interesting cut of wood when it was needed?

'Well, she's in a new relationship. With um…Pete Murphy.'

'Hmm. Good for her. Who's Pete Murphy?'

'Oh. Someone I worked with. Anyway, I should have followed up with Fliss and I didn't. Then, I was too caught up in my own world to notice my best friend was pregnant. I'm self-centred, like my mum.'

If he remembered Pete, Richard didn't react. 'Esther will be an amazing mother. And Bill must be so proud and excited.' He sighed. 'I'm happy for them.'

Louise reflected on their conversation at dinner. Esther's news had stirred something in her, not a yearning for a baby, but the possibility that she might become something more than a supporting role in other people's lives. 'Maybe I should consider training as a librarian,' she said. 'But it's expensive. And even if I could get a grant, it would mean losing paid work whilst I trained.'

The land rover slowed as they approached the entrance to their plot. Richard turned the wheel, and they bumped over uneven ground.

'Yes, but not a good time for you to commit to training,' he said.

The car stopped, and they gazed at their new home momentarily lit by the car's headlights.

'Bother, I forgot to bring a torch,' Richard said.

'Then it's lucky I did.' Louise felt around the well of her seat and held up her prize. 'See? I'm not completely useless.'

'Why would you say that? You know I think you're clever, beautiful, gifted.' He kissed her lightly on the lips, smoothing his hands over her hair.

'I know. But I feel bad, not being able to help fund this project. I know it would put off earning a decent income for a few more months––maybe years, I'm not sure––if I train as a librarian, but in the long term I would earn more money and have a secure job. I love books. I love the job.' Her breath quickened with excitement. But as Richard said, the timing wasn't great.

'Hmm. But what about our family?' he said. Words whispered into the darkness that now enveloped them.

'Our family?' Louise's mouth was dry.

'I know, I haven't asked you to marry me yet. And I'm not asking now, because when I do – and I will – I want it to be a romantic, memorable proposal. So, this isn't it. It's just, tonight made me realise how much I wanted a family. Our family. We aren't getting any younger. I thought when the house is finished.'

'When the house is finished, what?' Her voice sounded reedy.

'We try for a baby.'

Why had they never discussed this before? She had just presumed Richard felt the same way as her. He knew she was on the Pill.

'I'm thirty-five.'

'And I'm thirty-seven,' he said. 'So, we'd better not waste any time.'

'I thought with the holiday village… well, that will take up lots of our time and energy. A baby. I just didn't think…'

'Wouldn't it be great? You and me, a mum and dad?'

She couldn't tell him. It was the first time he'd seemed really happy and relaxed in a while. 'Maybe.'

7

SATURDAY, 18TH JUNE 1966

The next day, Richard was up and out before Louise opened her eyes. His eagerness to complete their home now felt like a cruel reminder of the gap opening up between them. She had to tell him how she felt. And if he can't live with that truth? Could she bear to give him up? The answer was no. She had tried once before, twenty years of being apart; she had felt as though a part of her was missing. But what he was asking of her was too much. She had grown up with tales of her grandmother, how she had favoured her Aunt Emma, Mum's younger sister, to the point of cruelty; taking only Emma to the circus and leaving eight-year-old Pearl at home alone. There were three years between the sisters, and although Aunt Emma said she had always adored her older sister, it seemed that their mother's unfair treatment of the girls drove a wedge between them. Louise's grandmother had died years ago; a distant figure to Louise, known mostly through anecdotes from her mum or Aunt Emma. Not a good mother, Louise had surmised. But her own mother wasn't much better. Sending back Ma's letters and Richard's was unforgivable. Louise had some happy memories of time spent with her mum before she was sent to Yorkshire as an evacuee, and before the weaselly Joe slid into their lives. Her mum was alone now, living in London, in a council flat. She ought to take pity on her, respond to her pleas to reunite – to forgive – but she couldn't. Her mum had rejected her when she needed her most. Bad parenting ran in the family. Louise didn't even know the identity of her own father. The idea that she too might one day be a mother frightened Louise. What if she screwed up? Disappointed their child by falling short of expectations. And that was the problem; she didn't know what was expected of her. It felt like an impossible task, raising a child. Keeping them safe, helping them fulfil their potential. Richard's child deserved better.

Bacon was sizzling in the pan, a Sunday treat. Through the window, she could see Richard talking to a dog-walker. A man he knew, by the way they were laughing together. What if it was the same dog-walker she'd spied along the bank from the farm?

Richard put his head through the door. 'That smells good. Give me thirty minutes.'

Thirty minutes. Time enough to sneak a look at the diary and ledger. Louise grabbed them both and settled herself on the bench seat with her notebook and pen. The ledger was huge; when opened, it would have taken up the whole desk. She imagined Ma filling her pen with ink, then gazing thoughtfully out of the window, organising her thoughts. Louise had never seen Ma writing in the ledger. She hadn't even known of its existence when she had stayed on the farm as a child. At what hour did Ma write? Maybe in the evening when Louise had gone to bed and Pa was dozing in his armchair, or early in the morning before milking. Louise turned the pages, every now and again tracing a finger over

Ma's words. There were inventories of dairy produce, records of what had sold at market, orders: half a dozen eggs for Mrs Hampton, half a pound of butter, and two pints of milk. The first entry in the ledger was dated 1918. The writing was small and neat, unlike the relaxed scrawl in later years. Ma had recorded her daily timetable, the times for milking, collecting eggs, working in the dairy.

'Another order for a table. Maybe we should forget the holiday village and just make furniture.' Richard laughed. 'Shall I make our butties?'

Louise cast one more glance over the neat recording of Ma's life in 1918: the method for making butter and cheese, a recipe for fruit cake. She wondered whether 1918 was the year Ma had come to Beck's farm as John Beck's wife. She made a note of the date, and then sprang to her feet. 'No, sit down, I'll make them.'

'Smells like rain,' Richard said, as he took a bite from his bacon sandwich.

Louise was about to protest when a steady thrumming on the roof of the caravan confirmed his prediction.

'I timed that well,' Richard said.

The noise increased. Hailstones like bullets were coming at them from all sides. Louise felt as though she were inside a tin being used for target practice. It was too noisy to talk, and so they ate in silence until the drumming of rain calmed to a gentle downpour.

'Bill was over the moon about the baby,' Richard said, when he had finished his last mouthful.

She didn't want to have this conversation, but if not now, when? 'Yes. It must be exciting for them,' she said, stacking their plates.

Richard put his hand over hers. 'Leave them. I'll wash up.'

'So, what's next for our house?' Louise said, hoping to change the subject.

Richard sighed. 'I've been thinking. Maybe I should go back to work, now our plans have changed. We'll manage eventually, but we do have a bit of a cash-flow problem.'

'I wrote to the to the Corporation. Told them I was outraged to hear they had lost the body in the relocation of graves, but I don't suppose it will make much difference,' Louise said.

'No. You know how I feel about the Corporation issuing compulsory purchase orders when house prices fell?'

'I do,' Louise said. 'Let's just hope Somerset House send the death certificate quickly and then we'll be back on track.' Water was seeping into her slippers, soaking her socks. She pulled her feet up onto the bench seat. 'Oh no. I should have emptied the bucket.'

'I don't think that would have made much difference,' Richard said. He squelched over to the full bucket. Water was falling in a steady stream through a split in the roof, the weight of water widening the gap as the roof caved-in.

Louise jumped up to collect saucepans and mixing bowls, placing them in a huddle beneath the leak. Outside, the rain picked up pace as though the heavens had opened. They worked together collecting and emptying water, but it was hopeless; water sloshed around their ankles.

A crash of thunder. Lightening. The caravan rocked, bringing back memories of the mudslide. 'Let's get out of here,' Richard said. 'We'll come back later and salvage what we can.'

Louise nodded. She took the ledger and diary, wrapping them in a towel. Then, they made a dash across the muddy field to the land rover.

In the car they sat in silence, each lost in thought. Louise's were of young Elizabeth Beck, new to farming life. Had Pa's mother been alive then? Who would have taught her how to split the curd from whey, to churn butter, and to make cheese?

'This isn't what I wanted for you – for us,' Richard said.

It took a few seconds for Louise to tune in. He held his head in his hands as he leant over the steering wheel.

'It'll pass,' Louise said. She stroked the back of his head. 'If we made a few holes in the bottom, we could drain out the water. What we need is a humongous can opener.' She laughed.

'I thought the house would be ready by now. I'd planned on proposing this summer. Celebrating our first Christmas together in our new home. There's no way we can carry on living in that old tin can. We won't survive the winter. I'll get a proper job.'

'Whoa. Slow down. It's June. We've got months until it gets too cold. We might even have a mild winter. If I'm covering for Esther's maternity I might get a bit of a raise, and I could ask the Corporation to pay me to get the museum barn set up quickly so that it's bringing in money for them. They've got to hand over my inheritance soon. You're giving up too easily, Richard. We can do this.'

'No. I'm sorry, Louise. I've decided.'

His face was stern. She'd seen that expression before. When Richard set his mind to something, there was no stopping him.

'What have you decided?' she croaked, fearing his response.

'I'm going to ask Fiona to give me back my job.'

'No,' Louise yelled. Fiona Simms had done everything in her power to frighten Louise away from Thorncrest, and from Richard, when she had returned last year. 'You can't. Please don't, Richard. We'll find a way to make this work.'

Richard turned in his seat to face her. He took her hand in his. 'I would just be working for a wage. Not as a business partner. Strictly business. Fiona would be my boss, nothing more. You know I love you, Louise. I'm doing this for us, so we can build our home. Get married. Raise a family.'

Those words again. A family.

'I don't know, Richard. I love you too. So much. But if I'm honest…' She had to tell him. Louise waited, watching his face. 'I'm not ready to be a mum.' A lump formed in her throat. 'I thought we could take our time. Get the holiday village established first.' She sighed.

'Are you saying you don't want to marry me?'

'No. Of course I want to marry you, Richard. How could you say that?' Her voice broke, and tears stung her eyes.

'But you don't want to have my children?' He was staring ahead, his hands tight on the steering wheel.

'I didn't say that. I do. One day. Just not yet.'

'When? Next year? We can't leave it too long. We don't even know if we can have children. It might take months to conceive.' She could hear the desperation in his voice.

'What makes you think I would be any good as a mother?' A hint of laughter in her voice masking her fear.

'You love children. They love you. Everyone learns as they go along. I would be a brilliant dad.' He was laughing. Excited.

'Maybe. Can you give me time to think? It's not something we should rush into. Let's get the house finished and our business set up first.'

'We can wait a while, but no more than a year or two.' It wasn't a question, more a statement, and Louise knew the topic was closed for now.

It wasn't that she didn't want to have children; Richard would be a wonderful father, but he was wrong, she would fail them, repeat the pattern started by her grandmother – a disappointment – and she couldn't bear that.

Richard started the engine.

'Where are we going?'

'Simms Emporium.'

'Do you mind if I don't go with you?' Louise said, a lump in her throat. 'It would be better if you approach Fiona alone, and I could use some time in the museum barn.'

'Are you sure?'

Louise nodded.

'Okay. See you later? Back here when the rain stops.'

'We'll have a job on our hands drying it out,' Louise said. Her voice sounded false. She was playing a part, like an actor reading her lines. Something had shifted; fault lines appearing in the ground between them.

He blew her a kiss before driving away – to Fiona.

In the museum barn, Louise tried to lose herself in the task of uncovering Ma's past. She sat at the desk where Ma would have written her ledger and turned the broad pages of tiny print spanning thirty years. It was a joy to read and a distraction from her misery, but there was nothing in there about Ma's illness. Just the last entry dated 2nd October 1951. *Write letter to Louise re will. Susan Jeffreys visiting to clear out cow shed and dairy. I'm going to miss my cows and chickens.* The ledger had begun with Ma, a young bride, and finished as she closed for business. The selling of cattle and farm stock would be recorded within its pages. The birth of each calf. Louise's arrival on the farm. Pa's accident.

Louise turned her attention to the Parish diary for the year of Ma's passing. *November 12th. Letter from Miss St Clair, Leeds re: Elizabeth Beck funeral.* It was a name Louise wasn't familiar with, but she knew very little about Ma. She turned the pages slowly, searching for an entry to tell her the date of the funeral. In the final month. December 18th Elizabeth Beck funeral 11.00 am. There had been a funeral. Surely that was sufficient evidence of Ma's death. It would have been helpful to have a date, but the death certificate when it arrived would provide that.

Exhausted by grief and worry, her eyes tired from reading tiny print, Louise took a blue cloche hat with a feather from the shelf and sank into Ma's armchair. She stroked the hat, a thing of beauty. Had Ma worn it somewhere special? She closed her eyes, trying to imagine a young Elizabeth.

8

MARCH 1915

It had become a routine she could have done in her sleep, and very often Beth felt as though she was sleepwalking. Her shift was from six in the morning until two in the afternoon. It meant getting up at four-thirty, washing in cold water as she wouldn't let Clara the maid rise any earlier than her, and then taking the train to work where she dozed until they jolted into the factory stop.

'Hair pin.' The policewoman pointed to a clip Beth had forgotten to remove. She handed it over.

Rosie tutted behind her. 'Trying to get us all killed, Beth Hardy?'

A forgotten hair clip was not a real risk to safety, but working in the munitions factory was dangerous. Far more dangerous than Beth realised when she signed up. Shells were delivered fully loaded, with only the fuse and cap to be added. It was a job that Beth had avoided, but she'd had her turn working in the room handling propellant for the shells. It wasn't the hardest job, or the most strenuous, but the chemicals they used turned the girls' skin yellow. This was what Daisy St. Clair meant when she said Beth was a Canary Girl.

Satisfied that Beth was wearing a regulation smock over her underwear, rubber-soled shoes, and her identity disc, and not carrying any forbidden items, security waved her through to begin an eight-hour shift.

The factory was noisy, the work repetitive, but the atmosphere was one of camaraderie and friendship. Beth had come to love these women. There was nothing she wouldn't do for one of them in need and knew that sentiment was returned.

'We're going out tonight,' Rosie shouted to be heard over the roar of machines.

'Where to? A grand ball?' Beth humoured her.

'I'll join you. Wear my taffeta and silk,' Connie chimed in.

'Ooh lovely. I'll ask the butler to arrange a carriage for me.' Iris giggled.

A conversation over breakfast a few days ago came back to Beth, and she let out a groan. 'Rosie! I hope you're not talking about Daisy's fundraising event at the Crown hotel.'

'The very same.'

Activity slowed as Connie and Iris waited to hear more.

'Concentrate on the job please, ladies,' Hamilton, the only man on the factory floor, said, as he patrolled the assembly line.

Beth rolled her eyes at Daisy. 'We're not invited. Daisy doesn't want us there. Besides, it will be full of toffs and I've nothing suitable to wear.'

Hamilton thumped his walking stick, unnecessary as a walking aid––although he claimed to have sustained an injury rock climbing––it was, however, a useful means of communicating. And today his message was clear.

Beth glared at Rosie. But Rosie just shrugged.

. . .

Rosie was determined that they should go to the ball. When Beth exclaimed for the umpteenth time she had nothing to wear, Rosie manifested a fairy godmother in the form of Daisy St Clair.

'If you must come, and I cannot say I welcome the idea, then wear something of mine. I don't care what you choose. Just remember this is a fundraiser. There will be aristocrats, some of them royalty…' The girls gasped before Daisy continued, 'and artists – bohemians. If you are to fit in wear something tasteful. Elegant not showy.'

If Beth had reservations before, she was certain now that she didn't want to go. 'I'm really tired. If you could just take Rosie with you.'

'No. We're both going.' Rosie stamped her foot, and Beth imagined her as a child. With her pretty face and curls, she was no doubt used to getting her own way.

'Be ready to leave at eight-thirty sharp,' Daisy said, dismissing them with a wave of her hand. 'Now go. I've important business to attend to.'

Rosie grabbed Beth's hand and almost ran with her to Daisy's dressing room.

'It feels wrong, helping ourselves to Daisy's wardrobe. Are you sure she's happy for us to just help ourselves? We don't even know what she plans on wearing herself,' Beth said.

'Honest to God, Daisy doesn't care a fig about clothes and frippery. Ooh, look at this boa.' Rosie tossed a luxurious feather boa across her shoulder and slunk around the room.

'Too showy,' Beth said. 'What do you think of this?' She pulled out a three-quarter length dress, silver-grey, it was embellished with a gold embroidered net ruffle, repeated at the shoulders to form cap sleeves. A spray of pastel rosebuds with velvet foliage completed the design.

Beth held the dress to her and admired her reflection in the long looking glass. The silver-grey went well with her auburn hair. The thought of wearing the dress was enough to change her mind about going to the ball.

'I bet it will fit you. Unfortunately, none of Daisy's dresses are big enough for me.' Rosie had a curvy figure. Heyden had described her as Rubenesque when he was trying to persuade her to pose nude. 'I'll just borrow this silky shawl and a pair of long gloves. I've got a long dress that can be made good with a bit of imagination, and a needle and thread.'

That evening, Daisy drove them in her Rolls-Royce, the cold air buffeting their hair, which was of no concern to Beth, but Rosie had spent an age creating ringlets around her face. Daisy left the Rolls-Royce at the front of the hotel for a man in livery to park. She was already in business mode, her eyes scanning the few guests who had arrived early.

'The works of art for auction are to the right of the stage,' a handsome woman, older than Daisy, said. 'We've given each of them a generous reserve price.'

'Thank you, darling. Let me introduce my two charges for the evening: Rosie Barton and Beth Hardy. They're lodging with me whilst working at Benbows. Rosie, Beth, this is my good friend Lady Hannah Whitely.'

Lady Hannah nodded at the girls. Beth didn't know the etiquette. Should she extend her hand? Curtsey? Before she had a chance to do either, Lady Hannah said, 'Oh, there's the captain. Where are the waiters? They should be circling with glasses of champagne,' and strode across the room to greet a couple of men in military dress.

The Canary Girl's Secret

Daisy seemed tense, her eyes flitting about the ballroom, which was now beginning to fill up with couples in formal dress, and others in more outlandish clothes: silk turbans, shawls, and flowing dresses for the women; the men favouring colourful waistcoats beneath their tailcoats. It wasn't hard to distinguish which of the guests were artists.

'It's time I left you to attend to business, but first a few rules.' Daisy gave the girls a stern look. 'Rule number one. Dance, love, and live, as though it's your last day on this earth. Two. Don't try to engage with me, if I'm in conversation. Three. Behave outrageously with no regrets. And be ready to leave at two-thirty if you want a lift home.'

'Two-thirty?' It was nine o'clock and Beth was struggling to keep her eyes open.

'I won't come looking for you. But I will leave at precisely that time. The auction starts in an hour. Time to warm up the buyers with some bubbly. Have a wonderful evening.' Daisy blew them a kiss before gliding across the room, her attention turning from one guest to another. The perfect hostess.'

A waiter paused with a tray of filled champagne glasses. Rosie took two and handed one to Beth, then she grabbed another. 'For later,' she mouthed to Beth behind the waiter's back. Rosie downed her first glass of champagne in a few gulps. 'I'm just following the rules. Drink up.'

Beth took a sip. It was her first taste of champagne. The bubbles tickled her tongue and made her smile.

'That's better,' Rosie laughed. 'We've worked hard all week – all month! All year. You heard, Daisy. It's time to have fun. Knock that back and we'll take to the dance floor.'

'With whom?' Beth took a few more sips.

'We can dance together. Why not? Can you Waltz? Tango?'

Beth giggled. Rosie's cheeks were pink, her eyes shining. It was good to see her friend relaxed and happy. 'Not very well, but I'll have a go.'

A trumpet sounded. Everyone cheered. 'Ragtime,' someone shouted.

Rosie and Beth discarded their empty glasses onto the tray of a passing waiter and wove their way to the dance floor. Couples were dancing energetically: hands flailing, bottoms jerking; they strutted and twirled, expressing themselves in a way that would have been frowned upon by her former mistress, Mrs Edgerton.

Rosie held out her arms, preparing to waltz. 'Who will lead?' She shouted to be heard.

Before Beth could reply, a man in military dress swooped in and took hold of Rosie's outstretched hands. He nodded, grinned, and together they fell into step, dancing across the floor. It looked so natural and carefree. Would he have dared to be so bold if not for the war? The fragility of life had made them all a little reckless. Beth followed their movements, delighted by her friend's untethered joy until bodies obscured her view – all of them having a wonderful time as they danced like crazy, blocking out for a few precious moments the atrocities of war. Beth wanted to join them, but she didn't feel the same energy. Her body was tired, and her head hurt from lack of sleep. A few women danced alone, moving their bodies in fluid movements as though unaware of anyone else. Beth wished that she too could retreat into an inner world, but the only way she would find peace was under her bed covers, fast asleep.

Alone on the edge of the dance floor, Beth felt self-conscious. She caught a few of the women and several men taking in her appearance. Could they tell she was out of her depth? A housemaid dressed up as a lady? Beth shrank into the wall, wishing she were at home snuggled beneath her bedcovers.

Rosie and her gentleman were making their way back across the dance floor. He must be hot in his military jacket, Beth thought. Her friend's face glowed pink from exertion, excitement, and two glasses of champagne.

When they joined her, a little breathless, Rosie said, 'Captain Geoffrey Palmer, I would like you to meet my very good friend Miss Elizabeth Hardy.'

Captain Palmer kissed Beth's hand, and she was embarrassed not to be wearing gloves, as the other women seemed to be. 'My pleasure. Miss Hardy. And now, after that excellent dance, I must take my leave to join Daisy St. Clair on stage. The art auction's about to begin.'

'Isn't he handsome?' Rosie said as they watched the captain retreat to the stage. 'A captain of the Flying Corps.'

'I wish I could join the Flying Corps. Maybe your captain could find me voluntary work on the airbase, looking after the planes or something,' Beth said.

'He's not my captain,' Rosie sighed. 'At least not yet. Maybe…'

'Ladies, gentlemen, honoured guests, distinguished artists…' Daisy's voice, clear and confident, filled the vast room. She spoke about her time working in Switzerland for the Red Cross, nursing injured soldiers and airmen. 'Proceeds from this auction will go to the Red Cross. Captain Palmer and Lieutenant Winterton are here on behalf of the Red Cross to thank you for your generous donations. In fact, Lieutenant Winterton and I met when he was a patient in Switzerland following a plane crash. A round of applause, please, for these courageous airmen.'

Captain Palmer and Lieutenant Winterton came centre stage to take a bow.

'And now, let the auction begin.' Daisy assisted by Camille––her hair in a long plait, her outfit simple but stunningly elegant – held up the first painting for auction.

'Daisy frames a lot of the paintings herself,' Rosie whispered to Beth.

Beth was finding out a lot about her landlady this evening. 'Did you know, Daisy was a Red Cross nurse in Switzerland?' she said.

'No. But I wouldn't mind nursing Lieutenant Winterton. He's gorgeous,' Rosie said.

Beth had noticed the lieutenant's startling blue eyes. She'd had to make herself look away in case he caught her staring.

'Lot thirty-three. An oil painting by William Chambers. Mother and Child. We have a reserve of twenty-pounds. What am I bid?'

There were a few bidders in the room. Beth paid little attention as she struggled to stay awake. 'Thirty,' the Lieutenant said. Beth sat up in her seat. It was the first time he had made a bid.

'Thirty-two, from the back of the room.'

'Thirty-five,' Lieutenant Winterton said.

'Going, going, gone at thirty-five pounds to the Lieutenant.' Daisy rapped the table.

The band started up again as paintings and other works of art were collected by bidders gathered around the stage. Intrigued by the Lieutenant, Beth found herself drawn to the cluster of people admiring his painting, Mother and Child. It was a pleasing enough image, but she was intrigued as to why he had only shown an interest in this particular piece. Too shy to address him, she spoke instead to Camille, who was at his side.

'Hello, Camille Beaufont. I recognise you from the other day. I saw you leaving our house. Daisy St Clair's house. I'm her lodger, Beth Hardy.' The Lieutenant turned his head, and Beth blushed, aware of his scrutiny. 'I was impressed to see you riding a bicycle. Daisy said you might help me acquire one.'

Camille grinned. 'Highly recommended. And once you start wearing bloomers instead of a skirt, you'll find any excuse to do so. Men have it easy. No corsets and stockings to impede them.'

Daniel laughed. 'I don't think anything could impede you, Miss Beaufont. From what I've seen, you're unstoppable.' He had an American accent. It was exotic. Delicious. Beth's arms prickled with goosebumps.

Camille stopped a passing waiter to request a carafe of red wine. Beth declined another drink; one glass of champagne was enough for her.

'If you will excuse me ladies, I'm going to store this precious painting somewhere safe.' Daniel lifted Mother and Child and held it at arm's length to admire the work.'

'Why that particular painting?' Beth said, surprised at her courage in addressing him.

'Um. Well, it's…' the lieutenant seemed lost for words, and Beth was embarrassed she had put him on the spot. They were saved by the waiter arriving with a carafe of red wine.

Daisy glared at them from the stage. Red wine near precious works of art was not advisable. Beth was surprised at Camille. As an artist and Daisy's assistant, she should know this. Beth turned, and in that second, the carafe seemed to fly in slow motion, turning mid-air, falling, falling… Beth stepped back but it came in a wave of red, soaking the front of her dress. *Daisy's* beautiful dress.

Beth gasped. Her eyes flew to Mother and Child. 'The painting?'

'Don't worry about the painting, it's fine, but your beautiful dress is ruined. I'm so sorry,' Camille said. 'I would drive you home to change, but I'm needed here.'

'It's okay. I'll get a carriage,' Beth said. Daisy's dress. She'd ruined Daisy's dress. Tears pricked her eyes. Everyone was staring at her now.

'Why don't you drive Beth home in Daisy's car so she can change then return here?' Camille said to the lieutenant. 'Her friend can accompany you as a chaperone.'

The poor lieutenant looked discomforted. He clearly didn't want to drive Beth home. The wine was soaking into her skin. She looked as though she had come straight from the battlefield. 'There's no need. I'll….I'll…' Unable to hold back, Beth let out a strangled sob.

'Okay. I'll have a word with Daisy,' the Lieutenant said.

'No need. If you escort Beth to the front of the hotel, I'll let Daisy know you're taking her car.'

'The painting…' the lieutenant said. 'I'll take it with me.' He looked around, but the painting had gone. Camille was making her way over to Daisy her hands free. 'I can't leave without it.' The lieutenant looked distraught.

'I'm sure it's safe. Someone would have moved it for you, away from the risk of wine spillages.' Beth gave a half-hearted laugh. 'I'm sorry to inconvenience you. If you don't want to drive me home it's okay, I'll ask the concierge to summon a carriage for me.'

'We weren't properly introduced. Lieutenant Daniel Winterton. I'm happy to drive you home where's your friend?'

'Last I saw she was dancing with your captain. I don't need a chaperone. If you're happy to risk being unconventional,

The Canary Girl's Secret

and I won't return to the ball. To be honest, I'll be glad to get home and sleep. I was up before dawn for work.'

'If you're sure? Okay. Let's go.'

As they left the ballroom, Daniel kept peering into dark corners. He stopped a man who was leaving with a wrapped painting under his arm. 'Which painting is that?' he asked.

'Rebecca Reclining by Heyden,' the man said. 'Pleased to raise money for a worthy cause. We're proud of you Lieutenant and grateful for your service.' He looked quizzically at Beth's wine-stained dress.

Daniel nodded. 'Thank you. Good evening.' He steered Beth away without giving an explanation.

They drove home in silence, each lost in thought. Beth was calculating how many week's wages it would take to pay Daisy for the dress, although it wasn't her fault it got ruined.'

A plane flew overhead. 'One of our men, patrolling the area,' Daniel said.

'That's what I want to do,' Beth blurted. 'Fly planes.'

Daniel laughed. Then he turned to look at her. His eyes. Blue as a summer sky. 'It's all I ever wanted to do,' he said.

'What's it like?' Beth said, a little breathlessly.

'It's like being a bird. Moving with the current of the wind. Just you and nature. My father had a biplane. We were both barnstormers – travelling county fairs in Ohio where I grew up.'

'What's a barnstormer?' Beth said. She was in awe of him. What she wouldn't give to live a life of adventure, flying a biplane.

'We took people for a ride in the plane. Me or my pa. Just one passenger at a time. It was popular and we did well.'

'I wish you could take me up in your plane,' Beth sighed. 'It's been a dream of mine since I first saw a plane.'

They were approaching Daisy's house. Daniel slowed the car.

'I grew up knowing how to fly. Up there, nothing matters. It's like stepping outside of time. Away from the world. I could leave behind my worries and soar free from thought, just me and the plane. It's a bit different now, with the war.'

'You're very brave,' Beth said. 'I wish I could do more than factory work.'

'Munitions?' Daniel said.

'Yes. Like you, we don't get much free time. But I'm glad I came tonight. I hope you find your painting when you return. I'll feel terrible if it goes missing because you were attending to me. But surely nobody would steal it?'

The idea was crazy and Beth laughed. 'What was Camille thinking of ordering a carafe of red wine when we were surrounded by art work?'

Daniel let out a long breath. 'Do you think she did it on purpose?'

'No,' Beth exclaimed. 'Why would she?'

'You're right. Forget I said that. Now, are you okay getting in the house and are you sure you don't want to get changed and return with me to the ball?'

Beth smiled. 'I'm fine. Thank you.'

It was hard leaving Daniel Winterton. In his company, she felt alive – tingling with energy. In fact, having felt sleepy all evening, she now wondered whether she would lie awake. An airman with blue, blue eyes. A lieutenant. She hoped his painting was waiting for him at the hotel. Should she soak the dress or wait until morning and consult Mrs Kavanagh?

Despite her fears, Beth fell asleep soon after her head touched the pillow.

9

MARCH 1915

The memory of Daniel Winterton had stalked Beth's every thought since the night of the art auction. The morning after – well, the afternoon, as no-one in the St. Clair household emerged from their room until after midday – Beth apologised profusely to Daisy about her ruined dress.

'It's not a problem, darling. I'll give it to Mrs Kavanagh. If she can't remove the stain, then she can use the material to make something for her granddaughter. What I want to know is how exactly it happened?'

Beth felt disloyal blaming Camille, especially as she and Daisy seemed so close. 'It was an accident. The carafe of wine just flew up in the air and landed over me. Maybe someone bumped into Camille or she tripped. We shouldn't have been drinking red wine whilst standing so close to the paintings.' Beth bit her lip.

'No. I'm surprised at Camille.' Daisy frowned. She picked up her toast and then returned it to the plate uneaten. 'Was

Lieutenant Winterton standing with you and Camille at the time?'

Beth blushed at the mention of his name. She nodded her head. 'In the commotion his painting went missing. Do you know if he found it?'

Daisy put a hand to her chest; her face paled. 'I've a headache coming on. I'm going to have a lie down. When Mrs Kavanagh pops in with our supper, give her the dress Beth. She can do with it as she pleases but please ask her not to disturb me.'

'It's okay. We'll sort everything, Daisy,' Rosie said. 'It was a great auction. You should be proud. Captain Palmer was very impressed.'

Daisy left them as Rosie warmed up to her theme of the charming, dashing, and swoon-worthy Captain Geoffrey Palmer. Beth listened, making all the right noises. He was a good-looking man and seemed to be captivated by Rosie. Who wouldn't be? Beth smiled to herself. Her friend was warm, vivacious and, most important, kind. Who wouldn't love her?

And then her mind wandered again to the blue, blue eyes of Daniel Winterton.

'Do you know if Daniel – I mean Lieutenant Winterton – found his painting?' Beth said when Rosie eventually paused in her adulation of the captain.

'We barely saw him after he left with you. Obviously, he returned Daisy's car but he didn't make a reappearance at the ball. I danced so much last night, my feet hurt. Geoffrey's a wonderful dancer. Did you see us waltzing together? Later in the evening, they played ragtime again. We went wild. I had to tell Geoffrey to remove his jacket before he passed out with the heat. He's so proper.' Rosie giggled.

Beth sighed as she thought of Daniel. She could have talked to him all night.

The Canary Girl's Secret

Rosie's eyes sparkled. 'Geoffrey's going to send a message or write. He wants to see me again.'

And with that comment, a seed of hope was sown in Beth's heart. Maybe she would see Daniel again. There was so much she wanted to ask him about flying a plane. Imagine his father having a biplane. To own a plane. It was the height of decadence and glamour. She imagined herself flying solo. But soon the image of Daniel Winterton invaded that dream, and they were flying together, soaring over fields and villages in a biplane. There was no war in this imagined scenario. Would Daniel return to America when the war was over? She imagined herself with him in that vast country.

'Miss Hardy.' Hamilton's stern voice broke into Beth's thoughts, and she realised a couple of parts were still awaiting her attention. Her hands had slowed as her mind wandered. 'Take a break. You can collect today's milk from the dairy.'

Rosie turned her head as Beth left the assembly line, and she felt like a naughty schoolchild being sent out of the classroom for bad behaviour. But she welcomed the break.

It was the first time Beth had visited the dairy. She knew the factory site incorporated a mini dairy farm to ensure a plentiful supply of milk for the workers, but its exact whereabouts were unknown to her. Pointed in the right direction, Beth stepped cautiously across a field, avoiding puddles of wet mud. The low of cows came from a corrugated-iron outhouse ahead of her.

'Dairy's over there,' a girl in breeches said. Louise envied her working on the farm. Being outdoors was preferable to the noise and monotony of the factory.

A young man with rosy cheeks and a mop of sandy hair greeted her. 'You're in luck this morning. The girls have served us well. Must be something in the air making them produce more milk.'

'Really? What might that be?' Beth asked, genuinely fascinated.

'Oh.' The man seemed a bit taken aback. 'I don't rightly know. Better diet. Rested. We've changed the milking routine. I've been trying to increase milk yields. I'll get one of the farmhands to help you carry the churns back.'

Beth followed him to the dairy. A long, low building across from the cowshed. Louise wanted to ask if she could see the cows, but didn't like to be a nuisance, keeping him from his work. As if reading her mind, the man stopped in his tracks.

'I'm sorry, I didn't introduce myself. John Beck.'

'Beth Hardy,' she said.

'Miss Hardy?'

Beth nodded.

'Would you like to meet the cows to thank them before I set you up with the trolley of milk churns?'

Beth laughed at his whimsy. 'I would indeed like to thank them.'

John Beck was easy to be with. He reminded Beth of her youngest brother, chatty, with no pretensions, just warm and kind. He obviously loved his cows, and she enjoyed listening to him as he explained the science of dairy farming. Unable to find anyone else to help her, John Beck assisted Beth, pulling and pushing the loaded trolley across the field. When it was on a paved path, they parted.

The rest of her shift passed quickly. In future she would keep her mind on the job, not on Daniel Winterton. There it was, his name again, and with it came the memory of eyes as blue as a cloudless sky.

'You must be Hamilton's favourite, getting off work to collect the milk,' Rosie said as they boarded the train home.

'I don't think so. If I slack like that again I don't think he'll be so kind.'

'Yes. I noticed you got distracted holding up production. You couldn't go to bed any earlier than you do.'

'Is that Camille's bike?' Beth said, as they approached the house. She would ask Camille if Daniel had found his painting.

'I don't think so. Camille's bike is shiny and new looking, that one's seen better days.'

'There's a letter in the basket,' Beth said. 'It's addressed to me.' She tore open the large buff envelope. Inside was a smaller lilac one addressed to Daisy.

'Dear Miss Hardy, My sincere apologies for ruining your beautiful dress through my carelessness. Please accept this bicycle as a gift. I would be grateful if you could pass the enclosed letter to Daisy St Clair. Yours sincerely, Miss Camille Beaufont.' Beth read aloud. 'A bicycle. This is going to be so useful,' she exclaimed. 'I'd prefer a bicycle to a fancy dress any day. Not that it was my dress to exchange. Maybe I should offer Daisy the bike as it was her dress.'

'If Daisy wanted a bike, she could buy a dozen. You'll have to learn how to ride it. And get some bloomers or a split skirt. Daisy must have been out when Camille called.'

Beth tucked her skirt into the legs of her knickers and climbed onto the bike. 'My brothers had one.' At first the bike wobbled, or was it her legs? Beth was out of practice.

'Watch out,' Rosie shouted as Beth narrowly missed a lamppost.

Beth dismounted. 'I'm a bit out of practice. I'll take it to the park and ride around until I feel confident. This is so exciting.'

'If you say so,' Rosie said, shaking her head. 'I can't think of anything I would hate more. All that oil getting on your clothes and a nasty bicycle chain to catch your skirt.'

'I'll wear bloomers like Camille.' Beth imagined herself looking modern and chic like the pretty artist. 'Shame Daisy missed her.'

They manoeuvred the bike up the steps to the house and settled it against the wall in the hallway. 'I'll store it in the back yard after my practice in the park.'

'You're going back out?' Rosie said. 'I thought you were tired.'

Beth grinned. 'I was but not now. First, I'll leave this letter for Daisy.'

Daisy wasn't in the salon, or the kitchen, so Beth knocked on the door of the library, a room used by Daisy for writing correspondence and more formal meetings. There was no reply, and so Beth tentatively opened the door, intending to leave the envelope on Daisy's desk.

'I'm sorry, I thought you were out,' Beth said. Daisy was pacing up and down, a hand held to her face. 'Camille...' before she could continue, Daisy interrupted.

'Camille? Have you seen her? Where is she?'

'No. She must have come by when you were out. She left this note for you. And a bicycle for me.' Beth proffered the lilac envelope.

Daisy swiped it from Beth's hand and tore it open. 'No. No. When? When was she here?' Daisy threw up her hands. She tore through the house and opened the front door.

Beth followed, keeping her distance. 'I'll move the bike,' she said.

Daisy let out her breath. 'Can you ride that thing?'

'I think so. I'm out of practice but I learnt on my brother's bike.'

Daisy nodded and swept past Beth back to the library, closing the door loudly behind her.

. . .

Sunday was the only day Daisy, Beth and Rosie ate breakfast together. The girls' shift pattern meant they got up long before Daisy, and as she was often out in the afternoons, they rarely saw one another, so Sunday breakfast was a noisy affair as they exchanged news from the week.

'Was Captain Palmer pleased with the money raised for injured airmen?' Rosie said, helping herself to another devilled kidney.

'The Red Cross sent a letter of thanks. It's on the sideboard if you would like to read it,' Daisy said. She winked at Beth. They both knew Rosie was fishing for news of the captain.

'Oh. Of course. Well done.' Rosie chewed her lip , a frown creasing her forehead, and they waited for the inevitable question. 'So, have you heard from him, Captain Palmer?'

'No darling. It's only been a week. He does have a squadron to command and given we're at war, he might be a tad busy.'

Rosie blushed. 'Of course. It's just that I thought he might have sent a note to me. Or something.'

Daisy glided over to the sideboard and plucked an envelope from where it was propped behind the toast rack. 'Like this?'

Rosie jumped up and waved her hands. 'Quick. Let me see. Why didn't you say?'

'A messenger delivered it this morning.'

Beth observed Daisy closely. She had dark rings under her eyes. Earlier, when Beth had found her in the kitchen assembling the dishes prepared by Mrs Kavanagh, she wondered whether she had been crying, as her eyes were red and swollen. As soon as Daisy saw Beth, she had switched into Daisy-mode. 'Devilled horse kidneys, and roast sparrow? Mrs Kavanagh is most inventive. Carry these through, darling.'

'Can I be excused?' Rosie clutched the unopened letter to her breast.

'Go. Go.' Daisy waved her away and sat down.

Beth bided her time, unsure of the right approach. Eventually she said, 'Have you spoken to Camille since the auction?'

Daisy shook her head and bit her lower lip. Beth felt partly responsible for the wine spillage that had ruined Daisy's dress and resulted in a valuable artwork disappearing. 'It's a pity you were out when she called on Monday.'

'I wasn't out.' Daisy tutted and shook her head. 'It's too late. She's gone. I've been a fool. A stupid fool.' Her eyes glistened with tears.

'Is there anything I can do?' Beth said.

'Yes. There is.' Daisy stood up. 'How are you on that bike of yours?'

10

BETH MARCH 1915

It was a curious arrangement, and one that Beth couldn't fathom. There must be an easier way to deliver a painting than to have her cycle into the country with it strapped to her back so she could meet Daniel in a farmer's field. She had only cycled to the local park and made a few precarious circuits, so the idea of cycling on main roads was daunting.

'I thought Mother and Child was much bigger than this?' Beth said as Daisy checked the brown parcel was secure on her back.

'It's a watercolour by Camille. Tell Lieutenant Winterton that it's a gift.'

'Does he know I'm meeting him in this field?' Beth said. The request was peculiar even for Daisy, and Beth was getting used to her landlady's eccentricities.

'Yes. It's the best arrangement. Farsley, the nearest airfield is too far away and I don't have time to drive you. Besides, I thought you might like a reason to see Daniel Winterton again.'

Blood rushed to her cheeks. 'It's hot wearing all of this gear, and carrying the painting,' she said.

'You look charming in Camille's bloomers. Now, make haste. Lieutenant Winterton can't park his plane in the middle of a field for more than a few minutes. You've got to be there waiting for him. Are you sure you know which field?'

Daisy was making Beth feel anxious. They had gone over the route she would take to find the field several times. 'Yes. But if I miss him, can't you just get it sent to the Flying Corps station?'

'Yes. Yes. Now quick. And be careful not to ride too close to horses.' Daisy waved her arms, shooing Beth out of the door.

Horses. What if she spooked a horse and caused a runaway carriage? It's only five miles away, Beth reassured herself, and mostly footpaths. Difficulty accessing the field by car had been Daisy's reasoning for sending Beth on her bike. I don't see why Rosie couldn't pass it to Captain Geoffrey Palmer when she meets him next week, Beth thought, finding her balance as the painting skewed her weight. And she was off.

Thankfully, the roads were quiet; she kept her distance from the horse and carriages she encountered. A messenger on a bike rang his bell as he passed Beth at speed. As she approached the footpath where she left the road, Beth felt exhilarated and proud of herself. She was a modern, independent woman. The bloomers felt great––so freeing. It was fortunate Camille had left a pair following one of her stays at the house. Beth climbed off the bike to push it through the hedgerow. Her legs felt like jelly, unused to the exertion. A rabbit darted from the undergrowth and observed Beth for a few seconds before continuing across the path and into a wooded area on the opposite side.

The field she was to meet Daniel Winterton was across

The Canary Girl's Secret

country for another mile or so. She scanned the cloudless sky searching for his plane. Nothing yet. She hoped he wasn't already parked in the field waiting. It would take her at least fifteen minutes to cut across a couple of fields. The footpath was too narrow and muddy to cycle, so she pushed her bike around the fallow field, and then on into a copse, where wild garlic grew between the trees. Here, beneath an ancient oak, she could almost forget there was a war, that men – her own brothers – were fighting for their lives and country. No time to dawdle, she pushed her bike onward.

Beth heard the propeller as Daniel's biplane soared overhead. She shielded her eyes to follow its path across the sky. When it disappeared from view, she hurried herself, scraping a bike pedal against her shin. Ouch. It was impossible to move quickly; cloggy mud slowed the wheels, and she was mindful of stinging nettles on both sides of the path. Daisy said he wouldn't stay long. Hopefully, he had spotted her from the sky and knew she was minutes away. Minutes away. Beth stopped pushing the bike to tidy her hair. Camille's bloomers looked cute on the elfin-faced artist, but Beth was afraid they were unflattering on her. Her heart began to race; her hands clammy. It was just the exertion. Not the airman with blue eyes. Maybe once she saw him again, she would get over this silly infatuation. It was his plane – a fascination to see a biplane up close – that was all. If she didn't hurry, she might miss him. Beth dragged her bike over a tree root and almost slipped in the mud. She took a deep breath and reprimanded herself. As Daisy St Clair's representative, she was delivering an artwork. A business transaction. No need for silliness.

Beth emerged from the copse to find Daniel's biplane parked in the centre of a meadow. Even from a distance, it took her breath away. He climbed out of the cockpit and jumped down. Beth propped her bike beneath a tree and with the painting strapped to her back, strode across the field to meet him.

Daniel wore a flying jacket and leather helmet with goggles pushed up to his forehead. Her stomach did a tumble.

'She's magnificent,' Beth said, catching her breath.

'Ain't she just?' Daniel stroked the plane's strut. 'Don't be fooled. She looks as delicate as a dragonfly but this baby's tough. Designed for strength and speed.'

Beth touched the cool metal of the plane with reverence. The wings were made of plywood. 'Is that linen?' she asked, stepping closer to get a better look.

'Sure is. It's used to protect the delicate parts of the plane. Have you got something for me?' Daniel reminded Beth of her mission.

'Yes, sorry. It's on my back. If you could help me take it off? Daisy secured it tight with bandages. It's a watercolour by Camille Beaufont. I'm sorry you didn't find Mother and Child. Hopefully, it will still turn up. But Daisy wanted you to have this. '

'Any news of Camille Beaufont?' Daniel asked as he loosened the strapping on Beth's back. She felt his breath on the back of her neck, and her knees wobbled.

'I'm not used to riding a bike,' Beth said, afraid he might notice. 'Camille left a note for Daisy when she delivered this bicycle for me, but I don't think Daisy has seen her since the art auction. Have you?'

'No.' Daniel sighed. He bit his lip and looked away into the distance. 'Okay. I'd better be off.'

Beth's heart sank. 'Could I just look inside your plane first? I've never been this close to one.'

Daniel grinned. 'That's right. I forgot. You're interested in aviation. I guess it's the least I can do as you've come all this way.'

Beth stood on tiptoe to see into the cockpit, but it was too high.

'Climb up,' Daniel said. He took her hand and helped her into the seat behind the pilot's. Then he climbed into the pilot's seat.

Beth sighed with delight. 'This is amazing. I can almost imagine what it would be like to fly. To really fly.'

The engine started up. The propellers slowly turned. 'Hold on tight. I'll take her up,' Daniel said.

Beth shrieked with delight as the plane sped forwards and then glided effortlessly up and up, soaring above the field, the footpath she had tramped across soon lost, as they went higher and higher. The plane tilted to one side as it circled around, and Beth gasped. The wind blew her hair across her face; her eyes watered. She was actually flying. Never had she felt so free. It was over too soon. They were landing. Like a great bird, gliding down gracefully. Then bump as the plane's wheels touched down.

It would have been impossible to hear one another when they were in the air. When the propellers stopped and Daniel turned around in his seat to face her, Beth clasped her hands to her breast. 'Thank you. That was the most amazing experience of my life. I've always wanted to fly.'

'Pleased to be of service, ma'am,' Daniel said, giving a mock salute.

'I envy you, flying every day.' Beth caught herself in time to add, 'I mean it's terrible being at war. And you're brave fighting for the Allies when your country hasn't joined the war.'

'It will,' Daniel said, climbing out of the plane to help Beth down. 'I was flying with the Lafayette Escadrille as a volunteer pilot in the French Air Service before joining the Royal Flying Corps. It seemed like the right thing to do.'

He was waiting for Beth to take his hand and dismount, but she was reluctant to leave. 'Your family must be afraid for you. I worry about my brothers. They're fighting on the Western Front.'

Daniel looked over his shoulder, and Beth, picking up on his anxiety, clambered out of the plane. Of course, he was in a hurry to leave. His hand was still in hers as she stood alongside the plane. Their eyes met, and Beth felt a jolt of energy shoot through her, tingling her palm. She blushed as he released her hand.

'My father died a couple of years ago. Before I volunteered to fly for the French Air Service. I've a step-mother but we never got on and when my father died…' his voice trailed off. 'Anyway. Thank Daisy for the painting.'

'Will I see you again?' Beth blurted, unable to stop herself.

'I sure hope so, but if not – keep safe.' He saluted.

'And you, because now, I'm going to worry about you as well as my brothers.'

'It will be good, knowing someone cares about me enough to worry. Home defence isn't too risky, just patrolling the area to keep Yorkshire safe from Zeppelin bombs. And now I'd better get going. It's not safe to stay stationery in a field. Glad you enjoyed the ride. It took me back to my barnstormer days.'

Beth watched Daniel's plane take off. He waved from the cockpit as the propellers spun, then he was up and away. She craned her neck until he was a dot in the sky.

11

SUNDAY 19TH JUNE 1966

Richard arrived back at the caravan before Louise returned from the museum barn. He had done a good job sweeping away the water and tearing out the sodden carpet.

'Is there a lot of damage?' she said, peering in.

'We got off lightly. The carpet's ruined and our bedding will need a wash but apart from that it's fine. That is until the next time it rains. I'll fix a tarpaulin over the roof but we'll have to find somewhere else to live until the house is ready.'

Louise sighed. 'Can I boil a kettle and make us a cup of tea?'

Richard stepped back to make room in the kitchen. 'For now. But we need to make other arrangements.'

'I know.' Louise didn't like to ponder what those arrangements might be. 'How was your meeting with Fiona?'

'Good. She's more than happy for me to take over as manager so she can focus on building the business. And she made a generous offer with regards to my salary.'

'So, you said, yes?'

'I did.'

'That's that then. Where are we going to live?' The kettle sang on the stove, and Louise switched off the gas.

'I can live in our house, now the roofs on. I don't need water and electricity. I can get by camping out in the front room. Would Esther and Bill let you stay with them?'

'No. I mean, yes. I'm sure they would, but no. I don't want to live away from you. If you can camp out, so can I. That's exactly what we've been doing for the past few months.'

Richard gave her a long look. It said, I won't argue with you now, but this conversation isn't over. She poured the tea into mugs and handed one to him.

'Thanks,' he said. 'Oh, I picked up our post on the way back. A bill from the timber merchant and two letters for you.'

She sat down with her tea to read the letters. 'This one's from Aunt Emma, and the other looks like it might be from Somerset House.' The reassurance of having a death certificate for Ma lifted Louise's spirits. She tore open the envelope.

Dear Louise Pearson,

Thank you for your enquiry regarding Elizabeth Beck 1890-1951. We have searched the records available to us and regret to inform you that a death certificate cannot be located at this time. There could be several explanations for this: An administrative error – unfortunately these do occasionally occur. It could have been lost in transit from the local registry. Misfiled. Or, incorrect details if the death was recorded under a different name, spelling or date.

'They can't find it,' she said in response to Richard's questioning look.

'Bugger.'

'I'm going to visit High House again, talk to Formoy. He forgets, I was working for the Corporation when the fiasco of moving the graves took place. They were working to a tight deadline. I'm pretty sure corners were cut. If we were to insist on an enquiry the Corporation wouldn't come out of it well. I've found a record of the funeral taking place. They'll have to be content with that. Perhaps you should hold off on accepting Fiona's offer?'

He seemed to be giving this some thought, and for a heartbeat Louise was filled with hope. They could get back on track.

'No. I won't mess Fiona around. She's been incredibly generous and forgiving welcoming me back. Why don't you read your aunt's letter and I'll raid the cupboard for tins that might make a half decent meal.' He started to rummage in the cupboard above her head. 'Baked beans. Spaghetti hoops. Spam. Corned beef. And some marrow fat peas. A feast!' He stopped his inventory when Louise didn't respond, and sat back down. 'What is it? Bad news?'

'Yes.' Louise let out her breath. 'It's my mum. She had a fall and is in hospital. Aunt Emma says its nothing serious but they want to keep her in for checks.'

'How long has it been since you last spoke to your mum?'

'Last year, when I found out she'd kept Ma's letters from me.'

'Maybe it's time you forgave her. Go and visit her in London, Lou Lou.' He spoke softly, taking her hand in his.

'Aunt Emma wants me to visit mum in hospital. She's probably fallen out with her again. I suppose I could go. I'm due some leave. But I'll visit High House first.'

'Will you stay in London?'

'Yes. I've got a key to mum's flat.'

'And when you get back? Will you ask Esther and Bill if you can stay with them?'

He wasn't going to give up. 'Okay. But I'll miss you.'

'I'll miss you too but it won't be for long. We can go out on dates. The cinema. I'll take you out to dinner.'

'Maybe.' She was warming to the idea. They had gone from best friends to live-in lovers, missing the usual ritual of dating. 'Okay. But please don't start popping in to Simms Manor for a bath, or meal whilst I'm away. I know Fiona will offer you the comfort of her home, because she's kind and generous.' She gritted her teeth. 'But I wouldn't feel comfortable with that arrangement. Not that I don't trust you one hundred percent but …'

'You know how desirable I am and don't want to put temptation in her way,' Richard laughed.

Louise threw a cushion at him. 'Ha. Ha. If you want a bath, I'm sure Esther and Bill will oblige. They live next door to Fiona, anyway.'

'Okay. Message received. Glad we got that sorted. Now are you ready for a bean and spam hot pot?'

It was eight-thirty in the evening when Louise arrived in London, too late to visit the hospital, and so she took a tube and bus to the housing estate where her mum lived. Tired from the journey and the emotions of that day, she looked out of the bus window: grey buildings, and pavements; the occasional splash of colour – a gold and pink sari, a child's red umbrella. London had been rebuilt since the war, but to Louise it felt as though it was in recovery, the memory of bombed-out buildings still vivid in her mind.

The bus stopped at a parade of shops. Louise peered out of the window. It was getting dark. If these were the shops closest to Wandsworth House, she ought to get off the bus to buy a pint of milk, but she was unsure. Her landmark was a

BP garage on the left a bit further up the road. If she got off now and it wasn't the right parade of shops, she would have to wait for another bus.

'Excuse me,' she said to the man sitting beside her. He mumbled and looked the other way.

The bus was getting busy as passengers crowded the aisle. She made a decision to get off, but before she was on her feet, it pulled away. Louise pushed her way to the exit and watched out for the petrol station. There it was. She rang the bell.

Her mind was turning over the events of that day as she crossed the road and headed for the estate. There had been a moment when she felt Formoy wavering. She'd laid it on thick about the mismanagement of the cemetery relocation project.

Formoy said, 'There were bound to have been a few unavoidable mishaps in managing the relocation of the church in such a short time span. And of course, being one of the project management team you'll know that better than me.' Her heart had lifted with an excited skip. She and Richard would have their happily ever after. When she told him her inheritance had come through, he would give up on the idea of working at Simms. She knew Richard. He was being responsible, making sure they had a steady income. Louise smiled remembering Richard's clumsy declaration, I'm not asking now, because when I do, and I will, I want it to be a romantic, memorable proposal. He loved her.

But then Formoy had shaken his head. 'It's possible that you're correct. However, the facts remain undisputed. Elizabeth Beck's grave was found to be empty. As an abandoned property, Beck's farm belongs to the Corporation. I'm sorry, Mrs Boyd, Louise. I wish I could tell you otherwise.'

How could the grave be empty? There must be a clue somewhere. But now, it was time to make amends with her mum.

There it was, Wandsworth House. Damn it. Why hadn't she walked back to the shop to buy a pint of milk? It was too late. She was tired and couldn't be bothered to retrace her steps.

A pile of mail caught under the door as Louise pushed it open. Mostly bills. She scooped them up before kicking off her shoes. The flat was cosy and welcoming; an oasis in the grey concrete tower. There were three rooms: a living room with kitchen, a bathroom, and a bedroom with floral wallpaper and a candlewick bedspread. Louise's old teddy sat on the pillow. Charlie. She hadn't seen him for years. A little threadbare, the same silky blue ribbon around his neck that, as a child, she had loved to stroke. Charlie had been comforting her mum. Louise held him to her face and breathed in her mum's favourite scent, Coty L'aimant.

She lay on the bed and cast her eyes around the room. A smart dress hung on the outside of the wardrobe as if waiting to be worn. Louise realised she knew very little about her mum's life. Why hadn't she told Louise about her father? It was a topic she had avoided as a child. Apparently, he had disappeared from her mum's life before Louise was born. As a child, Louise had invented stories to fill the gap. He was a sailor from a faraway land. When she was older, she wondered if he was in prison, or the unthinkable––she was conceived through rape. It was a fear that silenced Louise from questioning her mum, and Aunt Emma was quick to shut down any discussion on the topic.

When Louise opened her eyes, she was surprised to find herself lying in the dark, fully clothed, on an unfamiliar bed. A time check told her it was three in the morning, so she changed into her pyjamas and climbed into her mum's bed, feeling like a child seeking comfort. The scent of the sheets, a trace of lavender from the airing cupboard, her mum's washing detergent, and Coty L'aimant, comforted Louise. Tomorrow she would make her peace with Mum.

There was something she had forgotten to do. The thought pulled her back from the brink of sleep. Take a contraceptive pill. Damn. She'd left them in the caravan. Nothing she could do about it now. Maybe take two when she returned home.

12

SUNDAY 19TH JUNE 1966

They had once been close, Louise and her mum. If she hadn't been evacuated to Yorkshire, maybe things would have been different. As she made her way to the trauma and orthopaedic ward, Louise tried to fill her heart with happy memories: feeding ducks at Victoria Park; the little gosling that had prompted a story from her mum of the Ugly Duckling. Louise had made her tell it again and again. Every time she saw a swan after that, she would ask, 'Is that the ugly duckling grown-up?' Mum seeing her off on the train to Yorkshire for the first time. She had clung onto Mum, not wanting to be parted, and her mum had shed a tear. A day at the seaside. Southend. They had paddled in the sea and built a huge sandcastle. Her mum found all the best shells, and they decorated it together. Richard was right. She had left it too long.

'Mrs Pearson is in the single cubicle over there,' a nurse said, pointing the way.

Louise didn't correct her. Pearson was her mum's maiden

name; she had never married. Pearl Pearson had survived a war, managed as a single parent, and lived with the knowledge that her own mother didn't seem to like her very much. She was a warrior. But when Louise stepped into the single room, her mum looked frail, the bed too big for her tiny frame. Hearing the door click, her mum shuffled up the bed.

'Is that you, Louise?' The hope and joy in her voice shamed Louise.

'Yes, Mum. What have you been doing? Falling over so you could get the attention of a handsome doctor?'

'If I'd known falling over would bring you to me, I'd have done it sooner. Come over here, let me take a look at my beautiful girl.'

Louise smiled through tears that blurred her vision. 'I hope you don't mind. I slept in your bed last night. You kept Charlie, my ted.' She sat on the bed and took her mum's good hand in hers.

'I think of him as my Charlie now. So, don't go thinking he'll go back to Yorkshire with you. It was a long way for you to come. If you'd waited a few more days, I could have entertained you in my flat. Made you a nice roast and an apple crumble. You're looking peaky.'

The door opened, and a female doctor entered the room, followed by a gaggle of young medics in short white coats. 'Good morning, Pearl Pearson. I'm Doctor Swithens, Mr Butler, orthopaedic surgeon asked me to visit you. Do you mind if some medical students join us?'

Pearl beamed at the entourage, obviously delighted to be the focus of attention. For a fleeting moment, Louise recognised in her mum the cheeky, flirtatious woman she once was.

'I'm Pearl's daughter, Louise Pearson,' she said. 'When will my mother be discharged from hospital?'

The doctor read her mother's notes and examined her.

When she had completed her assessment, she said, 'We're going to transfer your mother to a medical ward. She fell because she had a TIA, a minor stroke. I'd like to run a few tests, but if all is well, your mother could be discharged home in a few days.'

When they were alone again, Louise poured her mother a glass of orange squash. 'Was that a surprise to you, Mum? Hearing you had a stroke?' It had shocked Louise. Her mum always seemed indestructible.

'No, I'd had a few dizzy spells and my arm went a bit funny before I fell. I knew something wasn't right. Enough about me. Tell me all about your life in Yorkshire. When am I going to meet Dicky?'

'Richard.' Louise laughed. 'I had to stop him from driving me to London just so he could meet you.'

'I'm sorry, darling. I shouldn't have kept his letters from you. Or Mrs Beck's. I hate to admit it but I was jealous. All you talked about after being evacuated was Ma and Pa. I was your Ma. I was afraid she would take you from me and you were all I had.'

Louise leant in and gave her mum an awkward hug, avoiding the plaster cast on her arm. 'It's okay. I was angry but let's put it behind us. If you're staying in a few more days, what do you need me to bring in from home?'

Richard had been right as always. Louise took the bus home, stopping this time to buy sausages and instant mash for tea. On the estate, a couple of lads in parka jackets revved their bikes. She would stay one more night, visit the hospital tomorrow with the toiletries and clothes her mum had requested, then catch a train back to Yorkshire. Esther and Bill were happy for Louise to use their spare room, but she longed to be living with Richard. She didn't care if the roof was leaking, or living without electricity and running water, so long as they were together. Her mum didn't have a telephone, and there wasn't one in their new home, so she would have to find a telephone box tomorrow to call Richard at work. Simms Emporium. Louise shuddered. Bloody Fiona.

Louise found underwear neatly folded in the drawers of her mum's dresser. Slinky slips, rolled-up stockings. She selected a couple of nightdresses, knickers and a bra to take into the hospital the next day. The top drawers contained boxes of jewellery, perfume and make-up. And a box. It had once been a stationery box, notelets and envelopes. Louise remembered the letters her mother had sent when she was evacuated. How she had loved to see an envelope with her mother's writing. She opened the box to find letters. From her – Louise. Her mum had kept them all. Reading them brought back happy memories of her time at Beck's farm. Maybe she had praised Ma and Pa a bit too much and too often. She could understand why this might have made her mum feel insecure living in London during the blitz.

It was getting late, but Louise wasn't sleepy. She'd washed up her tea things, and hoovered the flat. How was Mum going to manage on her own with her arm in plaster? Louise looked around for a suitcase or bag in which to pack her mum's clothes and toiletries. The flat was tiny with not much storage space; just a broom cupboard in the kitchen and another in the wall of the living room. Louise got down on her knees to open the door. It was stuffed full of boxes, thick pen labelling what was inside: Books. Crockery. Toys. And wedged on top of the boxes was a vanity case, big enough to hold the few items Louise had gathered together for Mum.

The labelled boxes must have been packed before Mum moved into the flat, and remained there untouched. I really ought to clear out this cupboard and send anything she doesn't want to a jumble sale, Louise thought, as she pulled out the one marked Toys.

Her puzzle compendium with snakes and ladders, ludo, and draughts. Some wooden doll's house furniture but no doll's house. Did she have one? Louise couldn't remember. A skipping rope. A tin, which she opened. Lead farm animals. Louise smiled. Mum must have saved these old toys, expecting one day to have a grandchild. Louise sighed. She felt guilty depriving Richard and her mum. It's not that she didn't want children. Spending time with Susan's grandchildren when they visited the mobile library was fun, and Richard would make a great dad. Maybe she'd been too hard on her mum. She wasn't that bad a role model. Her mum's mother was another matter. Louise returned the toys to the box.

Books. Louise opened the box, interested to see the books her mum had kept. Maybe there was one she could read on the journey home. Good Housekeeping – a cookery book. Encyclopaedias. A world atlas. Nothing of much interest. Disappointed not to find a novel, Louise flicked through volume one of The Royal Britannica A-D. A folded note fell out. She opened it, curious to glimpse a nugget of social history from her mother's past. A shopping list or notes made from the encyclopaedia? It was a handwritten letter.

My darling daughter,

I hope that one day you will read this. I did not know I had a daughter; if I had, I would have found you sooner. My precious girl, I would give anything to be part of your life. Sadly, I cannot make any demands. I have asked for this letter to be passed on to you when you are old enough to make your own decisions. If, then, you wish to make contact with me, write to me at: Beetabon Ranch, Dubbo, NSW, Australia.

Your loving father.
Blake Sommerfeld

Louise covered her mouth. Shocked. Then, she read it again. *Her father*. It had to be her father; her mum had been brought up by both parents, unlike Louise. Her father and he wanted to be a part of her life. How could her mother have kept this from her? This letter was meant for her, Louise, his precious daughter. She let out a scream of frustration. What was the matter with her mother? Seething with anger, Louise was tempted to go straight back to the hospital to give her mum a piece of her mind. Then, she thought of the man who wrote this letter. There was no date. How long had he waited for her to make contact? He loved her. His precious daughter. The words were a balm to her soul. Keeping her father's letters from her was worse than sending back Ma's. She couldn't forgive Mum this time.

Paper. Envelope. She would write to him straightaway. Louise's heart thumped as she searched through her mother's drawers searching for stationery. She found a gift set of snowdrop notelets with matching envelopes still in the cellophane wrapper and tore it open. There was a fleeting moment of guilt before Louise remembered her mother's treachery. What should she write to her newly found father? The idea overwhelmed her. A father. She knew logically there had to be a biological father somewhere, but in her heart, she had believed herself to be fatherless. What should she call him?

Dear Father, she wrote. Maybe she should have started further down the page. By starting at the top there was too much room to fill, and she didn't know what to say. *I came across your letter today whilst clearing out one of my mother's cupboards. My mother is in hospital, so we have not yet spoken about your letter and why she did not pass it on to me.* Louise paused. She didn't want to betray her mother. Maybe she had her reasons for keeping them apart, but it wasn't something she wanted to dwell on. Whatever the reason, it was between her mother and father. She didn't want anything or anyone to stop her from making contact with this man who thought of her as his precious daughter. All her life she had longed to feel beloved by a father. And she was. She had a father.

I am thirty-four years old. Old enough to make my own decisions. And it is my decision to meet you as soon as possible. It won't be easy with you living so far away, but we will find a way. Please write and tell me all about yourself. Have I got half brothers and sisters? There is so much I want to know... She had almost reached the end of the page and wrote in tiny print to finish. *I'm going to post this letter first thing tomorrow morning, but I will write a longer one soon and enclose some photographs. Perhaps you could do the same? Your loving daughter, Louise.*

Maybe it was too much, but she couldn't cross out the word loving. It would look strange. She considered rewriting the letter but realised she would never be happy with the end result. Best to seal the envelope and post it.

Sleep was impossible as her mind created different images of her father and played out scene after scene of their first meeting. They would meet at the airport in Australia. She would arrive unexpected on his doorstep – a little cabin on a sheep farm. Maybe he owned the sheep farm. He would hotfoot it to Yorkshire on receiving her letter and surprise her. Except she'd given a PO Box number. Her mind scratched out that scenario. Maybe she should have given the address of their new house, or Esther and Bill's. When sleep evaded her, Louise got out of bed and made herself a cup of tea. She read and reread her father's letter until daylight leaked through the venetian blinds of the kitchen.

Too many secrets. But Ma never lied to her, or kept the truth from her. Did she? Could Louise really know Elizabeth Beck when they had only spent a few precious years together? She felt unsettled. Afraid. If nothing was what she believed it to be, how could she build a future for herself, let alone a family? Her foundations were shaky, maybe nonexistent. Ma had always been a positive force in Louise's life, offering stability and unconditional love.

'I've got a dad, Ma.' Louise whispered. 'Oh Ma. Where are you now and who is Miss St. Clair?'

13

APRIL 1915

'You went up in his plane?' Iris gushed in a loud voice to be heard above the machinery.

'How romantic,' Connie sighed. 'Nothing like that ever happens to me.'

'She's had that look on her face for days now,' Rosie said. 'And this is the girl who wasn't interested in romance.'

'What face?' Beth laughed. But she knew. From the day she met Daniel at the airfield, she couldn't stop smiling or dreaming.

'Eyes on your work, ladies.' Hamilton, the floor supervisor, walked along the row behind them.

'What was it like?' Iris hissed under her breath. 'Flying.'

'Breath-taking. Glorious. The freedom. The feeling of being so small and insignificant within the vast sky – and yet part of it all.' Beth sighed, her heart yearning to relive the experience. It was impossible to describe the amazing joy she felt flying free as a bird – hills, valleys, villages and rivers, playthings beneath them. Up there, they were above everything, and a part of everything. Beth tried to convince herself it was the incredible experience of flying that lit her up. That it had nothing to do with Daniel. But the blue of his eyes. The way they crinkled when he smiled, the scent of him – a soapy, masculine smell, mixed with the leather of his jacket and engine oil. She wanted to bury her face in the crook of his neck and drink him in.

'Elizabeth Hardy. Take a break.' Hamilton stood behind her.

Beth was mortified. She'd been caught daydreaming again. If she wasn't careful, she'd be given her cards and sent home. 'I'm sorry, Mr Hamilton. I'll pay better attention.'

Hamilton waved away her apology. 'You're entitled to a break, take it now rather than later.'

The girls closed in covering the space created by Beth's departure. Rosie threw her a questioning look and Beth grimaced her apology.

The fifteen-minute break they usually took together would have been spent in the restaurant drinking a glass of milk. Iris's tales of her big family, five sisters and a little brother, entertaining them all as she smoked her roll-up. Connie was engaged and planned on getting married as soon as the war was over, so conversation would also cover the perfect wedding, and the availability of silks and satins – who could get what and where. Today, Beth was glad to be alone with her thoughts. She stepped out of the building to breathe fresh air.

Daisy had been agitated for days now, pacing up and down her library – Beth had spied her through the open door, jumping when Mrs Kennedy rapped on the back door, or Rosie knocked over the letter tray. She was getting up later, but looked tired with dark circles beneath her eyes. The most animated she had been since the art auction was on Beth's return from her errand.

The Canary Girl's Secret

'Did you hand over the painting?' Daisy had said, pouncing on Beth the second she opened the front door.

'Yes, of course. I wasn't going to lumber back with that monstrosity strapped to my back, it was hard enough one way. I don't know why it couldn't have been delivered in a carriage to the Flying Corps barracks, or wherever he lives. Where does Daniel, I mean Lieutenant Winterton live?'

Daisy had ignored her question. 'What did he say?'

'When? He said lots of things.'

'About the painting? Did he have a message for me? He must have said, something.'

Beth tried to think of something Daniel had said that would appease Daisy, but he hadn't really mentioned her. 'Um, he said thank you.'

If Daisy hadn't been so preoccupied, Beth might have asked her about Daniel. Rosie was of no help. She'd arranged to see Captain Geoffrey Palmer, but it wasn't for weeks, with him being so busy, and Beth wanted more information now. How long was he stationed in Yorkshire? Was he single? Had she imagined an attraction between them or was it one-sided?

Beth had wandered into the field behind the factory. It was good to be outside away from the deafening noise of machines. A cow lowed, and Beth turned to face the dairy. As she did so, a man waved. John Beck. He was walking towards her with another man. Beth waited as they approached. The man accompanying John left him, stalking off to a horse and cart.

'Good afternoon, Miss Hardy. Were you planning to visit me?'

'No, sadly not. I would have enjoyed saying hello to your cows. I'm ashamed to admit I was sent out to take an early break because I was a bit distracted.'

'I won't be so bold as to ask what it was that distracted you.

But I'm grateful as it has given me the opportunity to see you again. Life can become a bit lonely with only cows for company.'

Beth laughed. 'I am sorry to hear that, Mr Beck. Although I would have thought cows the perfect company, they listen without offering judgement, and there's something calming about their presence.'

'Please call me, John. Mr Beck sounds so old. When you get fed up with factory life maybe you could request a transfer to the dairy. You sound as though you were born to be a dairy farmer, like me. Few people really appreciate the beauty of cows. You, Beth Hardy, are a kindred spirit.'

Beth grinned broadly. 'I take that as a huge compliment coming from you. But now, I'd better return for duty or I won't have a job at all. Good afternoon, John. I hope we meet again before too long. Give my kindest regards to your cows.'

John lifted an imaginary hat and bowed graciously. Beth laughed and turned with a wave, feeling refreshed and restored.

The following Sunday, whilst they were seated at the breakfast table, a horn beeped from the street outside. Clara came into the dining room. 'Miss St Clair, there's a gentleman outside.'

Rosie and Beth ran to the window. 'Wow, look at that car,' Rosie said.

But Beth was looking at the driver. He stood alongside the shiny green car, his eyes searching the front of their house as if waiting for someone to come out. Daniel. He was here to see her. Beth gasped. 'Tell him I'll be out in a moment, Clara.'

Daisy joined them at the window. 'What makes you think he's here for you?'

Clara looked uncertainly from one to the other, awaiting an instruction from Daisy.

Could he be here to see Daisy? Beth wondered. She felt a fool; she'd been living in an imaginary world the past week, one where Daniel returned her feelings.

'Okay. What's in the pantry?' Daisy stalked out of the dining room. Clara pattered after her. 'It's okay. I'll manage. Tell Lieutenant Winterton, Beth will be out as soon as I've packed a picnic basket.'

He was there to see her. Beth's heart leapt. Daisy knew all along and had been teasing.

'He's certainly a looker,' Rosie said, peering out of the window. 'Not as handsome as Geoffrey but he'll do. What are you going to wear?'

'I've no time to change. This, I guess. Do I look okay?' She was wearing a navy-blue day dress.

'Grab one of Daisy's hats from the coat stand on your way out. That should do it. You'll need your coat, it's a bit nippy to be having a picnic.'

Clara met Beth at the front door. 'Daisy said, to tell your young man she's packed a loaf of his favourite bread.'

Beth frowned a question at Clara, but Clara just shrugged. 'It's what she said.'

'Okay, thanks. I'd better hurry.'

She took her coat from the coat stand. Bought new by her mother when she left Knaresborough to work as a lady's maid. 'You don't want to be arriving at your new job all covered in soot and grime,' she had said. The coat had served Beth well but was plain and ordinary. So, she followed Rosie's suggestion and grabbed one of Daisy's beautiful hats – a blue cloche with a feather – and rammed it on her head. A quick glance in the mirror. She didn't look too bad, even pretty, with her hair curling about her face.

Daniel straightened up when he saw Beth and glanced nervously at the house. 'Is that the picnic?'

Beth felt awkward. He didn't seem excited to see her. 'Yes. Daisy said she's packed your favourite bread.'

'Oh. Okay,' Daniel said. 'So, I guess, Daisy's not coming out to see me?'

'I'll ask her to...' Feeling awkward, Beth signalled she would return to the house. What was going on between Daisy and Daniel?

'No. No. It's fine. So, um where are we going?' He looked properly at Beth, his eyes meeting hers. And her heart jolted.

Beth took a deep breath to calm herself. 'You mean Daisy hasn't instructed you on the location for this picnic?'

Daniel laughed. 'No. Unless she has. Did she?'

Now Beth was getting exasperated. Somehow, she was caught in a game between Daisy and Daniel that she didn't understand. 'We don't have to go anywhere. Just take your favourite bread, no take all of the bloody picnic and––'

Daniel laughed, then silenced her with a kiss on the mouth. His lips were soft and warm; the scent of him, intoxicating. Her knees wobbled, and she struggled to form words in her head.

'Sorry about that.' He threw a long stare at the windows of Daisy's house before opening the passenger door for Beth. 'I know the perfect spot.'

It was the first time she had been kissed – well, kissed like that. She wanted to be angry. He had taken a liberty. It was improper. Ungentlemanly. But that kiss. Why had he kissed her? He was acting as though nothing had happened.

When her heart stopped somersaulting and her breath was even, she said, 'Just so you know. I'm only interested in you for your plane and now, quite possibly, your beautiful car.'

The Canary Girl's Secret

'Is that right? My kiss did nothing for you?' He raised an eyebrow and laughed.

'No. Not a jot. But how can you compete with the experience of flying? And now this. I'm impressed.'

'Not mine, I'm afraid. But she's a beauty. On loan for the day. A Ford Model T. And now you've kindly reassured me that you have no feelings towards me other than a shared love of adventure, can I take you to one of my favourite beauty spots? It's not far, but spectacular views and an amazing waterfall.'

'It would be a shame to waste a hamper of food. Especially as Daisy has packed, the bread you like.' He didn't respond to this barbed comment. Beth tried another tack. 'What sort of bread? I've only heard of one sort.'

Daniel shrugged. 'The bread you have here in England is different to the one back home.'

Tired of trying to fathom what was going on between Daniel and Daisy, and wondering about that kiss, Beth relaxed into the cushioned leather seat and enjoyed the ride. People turned to admire them as they drove out of Harrogate, and Beth felt like a queen sitting alongside the handsome airman. His broad shoulders and square jaw were those of a man; his soft lips and long eyelashes, boyish. Strong and vulnerable at the same time. Daniel caught Beth staring at him, and she felt the heat rush to her cheeks.

'I've come to love Yorkshire,' he said, as they reached the open road. It was April, and the hedgerows knew it, with hawthorn bushes foaming with white flowers, and buttercups dotted amongst varying shades of green as if added by an artist's brush. 'It's a lot different to Ohio where I grew up.'

'Tell me more about Ohio,' Beth said.

'My great grandfather emigrated to America from France,

my ma's family. They had a smallholding which grew into a farm, just vegetables and apples. By the time my ma was born they were growing tobacco. My pa was learning the trade of a blacksmith when they met. I remember the farm. My grandparents lived in a two-storey log cabin. I spent a lot of time with them growing up.' Daniel seemed far away in his thoughts.

'It sounds idyllic,' Beth said, trying to imagine the wide-open spaces of America she had read about.

'It was.' He sounded sad.

'Tell me about your mum,' Beth said.

'Ah, Ma. She was very French, despite being born in Ohio. That's why I ended up volunteering for the French Air Force.'

'How old were you when she died?'

'Eleven.'

They drove in silence. A horse and carriage passed them on the other side of the road. They hadn't yet seen another car.

Beth berated herself for stirring up painful memories. That was her trouble — curiosity. Some would call her nosy. She had never been great at small talk, preferring meaningful discussion, but as her mother often said, not everyone was comfortable revealing information about themselves. No more questions, she told herself.

Eventually she broke the silence, offering information about herself. 'I have two brothers, Fred and Archie. I'm the youngest. My father works on the railway. Before moving to Harrogate, I was a lady's maid and companion. Before the war someone like me would have no place talking to a gentleman like you.'

'I'm not sure about being a gentleman.'

'No,' Beth said, reliving the kiss. 'But maybe you should be taking Daisy out for the day, rather than me.' There, it was said. Now was the time he should admit his feelings for Daisy. The sole purpose of that kiss was to punish Daisy, Beth was sure of it.

'Why? I don't understand the British obsession with class. If you're happy to be seen out with me, a badly behaved American, then I couldn't give a damn about what anyone else thinks. Now, are you ready to see what this baby can do?' He grinned at Beth. 'Hold on tight.'

Beth squealed as they took off. It was like being in a carriage that was out of control, the horses spooked – only much smoother. She held onto her hat and lifted her face to the breeze.

They had been driving for almost an hour when Daniel said, 'The turn off's along here somewhere. I spotted the waterfall from the air but it took me some time until I found the road. I hope you have suitable walking shoes; it's a bit of a trek but worth it.'

Beth only had two pairs of shoes – her everyday ones and her Sunday best. 'I'm not fussed about mud. These are sturdy enough,' she said.

They walked single file along a narrow track. Branches caught her hair as they stooped through tunnels of hawthorn and brambles. 'There's not many women who would appreciate a walk like this. It's a bit rough.' Daniel sounded uncertain of himself for the first time.

'I'm not any woman,' Beth said.

'So, I'm discovering.' He turned around and offered his hand. 'It's a bit muddy there. If you step onto that log.'

Beth took his hand. The sensation of his skin on hers sent a delicious shiver down her spine. When she was safely on the other side of the log, her hand was still in his. She ought to pull it away, but she couldn't. He looked into her eyes, and Beth knew that she was completely undone. This must be what it is to fall in love, she thought. If there was a way to detach herself emotionally, to hold back, then she would have as her head said, No. But it was too late.

They negotiated a slippery slope, Daniel holding her around the waist until she was on firm ground. 'We follow this river. The waterfall is just around the bend,' he said.

The waterfall was magnificent. A heavy curtain of water fell from a ridge high above. Dappled sunlight transforming the dark green and black of moss and rocks to shimmering rainbows shot with gold. The river gushed from one fall to another as steps of rock carried it forever downward. Beth settled herself on a broad stone and watched, mesmerised. A robin sang. Water gurgled. If only they could stop time.

Daniel sat behind her. 'It's a magical place.'

'It feels as though we've slipped through time. That there is no war,' Beth said, trailing her fingers in the cool water that trickled around her sitting stone.

'This looks like your natural habitat,' Daniel said. Beth felt the warmth of his gaze and turned to face him. He smiled, 'You're a water nymph. At one with nature.'

Beth was glad she had left Daisy's cloche hat in the car. Daniel was right. Here, she felt free and uninhibited. 'Would it be wicked if I removed my stockings to paddle in the water?'

Daniel laughed. 'It would be wicked not to!'

He wandered away from her, and whilst his back was turned, Beth rolled off her stockings, tucking them into her shoes. The earth was gloriously slimy between her toes. With a slip and a slide – an ouch as she tiptoed across a sharp stone – Beth waded in. She gasped as water lapped at her feet.

A dragonfly hovered just above the water. Beth sighed with pleasure. Without thinking, she lifted her arms and released

The Canary Girl's Secret

her hair so that it fell around her shoulders. She turned to see Daniel staring at her, his lips parted.

'I wish I could paint. You are beautiful.'

Beth smiled, aware of his scrutiny as she lifted her skirt and waded further into the water. It was glorious, the water tickling her calves as it cascaded, bubbling and sighing forever onward.

'Daniel?' She pivoted to look at him, almost losing her footing on the slimy stone. But he had disappeared. 'Daniel?'

He burst from behind the trees wearing just his long-johns and with a war-cry ran past her and splashed into the river. 'Woo hoo.'

Beth laughed. He was just like her brothers. It wasn't fair. Why did women have to behave with decorum? Could she? Before she had time to question her own daring, Beth peeled off her dress and threw it onto the bank. The water was freezing, but it felt so good to dip down, submerging her shoulders.

'Atta girl!' Daniel splashed her, and she screamed, splashing him back. He ducked under the water and emerged with his eyes closed, water droplets sprinkling his lashes. When he opened them, Beth felt the shock of his blue eyes. It was as though he could see her soul. He held her gaze for several seconds, and Beth wondered if he was about to kiss her again. As he approached, Beth prepared herself, licking her lips.

'Look,' he whispered.

His bare shoulder brushed against hers as he pointed to a kingfisher perched on a stone. Beth's heart stuttered. The Kingfisher? Daniel's proximity? She turned to say something, and her breast came into contact with his bare chest. Her nipples hardened beneath the wet cloth of her camisole, and she lifted her face, hungry for him. Beth kissed Daniel with a passion. There was no thought about what she was doing or the consequences; her body was making the rules.

His hands threaded through her hair as he held her face. Her fingers traced the contours of his torso. The tiny ridges between his ribs, the rounded swell of his buttocks. He pulled her closer, burying his face in her hair. She could feel his manhood pressing against her groin. She kissed him again, long and deep. This was like nothing she had experienced, and yet it felt right. As natural and inevitable as the river flowing about them.

'No.' Daniel stepped away from her, his hands held up as if in surrender. 'I'm sorry, Beth. I went too far. This shouldn't have happened.'

'You didn't make me do anything. I'm an independent woman.' Beth wanted to hold him. To feel his lips upon hers. To explore the wonder of his body with hands and mouth. She didn't care about convention. But it was too late; Daniel was climbing out of the river. Beth watched him, feeling cold and bereft.

'Shall we see what's in this picnic?' Daniel called from the bank as if they had not just experienced a sexually charged moment.

Beth held her arms across her chest, feeling exposed and a little foolish. He must think her brazen and inappropriate, throwing herself at him like that. She had no experience with men. Somehow, she had to appear cool and unfazed. Inside, she was dying a thousand deaths, mortified by her own behaviour.

As she dressed behind a tree, grateful for her travel coat, which protected her modesty in a way the dress could not, as it clung to her wet torso, Daniel kept up his cheerful banter. 'Daisy has put together a veritable feast. Cold meat. Pigeon? And, of course, a loaf of bread. Hope you don't mind; I've made a start on that. Nothing to drink, I'm afraid.'

Beth crept out from behind the tree, avoiding eye contact.

The Canary Girl's Secret

What must he think of her? It was Daniel's fault kissing her outside Daisy's house. She wanted to go home, to put some distance between them. He looked up and gave a warm smile.

'Come and sit down. Are you cold? There's a blanket in the back of the car. I'll wrap it around you on the drive home.'

Beth settled herself opposite Daniel and the picnic basket. She examined the bread. It looked as though a hungry bear had torn into it.

'Do bears eat bread?' she said.

'Sorry,' Daniel said through a mouthful. 'Did you want some?'

'No. I'm not hungry.'

'I'll peel you a hard-boiled egg.'

Beth watched his fingers as they deftly removed the shell, exposing soft white flesh. A lump formed in her throat; the beauty and emotion too much to hold in her heart. 'I can't bare the fragility of life. This is so perfect.' She gestured to the gurgling stream, the waterfall and the kingfisher who watched them warily from across the bank. 'But we're at war. Tomorrow…'

She didn't get to finish her sentence. Daniel gently turned her face to look at him. 'Don't think about tomorrow. Only now.' His kiss was slow and tender.

This time, Beth pulled away. It wasn't fair; he was playing with her feelings like a cat with a mouse. 'No. You were right. We got carried away. It's the magic of this place.' Tears blurred her vision. She wanted to run.

Daniel caught hold of her wrists but let go as though scorched when Beth glared at him. 'Sorry. Beth, I want the same as you. I didn't expect this. It changes everything. I'll talk to Daisy. I'll find a way.'

'Are you and Daisy? Have you and Daisy?'

'No,' Daniel said. 'Nothing like that. It's complicated.'

'Can we go home now?' Beth said.

'Sure.' Daniel packed away the picnic. He tore apart the remainder of the bread and threw it to the birds.

Don't fall for him. You are an independent woman. You don't need a man. But it was too late; Daniel Winterton had captured her heart.

14

MONDAY, 20TH JUNE 1966

The train was surprisingly busy for mid-morning as it rattled out of London. It was June, and judging by the number of suitcases crammed into the overhead luggage, many would be travelling north for their annual holiday. Louise had settled into an empty compartment, only to be joined by a family of five: mother, father, two boisterous boys and a crying baby. The boys sat alongside her, their parents and baby opposite. And then there was the luggage: three suitcases, the paraphernalia associated with transporting a baby – the pram was, according to the guard, safely stored in the luggage compartment – and two fishing nets, one of which came dangerously close to Louise's eye as the youngest boy kept waving it around.

'Sorry to disturb your peace, luv. This was the only compartment with five seats free and although she's a little'un I need the space to change her nappy.'

Louise would have moved to another compartment if the train had been less busy and it hadn't seemed rude. Instead, she opened her book, The Millstone, by Margaret Drabble. It was of course a library book. One she had been delighted to get her hands on. It was about a single, educated woman who became pregnant but didn't want to lose her independence or give up her baby. Why did women have to choose? Louise thought, gazing out of the window as fields of wheat and barley flashed by. Would she consider having a baby if it didn't mean giving up work? A heavy sigh escaped her. She'd felt terrible leaving her mum's vanity case with one of the nurses. 'I'm sorry but I really can't stop. Please explain to my mother and give her this; a change of clothes, toiletries and a nightdress. No. I don't have a phone number. Best keep her sister, Emma, as next of kin. My aunt will keep me informed.' And that was it. She had left the ward with a heavy heart – weighted with anger, hurt, and regret. It had been a joy spending time with her mother the previous day. But how could she forgive her this time? Did her grandfather know his daughter was pregnant? Louise dreaded to think what her grandmother's response had been. It would have caused a greater rift between mother and daughter. Had her father been married to another woman at the time? The words on the page blurred, as did the images of Margaret Drabble's protagonist, Rosamund, with those of her mother as a young woman.

'I need to go now.' The boy's voice woke her, and the book slipped from her lap.

'Can't you wait until your dad gets back from the buffet carriage?'

'No,' he wailed.

'Well, you'll have to because I can't leave the baby.'

The boy, the youngest, who was sitting next to her, was squirming in his seat.

The Canary Girl's Secret

'I'll watch the baby for you,' Louise said.

'Would you, luv? I won't be long. Why he couldn't go with his dad when he asked him to. Come on then Edward. What about you Harry?'

'Nuh.' Harry had his head in a book.

'Stig of the Dump,' Louise said. 'Good choice.'

The woman placed her swaddled baby in Louise's arms before chasing after Edward, who was already out of the carriage, hopping up and down in discomfort.

The baby opened its eyes. 'Hello little one,' Louise cooed.

The baby's mouth opened and closed as if seeking food, and then a tiny fist escaped the blanket. Louise rocked the warm weight of her in time to the sway of the carriage. But the baby wasn't to be fooled. She opened her lungs and wailed.

'Do you want your bottle, Janey?' Harry put down his book. 'I'll get it out of mum's bag.'

Louise soothed Janey. 'It's coming sweetheart. Your big brother is getting your bottle.'

He passed the bottle to Louise, and she settled Janey in the crook of her arm. In seconds, Janey was feeding contentedly.

'Thank you, Harry. Janey's lucky to have a kind and caring brother. Are you enjoying that book?'

By the time the boy's father returned to the carriage, with sandwiches and bottles of pop, Louise and Harry had discussed Treasure Island, Charlie and the Chocolate Factory, and tiddlers versus frog spawn as the prize catch when fishing with a net. Janey had finished her bottle, and after being burped – Harry instructed Louise on how to do this effectively – had gone back to sleep.

Harry's mother and Edward arrived soon after their father and chaos followed as they settled themselves back down and distributed sandwiches and drinks.

'You must share our lunch,' the mother said, passing Louise an egg and cress sandwich.

Louise accepted and thanked her.

'No, it's you we've got to thank. I can tell you're an experienced mother. How old are your kiddies?'

Louise blushed. 'I don't have any.'

'Then you've worked as a nanny?'

'No.'

'Well, you're a natural. You'll make a great mum.'

It was as if the train journey had been designed to relay a message. First the book, a woman's determination to raise her daughter without losing her right to work – challenging societal norms – and then baby Janey. Louise had to admit holding the baby had released a maternal instinct she didn't know was there. And little Harry was a delight. He reminded her so much of Richard when he was a boy. But The Millstone was fiction. And minding a baby for fifteen minutes wasn't the same as raising a child. First thing, when she got back, was a visit to the caravan to pick up her contraceptive pills. She screwed up her face as she thought back to when she had last taken one. Friday night and it was now Monday morning. Hopefully, missing two days wouldn't matter.

'Come on boys. Tidy up your mess. Next stop is ours,' the father said.

When the train pulled in to Harrogate, Louise was anxious to see Richard. She'd phoned him from a telephone box before getting on the train at Euston and he'd promised to meet her at the station. The news about her father had been delivered in a hurry before the pips went. So, she couldn't wait to tell him everything.

The Canary Girl's Secret

Louise stood outside the station, her eyes scanning the cars coming and going. Richard wasn't going to be happy, when she told him there was another rift between her and her mum. His objections played through her head. Her mother wasn't well and needed the support of her only daughter. She should have discussed the letter with her mum; given her the opportunity to explain why she hadn't passed it on to Louise. He was right. Not that Richard had said any of these things, but he was the voice of reason. 'Come on, Richard,' she muttered. It wasn't like him to be late.

A car beeped. An M G Midget sports car. At first, Louise ignored it, but when it beeped again, she took a closer look. Fiona. What the hell was she doing here? How could he send Ferocious Fiona in his place? Maybe she was here to collect someone else.

'Quick, get in,' Fiona said, when Louise opened the passenger door. 'Throw your bag in the back.'

'Where's Richard?' Scenarios rushed through Louise's mind like a fast film. Big Jim turning up at their caravan. Richard threatening him and then *Bam* Big Jim wiping him out in one blow. No, he wouldn't get his hands dirty. But if Richard seriously pissed him off. 'Where's Richard?' she yelled.

'Just get in. I'll explain on the way.'

Was it always going to be like this? Sharing their lives with Fiona? Richard was spending more time at the shop with Fiona than he was with Louise.

Fiona accelerated away. 'Richard's been taken in for questioning. He's at the police station. He asked me to collect you.'

Louise's heart hammered. Thank God she had come home early. 'Why? What's he done?'

Fiona flashed an accusatory look at Louise that said, how

could you even suggest Richard might commit a criminal act? 'It's about the day of the flood. Richard was the last person to see Eddie Boyd. They want to speak to you too.'

Louise covered her face with her hands. Beyond the grave Eddie was keeping a tight rein on her and with each tug of the leash her life unravelled some more.

15

MONDAY JUNE 20TH 1966

'It was kind of you to collect me from the station,' Louise said, composing herself.

Fiona drove like she lived, focused on where she wanted to be and woe betide anyone who got in her way. A Morris Minor scuttled out of their path into the slow lane. 'Richard asked.'

Okay, thought Louise, she's only doing this for Richard. Fine. 'Well, I appreciate it. When did Richard go to the police station? What exactly happened?'

'About an hour ago I got a phone call from him. Richard said a detective visited him at the house and asked if he would accompany him back to the police station as he had some questions regarding the day of the flood. Of course, I was upset on Richard's behalf, I know how traumatic that day was for him.' Fiona gave Louise a sideways look which she couldn't interpret. Was she suggesting Louise was the cause of Richard's trauma?

Fiona drove close to the car in front until it indicated and moved over. 'I asked if I could do anything for him. If he wanted me to sit with him. He asked me to meet your train from Harrogate station and take you back to Esther and Bill's house. Is that okay with you?'

'Yes. Thank you,' Louise said. 'Do you think they'll keep him in for long? Why do they want to question him?' *Had they found the shovel?*

'I wish I knew. I'm as worried as you are. Richard wouldn't do anything unlawful. He's the kindest, most honest person I know. I thought you might know what it was all about. You were there, the day Richard nearly drowned in the flood.' She didn't say the day Eddie died, but Louise knew that was what she meant.

'Maybe we should go to the police station,' Louise said.

'I don't think Richard would want that. Besides, you may want a bit of time to prepare yourself before you're called in for questioning.'

Louise's stomach lurched. How could she prepare? She'd tried to destroy evidence. There was no talking her way out of that. Please, God, don't let them find out.

Bill's car wasn't in the drive, and the door to the cottage opened before Louise had a chance to knock or use her key.

'Louise. Come in. make yourself at home. Hi Fiona,' Esther said, as Fiona followed, carrying Louise's overnight bag, which she had forgotten was in the back seat of Fiona's car. 'Lovely to see you, Fiona. Bill's at work so we can have a girl chat. You'd think being neighbours we'd see more of each other.'

The women followed Esther into the kitchen, where a Golden Retriever greeted them, pushing himself against Louise's legs. She made a fuss of him, stroking his ears.

'Sit Bouncer. Tea or wine?' Esther said.

'Better make it tea in case we need to drive anywhere, although I think I need a brandy,' Fiona said.

'Why? What's happened?' Esther looked from Fiona to Louise. 'You're both white as a sheet. Did something happen on the road? Where's Richard? I thought he was collecting you from the station, Louise.'

As a compromise, Louise and Fiona had a nip of whisky with their tea. Fiona waited for Louise to tell Esther what had happened.

'I thought it was accident by misadventure. An accident,' Esther said.

'Well, that's what we believe but there still has to be a post mortem. I was originally told the inquiry was of public interest because Eddie drowned when the reservoir was being flooded. Then Bill told Richard there was a police investigation regarding cause of death.' Louise had screwed the edge of Esther's tablecloth into a tight ball.

Esther stroked Louise's hand. 'Sorry,' Louise said, releasing the cloth.

'That might be all it is', Esther said. 'A formality. They have to be thorough and you and Richard were with Eddie at the end, just before he fell in.'

'There was a fight. Richard was protecting me,' Louise said.

'What are you saying?' Fiona barked. She glared at Louise as though she had just accused Richard of murder.

'I'm just stating fact. Eddie was fine when Richard last saw him. The mudslide put an end to their fight. I told the police at the time. Neither of us have anything to hide.'

Esther's hand covered Louise's. 'Then you have nothing to fear.'

If only that were true. There was a knock at the door. 'I'll go,' Fiona said.

Louise heard Richard's voice. It was upbeat, but she could detect an uneasiness. If only they could be alone; she couldn't talk to Richard properly in front of Fiona. Now that they had decided to move out of their caravan, life was going to be like this — snatched moments in public places, their interactions observed as if they were on a stage. As children, they could hide from the world in their secret valley – the deserted village. Now, Fiona spent more time with Richard than she did. Esther caught Louise's eye and gave a reassuring nod.

When they had greeted Richard and listened to his account of what happened in the police station – just a routine enquiry, he explained – Esther said, 'Louise you'll want to freshen up after your journey from London and I'm sure you and Richard will want some time alone. Why don't you take your things upstairs? Fiona, fancy a canter across the moors?'

Alone at last, Louise hugged Richard. 'I was so frightened. Why did they want to question you? You gave a statement at the time.'

He slumped into a chair and raked a hand through his hair. 'It's turned into a murder investigation.' Bouncer turned in a circle and whined. Richard stroked him, and he settled at his feet.

'Why? You didn't. He didn't.' Her mouth was dry.

'I told them everything I knew. You and I left the farmhouse together. They asked me what we were doing there and I explained about you reading a letter from Elizabeth Beck that said her will was under the floorboards and she had left everything to you. And, like me, they wondered why you hadn't waited until after the trial flood, especially given the storm that day.' Richard held up his hands and shrugged.

'I know. I probably should have waited but I was afraid it might be lost to me forever. What else did they say?' Louise asked.

'How I knew where to find you. I said, Peggy at High

House told me. You asked Peggy to let Pete Murray and Sean Fitzpatrick know where you were, in case they needed you.'

'Yes, I was meant to be arranging a press conference. But with the storm and mud slide...' Louise trailed off as she remembered that day. Pete had made it clear that he, on behalf of Big Jim, was keeping a close eye on her.

'Pete Murray,' Richard said. 'The Pete you worked with? Is that the Pete you mentioned the other day?' Louise held her breath as she watched the cogs turn in Richard's head.

He took a breath and continued. 'Anyway, I told them we were trying to reach the lane where my land rover was parked but with the mud slide it was a struggle. I'd pulled you up on to solid ground. Eddie was waiting for us. He told you to get in the car. When you refused, he took hold of your hair and tried to drag you. So, I punched him on the jaw. His left side. My knuckles bled; I showed the police when they took my first statement. He punched me hard in my solar plexus. I was doubled over when I heard you scream. When we realised, you'd been swept away, we stopped fighting. All I could think about was rescuing you. I ran to my car to get help. Thank God, I saw a policeman on a motor bike further along the road. He alerted the rescue service. I didn't bother reporting Eddie; he could look after himself and had a car.'

'So, you just told them what they already knew? Did they ask anything else?'

'Did I go back to the farmhouse? Did I see where Eddie went after I left him? Did I notice his car on the road following me?'

'And did you?'

'No. You know I didn't. Until I knew you were safe, I wasn't interested in anyone else. I should have jumped in to the reservoir to rescue you.'

Louise shook her head. 'I'm glad you didn't. I'm a stronger swimmer than you. Do you think that's the end of it?'

Richard sighed. 'I don't know. They didn't say why it was a murder investigation. I'm sorry I couldn't collect you from the station. I've been desperate to hear about this letter. What did your mum say when you told her?'

Louise couldn't tell Richard she'd abandoned her mother, again. She let out her breath. 'To think my dad's been waiting to hear from me all this time. I've sent him a letter. If he didn't live on the other side of the world, I would have gone straight to him. What if I'm too late? He could have moved or died. Oh God, Richard. I couldn't bear it, to almost find him and then lose him again.'

Richard put his hands on her shoulders, and Louise felt the ground firm beneath her feet. 'Slow down, Lou Lou. Why didn't your mum pass on his letter?'

'I don't know. I haven't asked her. I can't forgive her this time.'

He held up his hands. 'You've got to find out. There might be a very good reason and now you've invited him into your life without knowing anything about him or his past. I love your courage and passion, Lou Lou, but your impulsive – act before you think – nature has got you into trouble before. What did your mum tell you about him?'

Louise hung her head. 'I left this morning without seeing her.'

Richard shook his head. 'And you've already posted the letter?'

She nodded. Suddenly, she felt incredibly tired. 'I'm sorry about my inheritance, Richard. I really hoped Formoy would accept it was mismanagement. How can her grave be empty?'

'I don't know, Lou Lou. She rose from the dead, like Jesus?'

The Canary Girl's Secret

His half-hearted attempt to make her laugh fell flat. He sighed. 'I'm starving. Shall we eat at The Coach and Horses?'

'Do you mind if I have a bath first?' She needed to be alone with her thoughts, and her body felt too weary to do anything but lie down, preferably in warm water.

As she submerged her shoulders beneath the bubbles, Louise heard Bill's key in the door. Then his voice and Richard's. She closed her eyes. The police asked Richard whether he had returned to the farmhouse. Had they found the shovel? Why would Eddie go down there, anyway? It had been treacherous; the mudslide uprooting trees. Keep calm, she told herself. It was a routine enquiry, nothing to stress about. Was she too impulsive, writing to her father before giving it any thought? Yes. It had always been her downfall. In a way, it didn't matter what he had done. She would give him the chance to explain himself. Her mum would only give one side of the story, and he was her father. She repeated the words in her head like a mantra. My father. My father. I've got a daddy. And she felt as though she were eight years old.

The clinking of glasses downstairs. Bill and Richard would be drinking Bill's best malt whisky. She climbed out of the bath and towelled herself dry. Bless Esther for giving her some time alone with Richard. Maybe living here wouldn't be so bad. They would find time to be together. And she could assist Esther in the weeks leading up to the birth of their baby – her godchild. Today she had successfully soothed and fed a baby, so maybe she wouldn't be an entirely useless godmother.

As she dressed and brushed her hair, she imagined Ma looking over her shoulder. 'That's my girl,' she would say. 'Things may look dark but everything will work out for the best.'

But will they, Ma? Did everything work out for you?

16

APRIL 1915

Beth peeled off her wet clothes. There was no hot water, Clara finished early on a Sunday, and Beth was reluctant to visit the scullery as she was avoiding Daisy. Her landlady must have been waiting for her return as she pounced on Beth the moment she arrived home.

'How was Daniel?' she had said, her eyes wide.

Beth didn't want to talk about Daniel to Daisy. 'Fine,' she said, busying herself with removing her wet shoes and returning Daisy's hat to the stand.

'Did he give you a message for me? Maybe he told you to say something, specific?'

'No,' Beth spoke abruptly.

'Did you tell him I packed his favourite bread?'

'Yes.' Beth glared at Daisy. 'We had a wonderful time. Thank you for the picnic.'

'Oh no. Please don't tell me you've succumbed to Lieutenant Winterton's charms? I thought you were immune. A strong, intelligent woman.'

Beth looked directly at Daisy, expecting to see anger, but

her eyes were full of compassion. 'So did I. But it seems I'm not. I love him, Daisy.'

'No. You can't.' Daisy threw up her hands and paced the hallway. 'Oh, Beth. What have I done, introducing you to this man?'

'I don't know what has gone on between the two of you, Daniel wouldn't say, but he feels the same way as me. We're in love. The timing's not ideal but after the war.'

'Did he say that? Did he give you hope that you would have a future together?' Now Daisy was angry.

'Yes. He said, he wanted the same as me.' Then Daniel's words came back to her. 'He said, he would speak to you that he would find a way.' Had he said that? It was an odd thing to say unless Daisy and Daniel were betrothed. That was it – they had been promised to one another, an agreement made by their parents when they were born. Maybe Daisy's inheritance depended on this union. But Daisy and Daniel weren't in love. They were. Beth and Daniel.

'That was his message? He said, he would speak to me and find a way?' Daisy bit her lip and looked past Beth, narrowing her eyes.

She nodded and hurried up the stairs before Daisy questioned why she was still wearing her coat.

Beth had removed her outer garments when there was a gentle knocking on her bedroom door. 'Beth. Can I come in?' It was Rosie. She threw on a robe and opened the door.

Downstairs, Daisy was in full flow, the music loud and haunting.

'What did you do to inspire a rendition of Totentunz?' Rosie said as she entered the room. 'Liszt. The Dance of Death. Last time she played it was the day she had a set to with old Issac, the rag and bone man, in the street. It was a proper shindy. Caught him beating his horse with a whip.

Police didn't want to know, but Daisy was wild. I thought she was going to break her piano the way she thumped those piano keys.'

As if in answer, Daisy's rendition grew in intensity. The two girls froze. Then it ebbed to a slower tempo, and they laughed, letting go of their breath.

'Why's your hair wet?' Rosie said as Beth towelled it dry.

Beth sank onto the bed with a heavy sigh. 'It was a perfect day.'

'Where did he take you? Somewhere fancy, I hope. Did it rain?' Rosie looked out of the window. 'I can't see no puddles here.'

'A waterfall. It was incredible. A hidden paradise.' Beth hugged her secret to her, unwilling to share anything of their time together. It felt sacred. Intimate.

'Geoffrey didn't tell me Daniel had a car. Would he take me and Geoffrey to this waterfall? We could go together. Prepare a hamper of food.'

Beth smiled at her friend's happiness and enthusiasm. 'Maybe. But it's not his car. Just one he had on loan for the day. Is it wrong to feel so gloriously blissful when we're at war?'

Rosie curled up on the bed alongside Beth, resting her head on her shoulder. 'Last I heard, joy wasn't rationed. We're doing our bit for the war, working bloody hard. So, I reckon we're allowed a bit of fun too. I knew Daniel Winterton was taken with you. He must like you a lot borrowing a car to take you out for the day. It's so romantic. Tell me everything. Did he take you somewhere fancy for lunch?'

'No. Just the waterfall. But something's not right. There's something he's not telling me.'

'Do you think he's got a wife, back home in America?'

'Maybe. But probably not. I think it more likely he's

involved with Daisy in some way. Something's going on between the two of them that they're not telling me.'

'Listen.' Rosie froze. The piano was silent. The front door opened and then closed.

'Has she gone out?' Beth said.

Rosie got up to look. 'No. There's a boy on a bike leaving. Expect he's delivered a message or a telegram.'

'I hope it's not bad news. If anything else upsets Daisy we'll have to contend with her playing the Dance of Death for the rest of the day,' Beth said.

Rosie laughed. 'You'd best get out of those wet clothes before you catch a chill. I'll go down and see what Mrs K has left us for supper.'

Alone in her room, Beth took her time undressing. Her body felt different, as if something inside her had been given life, unfurling, expanding. She brushed a hand over her nipple and closed her eyes, remembering. He said she was like a water nymph. Beth lifted her hair from her neck and gazed at her reflection in the looking glass above the washstand. She stood on tiptoe, trying to see her body, her breasts, but it was hopeless. So, she closed her eyes and ran her hands over her body, imagining they were Daniel's. Silky smooth skin. Breast. Stomach. Inner thigh. His body, in contrast with hers, was taut. Hard. How was she going to free her mind of him?

A knocking on her bedroom door. 'I'm still getting dressed Rosie. I'll be down in a mo.'

Daisy poked her head around the door. 'Could I see you in the library, darling?'

Beth sighed. Maybe it was just as well to have things out. Let Daisy tell her about this betrothal or whatever it was. 'Okay. As soon as I'm dressed,' she said.

. . .

The Canary Girl's Secret

When Beth knocked on the library door, half-an-hour later, Daisy wasn't there, so she sat in a chair opposite Daisy's writing desk to await her return. The grandfather clock ticked. Voices from the back of the house – Rosie and Daisy. Beth yawned. She wriggled in her seat to stay awake. A nap was needed on Sundays to make-up for lack of sleep during the week. As she fidgeted, Beth noticed a sheet of lilac paper peeking from beneath a book of poetry. Camille's note to Daisy? Beth slanted her head to try to read the elaborate scroll. It looked as though there was one line. She could make out *give* and *me*. Beth leant over the desk and slid the note out. Just two words. *Forgive me.*

Daisy opened the door, making Beth jump. It was too late to hide the revealed note.

'I'm sorry, Daisy.' Beth jumped to her feet.

'It's okay, darling. I got detained by the question of supper. Apparently, the pigeon I supplied for your picnic was intended for this evening. So, we'll have to make do with the remains of yesterday's potato and egg pie. Beth. Sit down, darling.' There was something in her tone that alarmed Beth.

'What is it, Daisy? You're scaring me.'

'A telegram came for you.' Daisy opened a drawer in her desk and handed her a yellow envelope.

It was addressed to Elizabeth Hardy. She felt the blood drain from her head.

Fred and Archie both dead. Come home at once.

Her throat was dry. 'No. No. It's not possible.'

The room came in and out of focus. Daisy was talking. A glass of water was held to her lips. Beth tried to swallow, but it was impossible, and the water came back as she choked. A keening wail came from somewhere.

She was lying on a couch, her legs raised on a cushion. 'No,

I've got to get up. Go home. They need me. My brothers.' She was the little sister. One of three. They were a family.

'Not now, darling; you need to rest. Here, take this sedative.'

She was too weak and tired to resist. 'When? When did they die?' Her brothers were dead, and she had been kissing Daniel Winterton.

17

BETH, MAY 1915

Beth had stayed in Knaresborough with her parents for four days. Long enough to attend church with them on the Sunday, when the names of Private Fred Hardy and Private Archie Hardy were called out as part of the weekly roll call of local lads killed in action. So many young men, one of them sixteen years old – Charlie Cartwright, Beth knew his sister – dead. A waste of life. Fred and Archie had gone to war as though off on a Boy's Own adventure. Fictional heroes. She hadn't seen them since the day they left, full of bravado. The bedroom her brothers shared still held the scent of them: hair oil, sweat, cigarettes, and comics. Beth had sometimes sneaked into their bedroom when she lived at home, and sat on the floor between their beds listening to them chortling as they read their collection of illustrated weeklies: The Comic Cut, and The Chips. The sacred piles of comic papers still stashed beneath their beds, along with an empty crumb-lined tin once used for midnight snacks. Beth buried her head in Archie's favourite bear, Mr Snuggles. But she couldn't cry. To cry would make it true, and without a funeral, or a body, it didn't feel real. Beth couldn't make sense of what had happened. Her brothers were full of life. Too young to die. They just had to make it through this atrocious war, and everything would go back to normal. Deep down, she knew it was a lie, but the reality was too painful. Her mum and dad put on a brave face, accepting all the words of condolence at the church service with dignity. They weren't the only family to have lost brothers and sons fighting for the realm.

It had been a relief to leave the little cottage in Knaresborough and return to Harrogate. Her important work in the munitions factory was a good excuse to cut short her stay. There was nothing she could do to ease her parents' pain.

Daisy urged Beth to stay away from work so that she could recover from the shock, but her advice, as always, fell on deaf ears. At least in the factory, Beth had Rosie, Connie and Iris to distract her. That morning, they were sharing their break in the canteen.

'When Harry's next on leave I'm not going to hold back,' Connie said, her eyes flashing with the audacity of her statement; a grin, as if imagining the pleasure.

'What? Make love?' Beth said.

All three of them laughed at her.

'You make it sound as though you've not done it before, Connie Drinkwater,' Elsie said.

'We was going to wait until after we was wed, but I don't see the point. I love him, and if it weren't for the war we'd already be married. The worst that could happen is I'll get pregnant and to be honest I'd be happy with that. He's the only man I'll ever love and if I lose him at least I'll have his child.'

They sat in silence. The mood now sombre. Rosie squeezed Beth's hand. Connie noticed and put her arm around Beth. 'I didn't mean to upset you, Beth.'

'It's okay. I know I should be proud of my brothers dying in action, but I'm just angry with them for going to war. It's not like they had a choice, but when they left, it was as if they were going on holiday. They didn't prepare me for this. We didn't say goodbye properly.' Fred had ruffled her hair. Archie a playful punch on the arm, they'd been bickering over something trivial – who had used up the last of the week's sweet ration or something. 'They were meant to be at my wedding. Uncles to my children. To share the care of our parents when they get old.' It wasn't fair. She felt angry and cheated. Then the tears came, and with them great sobs.

The girls enclosed her in a group hug. When Beth felt restored, she wriggled free. 'Thank you. And I agree, Connie. Give it your all! Break the springs on his bloody mattress.'

'Beth Hardy!' Rosie squealed.

The girls roared with laughter. It was a relief to release some of the pent-up tension Beth had experienced since hearing the news.

'Hold on. Beth Hardy. What do you mean – be at my wedding? I thought you planned on staying single,' Elsie said.

All eyes were on her.

'Maybe I changed my mind.' Beth grinned. 'I might even practice a bit of mattress bouncing myself at the next opportunity.'

This had the girls in hysterics. They thought she was joking, but there was an element of truth. Life felt tenuous. Anything could happen. Only now counted because who knew how many nows they would have.

A week later, Beth was enjoying a lie-in. She'd woken at the usual unearthly hour and snuggled under the bedcovers as she heard Rosie creeping across the landing outside her door.

Hamilton had asked one of them to cover the evening shift, and Beth picked the short straw. It would mean an evening followed by a morning shift, so she was going to make the most of lying in bed – all day if she chose.

She stirred when the stairs creaked, Clara delivering hot water to Daisy's room. Then, she drifted back into a long, deep sleep. Daniel was giving her a flying lesson. Below them, fields of corn, a fairytale castle high on a hill. The plane became a flying horse, and she was clinging to Daniel's back as they swooped over their kingdom. A man was shouting. He waved his arms at them. A woman's voice. Loud and angry. Beth tightened her grip on Daniel. She was in freefall, headed for the earth, where the fields were now ablaze.

A door slammed, and Beth woke-up with a start. Her mouth and throat were dry. She dressed quickly, guessing it must be mid-morning. Daisy and Clara didn't know she was home, but if she was quick, then she might be in time for breakfast. Maybe even a hot chocolate for a treat, she knew Daisy favoured these during the week.

Excited to surprise them, Beth hurried downstairs. The library door slammed. She stood still to listen. Clara was upstairs; Beth could hear her humming to herself and the rhythmic swish of a broom. It must be later than she thought. A man's voice.

'I can't. Not now,' he shouted.

'It's non-negotiable. You know that,' Daisy boomed.

Beth shivered as she remembered falling through the sky, certain she would die in the fire below. These were the voices that woke her. And then she had a sickening feeling. She recognised his voice. Daniel.

Beth didn't knock. Whatever it was that made Daniel beholden to Daisy, she was going to find out. They jumped as

The Canary Girl's Secret

if ready for action when Beth burst through the door. Daisy brandished a letter knife, and Daniel clasped a paperweight.

'Whoa. I come in peace,' Beth said.

Daisy let out her breath and slumped back into her chair. 'Sorry, darling. I thought you were an intruder. What are you doing home?'

Beth studied the expressions fleeting across Daniel's face. Surprise. Guilt? Discomfort. He didn't look pleased to see her. 'I'm on the evening shift,' Beth said.

'Beth. I am so sorry for your loss. Please accept my deep condolences,' Daniel said, extending a hand. 'I would have come sooner but it wasn't possible.'

'Have you had breakfast, darling?' Daisy said, her composure complete.

'No. I was about to but I heard voices.' She couldn't confront them.

'Lieutenant Winterton kindly called on me to deliver a letter of thanks from Captain Palmer and the Flying Corps for our generous donation,' Daisy said as she stood up.

'And to leave a message of condolence for you, Beth. It's an unexpected pleasure that I can do so in person.'

'I'll leave you two whilst I rescue what's left of breakfast for Beth. Daniel.' She gave him a meaningful stare. 'You know what you've got to do.'

When the door closed behind Daisy, Beth tried to compose herself. He was dressed in uniform and looked breathtakingly gorgeous. Those eyes. His lips.

'Come here,' he said, opening his arms to her.

She wanted to be aloof, to demand an explanation, but the temptation was too great. Beth allowed herself to be enfolded. It was what she needed; to be wrapped in his arms. Warm. Comforted. And relieved. 'Oh, Daniel,' she sighed. 'It's all so terrible. I can't believe they're dead.'

'Hush.' He kissed her hair and rubbed her back. 'I thought you would be at work. I'm a coward. It's not that I didn't want to see you. I've thought of nothing but you since the day we spent at the waterfall. But, Daisy's right.'

Beth pulled away from him. 'What did she say? I heard you arguing. Was it about you and me?'

'Yes. No. Kind-of.' Daniel rubbed his face. 'We shouldn't have happened. You and me.'

'Why? It makes more sense to me than anything else in my life. I didn't believe in love and marriage. I thought it was make-believe until I met you,' Beth said.

'Oh Beth. If we weren't at war. If I'd met you a few years ago. If———'

She kissed him, and when she released him said, 'It's because we're at war that we have to grab our happiness whilst we can. I have nothing to do all day. Let's run away. Unless you have to do army things?'

'Army things?' Daniel grinned. 'You mean fight this bleedin' war?' He mimicked a Cockney accent. 'It just so happens I have the use of a car. At some point today I've an errand to run, a man I've got to meet but I could sneak out for a while.'

'Then let's go now, before you change your mind or Daisy stops us,' Beth said, pulling him by the hand.

They drove in silence. Every few seconds, Daniel looked at her as though committing her to memory. She squeezed his free hand in hers.

'Where are we going?' she said.

'Knaresborough? I want to see where you grew up. I want to know everything about you. We can just drive around the area. We won't disturb your parents. Your pa might not approve of you dating an American.'

Beth sat back and enjoyed the ride. As they left the town

behind them, theirs was the only car on the road. Horse and carts from the farms, a carriage or two, and the occasional horse rider shared the roads with them. Daniel's Ford Model T attracted a lot of attention, and Beth was proud to be his passenger.

As they approached Knaresborough, Beth became nervous. Friends and neighbours would notice the car and Beth sitting alongside the handsome driver. Word would get back to her parents, and they would be hurt that they hadn't stopped for a visit. But it wouldn't be fair to surprise them. Her mum would be mortified if Daniel met them when she had no notice to prepare for visitors. Beth explained this to Daniel.

'Maybe don't drive through the high street. Just stick to the surrounding area. If all goes well you can meet my family - my parents,' Beth corrected herself. It didn't seem right referring to her family when it was just her, and Mum and Dad. Maybe coming back wasn't such a good idea. She sighed. 'After the war.'

Daniel glanced at her. He nodded. 'Sorry. I should have thought it through.' He drove past a turnoff signposted Knaresborough. 'Okay. Let's go on a mystery tour.'

Beth enjoyed pointing out landmarks to Daniel. The spot her family chose for the occasional picnic on days out, the blacksmith frequented by villagers for miles around because it was the best in the area, she told him about the pedlar who walked from village to village selling his wares.

They had left Knaresborough behind them. Although Beth was happy to spend hours on the road just being with Daniel, she was thirsty and hungry. Her stomach rumbled, giving her away.

'Message received. Next stop, lunch,' Daniel said. A road sign told them they were in Thorncrest. 'Keep your eyes peeled for an inn.'

'This is the village that's going to be flooded for a reservoir,' Louise said. The tragedy of losing Thorncrest, and the effect the Bill of Parliament had on people living and working in the valley, was a popular topic of conversation for miles around. 'The war delayed plans, but lots of people have already moved out. 'Oh, look. Beck's farm. I wonder if that's the farm belonging to the family of my friend John Beck. He works on the dairy farm at the factory.'

'Have I got competition?' Daniel said, slowing down the car so Beth could take a closer look.

'No. Maybe from the cows. They have beautiful eyes. I'd love to work in the dairy rather than the factory floor. But I would miss my friends, Rosie, Elsie and Connie.'

'How about here?' Daniel drew up outside a pub. The Coach and Horses.

Lieutenant Daniel and Beth were treated like celebrities. The landlord insisted they sit close to the fire and, despite the scarcity of good food, got the kitchen to prepare a platter of boiled beef and vegetables, followed by apple pudding.

'How is the reservoir going to affect people living in these parts?' Daniel said, when the landlord sat down with them.

'Not many folk living in the valley, nowadays. The mill closed down years ago. It's worth a look, the deserted village they calls it on account of so many cottages being uninhabited.'

Daniel was fascinated, and so after thanking the landlord for his hospitality and insisting on paying for their meal – he wanted them to be his guests as a thank you to the Royal Flying Corps, but Daniel wouldn't hear of it – they drove down into the valley. Beth had visited several times when living at home. One of the children at school, Mary Button lived there, and Beth had stayed over. Mary and her brother Simon had shown Beth into an abandoned cottage and played

The Canary Girl's Secret

with her in the ruins of the mill. Beth regaled Daniel with stories of her childhood as she led him over the packhorse bridge into the pretty village with the stream running through it and blackened stone cottages. Gardens, once neatly kept, were overrun with May flowers: bright red poppies, and cornflowers mixed in with cow-parsley; bluebells, and hollyhocks triumphing over the weeds. Beth sighed with delight.

'I wonder if Mary Button still lives here.'

Daniel was fascinated by the village. He asked questions Beth couldn't answer. When would the valley be flooded? How many people still lived in the village? What did the mill produce?

They held hands as they picked their way across the ruins of the mill. Daniel seated himself on a broken wall, and Beth settled beside him.

'It's kind of sad, seeing cottages empty and gardens overgrown,' he said. 'It would have been a beautiful place to live. I wish I could show you where I grew up, in Ohio.'

'Maybe you can. One day. When the war's over,' Beth said. 'I'm counting on you taking me flying in your bi-plane.'

'I will,' Daniel said. His face lit up as if realising for the first time, this could be a reality. 'Why not? To hell with them. We should be together. Nothing's going to stop me, Beth Hardy. Now I've met you, everything's changed.'

'There. You see. Anything is possible,' Beth said.

They kissed for the second time that day. A slow, lingering kiss that ignited each of her nerve endings, opening her like a flower to the sun. They paused, and Daniel cupped her face in the palm of his hand. If she were an artist she would use the same paint for the cornflowers, the bluebells, and Daniel's eyes. The palest pink for his lips and the petal tips of the daisy.

'I wish we could freeze time. Stay here. Right now. Forever,' she said.

'I love you, Beth. I've never felt like this about anyone before. I can't let you go. I won't.'

'I love you too, Daniel. I love you with all my heart. I love you so much, it hurts. Right here.' She took his hand and held it to her breast, where the thought of losing him was already causing a physical pain. 'I've lost so much. I couldn't bear to lose you too.'

'You won't,' he whispered. 'I promise.'

A raindrop fell on Beth's head. And another. Big, fat raindrops. She laughed. 'Time to leave.'

Thunder rolled, and the heavens opened. Beth shrieked, and Daniel held her hand. They scrambled up the little lane to where their car was parked.

'Damn. I should have covered the car,' Daniel said.

They worked together, struggling against the wind and rain to fasten the fabric roof. Beth's hair had come loose. Her travelling coat and dress were soaked. 'We seem to be making a habit of getting wet,' she laughed, when they were safely inside under cover.

'It suits you,' Daniel said with a wistful look on his face.

Beth checked her appearance and blushed when she realised that her clothes were clinging to her body. Daniel removed his jacket and draped it across her shoulders. She watched a droplet of water trickle down his neck and clavicle. Her lips parted as she followed its journey. His eyes met hers, and she wondered if he could read her mind. The passion in his kiss suggested he had been having similar thoughts.

'I'd better drive you home before I get carried away,' he said.

The engine started after several failed attempts, and they pulled out onto the partly flooded road. Water was seeping through the roof. It was hard to see out of the windshield. Beth kept quiet so Daniel could concentrate. She reminded

The Canary Girl's Secret

herself that he was a skilled pilot, so driving a car was child's play for him, whatever the weather conditions. They had been driving for ten minutes when the car came to an abrupt stop.

'Oh, no. I should have checked the petrol gauge,' Daniel said.

Beth sat patiently waiting for the car to start. When she realised that they weren't going anywhere, she frowned at Daniel. 'Is there a problem?'

''fraid so. Petrol's in short supply with the war. I didn't check how much was in the tank. And…' He shrugged his shoulders, holding up his hands. 'We're flat out. I doubt there's anywhere around here where I can buy petrol. I'll go and get help.' He looked as though he were going to climb out of the car.

'How? Where? It's tipping it down out there. In here a bit too,' Beth laughed.

Daniel sighed. 'I'm sorry, Beth.'

'The Coach and Horses isn't far. Let's make a run for it. At least there's a roaring fire and the landlord took a shine to you. I'm sure he'll help us if he can.'

Twenty minutes later, Beth and Daniel were back by the fire in the Coach and Horses.

'You'll not get anywhere tonight,' the landlord said. 'No carriages passing through here until tomorrow. I don't know where you can buy petrol in these parts. It was hard enough before the war but you haven't got a hope now. Has he Jack?'

An old boy on the other side of the pub looked up from smoking his pipe. 'Don't know anyone who has a use for it round here. You don't get that problem with a horse and cart. That there motoring fad won't catch on.'

'Sorry, Lieutenant Winterton. You and your missus want a room for the night?'

The landlord arranged for a fire to be lit in their room and a bathing tub filled with hot water.

'You'll want to get out of those wet clothes,' he said. 'I'll send up some soup and bread for your supper and a jug of ale. A carriage passes through here around eleven tomorrow headed for Leeds.'

When he left them to make arrangements, Daniel spoke softly in Beth's ear. 'He thinks we're married. I'll tell him we can't share a room.'

'No. It would be wasteful to light a fire in two rooms and we'll want to eat together.'

'I'll sleep in an armchair or something.'

The pub was quiet on account of the weather, and so there was nobody there who might recognise her. She used the landlord's phone to contact the munitions factory, explaining she couldn't get in to work until the following day.

'All ready for you Lieutenant and Mrs Winterton.'

Beth liked the sound of Mrs Winterton. They took the creaky stairs up to their room, passing a maid on the landing. 'Let me know if you need any more hot water, sir,' she said, her cheeks dimpling with a smile. Daniel had that effect on women, and with a wet shirt clinging to him, it was no wonder the maid was staring a little inappropriately.

The fire was crackling nicely. A bathing tub had been filled with warm water, and a rack supplied on which to dry their clothes. Alone in their room, Beth felt awkward.

'I could wait downstairs whilst you bathe and dry your clothes,' Daniel said.

'Why don't you sit in that chair and look the other way?'

So, Daniel sat in an armchair, his back to the tub, and Beth removed her sodden clothes.

'Throw them over here and I'll hang them up to dry,' Daniel said.

The water was pleasantly warm, but Beth was concerned it would have cooled when Daniel took his turn. 'I'll be quick so you can jump in whilst it's still hot,' she said. Peeking over the bathing tub, she watched as Daniel hung her chemise and petticoat in front of the fire.

She closed her eyes and sank deeper into the water. 'My mother used to soap my arms and legs when I was a girl,' she said.

'I could do that for you.' He paused in the act of hanging a stocking.

A heavy silence as Beth contemplated his words. Time was precious. Every moment with Daniel might be the last. He turned to look at her, his face flushed.

'You're beautiful.'

'Why don't you join me in the tub? The water won't stay hot for long. We can soap one another.'

Daniel kept his eyes on her as he pulled the wet shirt over his head. Beth drew in her breath. He was beautiful. Magnificent. A tight, toned stomach, a line of body hair from his navel to … He removed his trousers. His underclothes. Now, he stood before her. An Adonis.

'Come here,' Beth croaked, her mouth dry.

Daniel grinned. He knelt beside the tub and rubbed the soap with a cloth. 'Arms, please.'

Beth lifted both arms like a child. He took one and with a look of concentration on his face gently soaped from her armpit to her hand. She wanted to pull him to her. To feel his soapy body against hers. How could she endure this restraint?

'Next.' Beth lifted her other arm, then gasped as he caressed her with soap, moving from arm to breast. His hands replaced the cloth, cupping her breasts, his fingers teasing her nipples.

'My turn.' Beth made room in the tub, kneeling at one end.

Daniel stepped in. His legs enclosed her as he lowered his body into the water.

Beth soaped the cloth and washed his arms, as he had hers, then his chest, exploring the contours of muscle and sinew. She traced a finger along the downy line of body hair from his sternum, down beneath the water. Here was his root, a secret life-force throbbing beneath her touch.

Daniel gasped. 'Are you sure?'

Beth slid onto his lap, wrapping her legs around him. They kissed. She wanted him. Nothing else mattered. 'Yes,' she whispered.

Daniel stepped out of the bath and held up a towel. They stood naked before one another in the softened light from the fire. Beth took the towel and with great concentration dried his body, treasuring every muscle and bone. The hollow in his clavicle, the ridges of his ribs, the swell of his buttocks. His thighs.

Daniel grabbed her hand. He swept her off her feet and carried her to the bed. 'I love you, Elizabeth Hardy.'

'And I love you, Daniel Winterton.'

They made love in the firelight, reflections flickering across their bodies. 'Are you sure?' Daniel had said again, propped up on his elbows.

'Yes,' Beth almost wailed. She wanted him. For their bodies to merge as one. To absorb him so she couldn't ache for him any longer.

Later, as they lay watching shadows dance across the wall, Daniel said. 'It won't hurt the next time.'

'It didn't. Not really,' Beth said.

There was a knock on the door. Daniel jumped up and wrapped a towel around his waist. He opened the door ajar and called out, 'Thank you.'

When the coast was clear, he carried in a tray laden with

soup and bread, then a pitcher of ale with a couple of mugs. They draped a blanket around themselves as their clothes dried by the fire and enjoyed the supper provided.

'Will you marry me, Beth?'

Beth felt as though she were already married to him. He had her heart and soul. 'Yes,' she said.

'Good. I'll fix everything. We can live wherever you choose.'

'Can we have a plane?'

'Anything your heart desires.'

'Only you.'

'You have me. Whatever happens. I'll never stop loving you, Beth.'

'Daisy won't approve,' Beth said. 'Maybe she thinks you're too good for me. If there is something between you and Daisy, you have to tell me now, Daniel.'

Daniel stood up and turned his back to Beth as he pulled on his trousers. 'You're right. There is something we're not telling you but that's because we want to protect you. To keep you safe.'

'I'm not a child. If we're to be married there should be no secrets between us.'

'You're right.' Daniel pulled on his shirt. 'There won't be. I'm through with secrets and subterfuge. But first, I've got to sort out some things. I've got myself into a bit of a jam and yes, part of that does involve Daisy. So, let's keep our plan to get wed under the radar for now.'

'Can I tell Rosie?'

Daniel smiled at her with love in his eyes. 'Yes. You can tell Rosie. But let me talk to Daisy.'

18

TUESDAY 21ST JUNE 1966

The day Richard had been taken in for questioning he and Louise had been persuaded to share Bill and Esther's supper. Bill had been reading Dr Spock's book on baby and child care, so there was a discussion about picking up a crying baby, or as Esther's mother apparently argued, leaving it to self-soothe.

'There's no way I'm leaving our little one to cry his heart out,' Bill had exclaimed. 'Dr Spock says every baby is different and you can't give them too much affection.'

'I'm with you on that.' Richard had joined in the discussion with a passion and Louise felt as though she were the mother neglecting her loved one's needs – because that's what she was doing. Richard wanted to be a father and, if he stayed with her, she denied him that opportunity. Moved by the fierce love and protection expressed by the two men, Beth wondered whether her father had felt that way? He wanted to be part of her life and her selfish mother had kept them apart.

The conversation moved on to Esther's maternity leave. 'I'm worried about the local library service. I worked hard to establish it and with me being away on maternity leave, I'm afraid it won't survive. Can you imagine not having access to a supply of books? There are rural communities that depend on the mobile library,' Esther said, spooning portions of apple crumble into bowls.

'You don't have to convince me. I love working with you, taking books to the villages. And I'll carry on working whilst you're away. You know that.' Louise took a bowl of steaming pud from Esther. 'I can smell the cinnamon. Yum. Thank you, Bill. I'm going to be well fed living here.'

'She won't want to move back in with me,' Richard laughed.

'You know that's not true.' Louise squeezed Richard's hand. She was already dreading having to say goodbye to him again.

With all four bowls distributed, Esther sat down. 'Unfortunately, librarians are in short supply. Without a qualified librarian, the council might have to discontinue the service.'

'No. They can't do that.' Louise waved her spoon. 'It's too important. Not only do we provide books, we share information about public health, the reservoir project. We get information out there.'

'I know. Are you sure you don't want to train as a librarian? There are grants available,' Esther said.

Richard studied his dessert, avoiding eye contact with Louise.

'Maybe one day. But it's not just the money. I'm not qualified. I don't have a degree or anything.'

'I've been looking into that. You could do a part-time course. It would mean going to evening classes in Leeds. The basic certificate would be enough for you to take my place on our round.'

Louise laughed uneasily. 'Sounds like you've got it all planned.'

The Canary Girl's Secret

Bill threw Esther a cautioning look. 'There's a few more months before your maternity leave. We don't need to save the library service tonight. Another whisky, Richard?'

Later that evening, getting ready for bed, Louise remembered her pills. Why hadn't she driven to the caravan as soon as Fiona dropped her off? Tomorrow. She would take two a day for two days.

The following morning, Louise and Esther set off together in Mobi. 'I'll think about training as a librarian,' Louise said. 'It's just that there's a lot going on in my life right now.' That was an understatement. She was surviving on very little sleep; it was a wonder she could function at all.

When the mobile library came into view, a scattering of people gathered, like hungry seagulls following a tractor. 'This service means so much to so many,' Esther sighed. 'I can't bear the thought of letting them down.'

'Okay. I promise I'll think about it,' Louise said.

'Perhaps you could have a go at driving Mobi?'

'Perhaps,' Louise said, more to silence her.

Louise was kneeling in front of the children's section tidying the books back onto the shelf when Janine, Susan Jeffries's granddaughter, barrelled into her. 'Louise! I loved A Wrinkle in Time. I read it in just two days. Have you got another book for me?'

'I want a book too,' Dylan said.

Hooray! The Beano Annual she lent Dylan may have converted him to being a reader. That, or his sister's enthusiasm.

'It just so happens; I have saved a book for each of you.'

'You're good taking the time to find books that will excite

them,' Susan said, as she sat on the bench seat. 'Mobile library day is the highlight of Janine's week.'

'Don't you think Louise would make a good librarian?' Esther said.

'I thought she was already. I've known Louise since she was not much older than Dylan. About twelve when you came to live here as an evacuee, wasn't it luv?'

'That's right. I was a bookworm too.'

'You might have been. I wouldn't know as I only saw you about the farm, helping Ma and Pa Beck but I was going to say, you were a bright one. They were so proud of you. Top of her class, they said. Pa told me you made up stories about the people who lived in the village and worked at the mill, before it was deserted. Doesn't surprise me you ended up working with books.'

Esther winked at Louise; she would be chalking up another mark in favour of Louise training.

'Where are our books?' Janine said, as politely as a frustrated child desperate to get her hands on a new story could be.

Louise laughed. 'Right here. Harriett The Spy by Louise Fitzhugh. It's had excellent reviews. I'm sure you'll enjoy it, but I want to know your thoughts. I might read it myself.'

Janine took the book eagerly. She curled up on a bean bag and started reading.

Dylan eyed Louise as though gauging if she were to be trusted in finding something worth reading.

'And for you Dylan, Charlie and the Chocolate Factory by Roald Dahl. It's about a boy around the same age as you.'

'Is it about chocolate, too?'

'It is. When you've read your books, you might like to swap them as I chose books that would appeal to you both.' It wasn't true. Louise had picked two books for Janine, not expecting

Dylan to be interested. The fact that he was, had indeed persuaded Louise that she might have something to offer as a future librarian. She would find a copy of Stig of the Dump for his next visit.

Susan's remarks about the farm prompted Louise to say, 'I heard you were helpful to Ma Beck in closing down the farm before she went into hospital.'

'Broke her heart, the poor love, having to sell off the cows. They'd not been producing milk for a few years. But the farm was her life. Of course, she was never the same after losing John. I can't imagine what that was like. If it were me, and my Simon died sudden like that, I don't think I'd be as strong as her.'

'Did you go to Ma Beck's funeral?' Louise said.

'No luv. I wish I had. I went to John's but we were away somewhere. That's right. My sister's fiftieth. We stayed with her in Loughton that week for the party, and to help out. I went to John Beck's funeral. That was sad. Liz was in pieces.'

'But there was a funeral for her?' Louise said.

Susan screwed up her face as though Louise was mad. 'Of course. Didn't you see her grave, before it got moved?'

Louise nodded. She wasn't going to tell Susan that Elizabeth Beck's remains were reported missing. Her grave empty. 'The date of death wasn't on her gravestone, just the year.'

'Well, that's Liz for you. She wanted to arrange everything herself, even her own funeral would you believe? I told her she could pay to have her gravestone engraved but it would have to be done after her passing. But no, Liz said she wouldn't survive the year and arranged to have it partly done. I didn't see much of Liz after helping close down the business. Elsie Braithwaite was looking in on her. Elsie said the district nurse arranged her admission to hospital when she was nearing the end.'

'Did you meet Miss St Clair? I think she was a friend of Ma's?'

Susan shook her head. 'Never heard of her. Now, much as I'd like to have a good old natter, I've got to get these two back to their mum's for tea. Shame Liz isn't alive to see you. She'd have been made-over to have you back. They couldn't have children, Liz and John. It was something to do with the chemicals she had to handle in the war, made her infertile. That's why you meant so much to them. The daughter they never had.'

Janine looked as comfy as a kitten curled up on the bean bag but Dylan was kicking around a blue plastic dog––a toy intended for toddlers––as if it were a football. Susan chivvied them up and out as Esther and Louise prepared to get back on the road.

'You don't believe this nonsense about the grave being empty?' Esther said.

'Well, it obviously is now. But I dread to think how that happened. In a way I'd rather believe she wasn't buried there. I know,' Louise shrugged, 'it's ridiculous. Where else would she be? If only she were still alive.'

'We have to find evidence. What do you know about Miss St Clair? It's an uncommon name. I'll do some research. Maybe contact Leeds library,' Esther said.

'Would you?' There was still hope.

'There's no way I'm going to watch your inheritance go to the greedy Corporation. Now, are you ready to have a go at driving Mobi?' Esther said, climbing into the passenger seat.

'Crikey. No.' Louise took a deep breath. She knew that it wasn't really a question. Esther had decided it was time she had a go behind the wheel. 'Okay. But only on this quiet lane.'

Louise familiarised herself with Mobi's gear changes, the indicator lights and the pedals. Then, she adjusted the mirror.

'It's exactly the same as driving a car. In a way, it's easier, as you're high up and get a good view of the road. There's nothing coming, you can pull out.'

Mobi pulled away smoothly, although Louise's leg was shaking as she tried to control the clutch. Second, third gear. Fourth. A smooth drive. Louise let out her breath and tried to relax.

'Well done. You're a natural. Left at the top of the lane.'

'Really? It's busier on that road.' But Louise indicated and slowed down, shifting smoothly between gears. 'Okay. Here goes.'

A mile or so along the road, Louise was feeling quietly confident. Who would have thought she could drive this monster of a vehicle? She stroked the steering wheel. 'Well done, Mobi.'

'Oh, you'd better pull over,' Esther said a note of panic in her voice.

'Why?' Then Louise saw police lights flashing in her rear-view mirror. She tried to change gears quickly as she slowed down and Mobi stalled. They came to an undignified stop at the side of the road. Louise wiped her forehead. 'Why don't they just go past?'

'I think they want us to stop,' Esther said. She opened the door and climbed out to greet the police officer.

Louise followed, her knees trembling, after her ordeal. Until the police pulled them over, she'd been doing okay. Surely, they hadn't stopped them because of her driving?

'Louise Boyd?' The police officer flashed his ID card.

'Yes, but I use my maiden-name, Pearson.'

'Sorry to disturb you at work. We're here to escort you to the police station where you're wanted for questioning.'

Louise's heart hammered; her knees were jelly. 'Why? If it's about the day of the flood, I've already told you everything I know.' Keep calm. It's just routine. They don't know about the shovel.

'I think it's best if you come with us.' The policeman said, nodding at the traffic which was slowing down as people stared out of car windows curious to know what was going on.

'Don't worry about me,' Esther said. 'I'll be fine. Just go.' She gave Louise a reassuring nod, conveying love and calm with her eyes. "I'll catch up with you later.'

Louise climbed into the back of the police panda car, surprised that a policewoman felt it necessary to sit alongside her rather than in the front passenger seat.

'I'm guessing this is just a formality,' Louise said, a smile in her voice. There was no reply.

By the time they reached the police station, Louise was jittery. This wasn't a routine enquiry; she could feel it in the police officers' silence. She was escorted to an interview room and asked to wait there for DI Jenkins who had a few questions.

Alone, in the room Louise removed her jacket. It was too warm – airless. Her hands were sweaty.

'Good afternoon, Mrs Boyd.' DI Jenkins was a tall man with thick rimmed spectacles. He wore a suit, and beneath that a white shirt, the top button undone – no tie.

The door opened and a younger man in police uniform joined them.

'PC Williams is here to take notes,' DI Jenkins said.

'What's this all about? Do I need a solicitor to be present?' Louise asked.

'I don't know. Do you?' DI Jenkins said.

Louise's mouth was dry. 'I gave a statement that covered everything I remembered about the day of the flood. I'm presuming that's why you want to talk to me?'

'You did. But something has recently come to light. PC Williams?'

The young policemen stepped out of the room and returned carrying the shovel wrapped in polythene. Louise gasped before she could stop herself.

'It sounds as though you recognise exhibit A,' DI Jenkins said.

'I can see it's a shovel.' Louise tried to compose herself.

'Yes. We found it below Beck's farm when the reservoir level dropped.' The detective paused. He looked directly at Louise and she felt her face flush.

'Please could I have a glass of water?' she said.

'In a moment. On the morning of Sunday 12th June, a bird watcher using binoculars witnessed a woman matching your description throw this spade into the reservoir. Would you like to tell us the reason for this?'

Louise shook her head. 'I think I might need a solicitor.'

19

JUNE 21ST 1966

Louise was allowed to make one phone call, and so she telephoned Richard at Simms Emporium. Esther would have told him she had been brought in for questioning, and Richard would have assumed it was a formality. She hadn't told him about the shovel. Now, she wished she had. She wished a lot of things – not throwing it into the lake for one. How could she have been so stupid?

'Simms Emporium. Fiona Simms speaking.'

Louise's heart sank. 'Is Richard there?'

'No. Sorry, Louise. He's out on a delivery. I can take a message for him.'

'When are you expecting him to return?' she said. A policewoman stood close to Louise, timing her call. 'Never mind. I've been taken in for questioning. Fiona …' Panic seized her. Louise gulped. 'Fiona. I think I need a solicitor. I'm about to be questioned and I'm frightened.'

She could hear Fiona's intake of breath. 'Okay, Louise. Keep calm. I'll send over the family solicitor, Evans. He deals with all of our business. Don't say anything until he gets there.'

'I don't know if I can afford him,' Louise said. 'Maybe I'm over-reacting. I'm innocent. I'll just explain.'

'Trust your instincts. Don't worry about the cost. He has a contract working for my family's business. I'll let Richard know as soon as possible. Be brave. Look, I'll get off the phone so I can call Evans. Keep strong, okay?'

This was a side of Fiona Louise hadn't seen before. But then, they had always been in combat. When she had returned to Thorncrest, Fiona guessed who she was and knew of her history with Richard. It was understandable that she had felt threatened. Until Louise arrived on the scene, Fiona had hopes that she and Richard would one day marry. Louise felt mean about the way she had treated Fiona. Richard and Esther held Fiona in high regard; it was time she made an effort to like her.

An hour later, when Louise was beside herself with anxiety, a policeman from the front desk said, 'Paul Evans of Wyatt, Evans and Evans Solicitors, is here to represent you.'

Paul Evans was younger than Louise expected. A good-looking man in his mid-thirties. He wore a suit and tie and his hair fashionably long so that it curled in a quiff, giving him the look of Cary Grant.

'Thank you for coming to my aid, Mr Evans,' Louise said, standing up to shake his hand.

They were given privacy so Louise could brief him.

'Why did you dispose of the shovel? Did you suspect it was evidence of foul play?' Paul Evans said.

'Maybe. Richard, my boyfriend, had a fight with Eddie before they got separated by the mud slide. But that wasn't on the farm. We were on the road, higher up. I fell in, so I didn't see how their fight ended.'

'So, Richard could have killed Eddie Boyd?'

'No,' Louise exclaimed. 'Richard wouldn't hurt a fly.'

'And yet, you obviously thought he might be guilty or why hide the evidence?'

Louise put her head in her hands. 'And that is why I asked for a solicitor. It looks bad.'

Paul gave her a long, cool look as though assessing her. 'Was anyone else present?'

'No. Just the three of us. Then I got swept away leaving them alone.'

'We only have your word and Richard's. It's possible you worked together. That you hit Eddie with the shovel on the farm and then threw him into the reservoir.'

'But we didn't. He was waiting for me on the road. His car headlights were on. Someone must have seen him. A passing motorist?'

Evans rubbed his chin. 'It's good you called me. I think it's best you say no comment to every question until we've had time to build your case for defence. I'll need to meet with Richard. Braithwaite?'

'Yes,' Louise said.

'Good. Are you ready?'

The police interview took fifteen minutes. Louise did as she had been told, but it was frustrating. She wanted to explain herself because she had nothing to hide, but she could see Paul's point. If Eddie had been murdered, and it was looking that way, then she and Richard were the prime suspects.

'I don't think they have anything other than the witness seeing you throw the shovel,' Paul said, when Louise had been given permission to leave.

'It makes me seem more guilty by not answering their questions.' It had felt uncomfortable refusing to co-operate.

'Is there anyone who might have wanted to kill Eddie Boyd?' he said.

'Yes.' Louise sighed. 'A line of people, I expect.'

He gave her his card. 'Let's see what they decide to do. You might have heard the end of it. They couldn't have found your fingerprints on the murder weapon or they would have detained you.'

Richard burst through the door. 'There you are. Thank God. Fiona told me. I got here as soon as I could. What's happened?'

Paul tilted his head, waiting for Louise's direction.

'It's okay, I'll fill him in. Unless you wanted to speak to Richard?'

'I don't think that will be necessary, for now. Let's sit tight and see how things pan out. You know where to find me.'

'Why did you want a solicitor?' Richard said as they climbed into his land rover. 'I told them what I'd said before. They're just confirming our statements. We'll have to pay Fiona.'

'I know. It was kind of her and of course I'll insist on paying.' She had to tell Richard about the shovel. 'Richard?'

'Ye-es?' he said, picking up on her tone.

'There's something important I need to tell you. But not here. Can we go back to our house? I've got to pick something up from the caravan, anyway.'

Richard pulled up beside the house. It looked complete from the outside. He had tidied away his workbench and stored the unused timber.

'Can't I just move in with you?' Louise said. She longed for the intimacy of sharing quiet moments; his hand cupping her breast as she slept; waking up beside him his hair tousled;

drinking coffee as they read the Sunday paper together; making up a story for him, her feet in his lap.

'I miss you too, Lou Lou. But you'd hate it. I wash in cold water from the reservoir and go to bed in layers of clothes to keep warm.'

'I'd keep you warm.'

'I know you would, darling.' He kissed the top of her head.

Louise was about to make a dash to the caravan to pick up her contraceptive pills when Richard took her hand. 'See what you think of my attempt to make the place homely.'

He'd created shelves in the hallway and lined them with framed photographs. Louise studied a photo of herself as a twelve-year-old evacuee.'

'I won't put in any more shelving or cupboards until we've had a chance to discuss what goes where. This is our home, Louise. I've just tried to make it feel less like a work in progress.'

She returned the photo of herself and picked up one of his parents outside Braithwaite's. 'They look so young and happy,' she said.

'It was taken soon after they married and took over the management from my dad's parents. Come into the front room and tell me this big news.'

The front room had been furnished with a couple of huge beanbags, an ethnic-looking rug, and a drop-down blind to cover the floor to ceiling windows that looked onto the reservoir. A double mattress made up with pillows and blankets was pushed against the wall. Louise took off her shoes and sat on it, curling her legs beneath her.

'Where did you get all of this? The mattress is new.'

'Just a few things to make it more comfortable. Our mattress was sodden. I had to throw it out. And we needed blinds as we're exposed from the reservoir.'

'Who would look in from out there?' Louise said, aware of the tone in her voice. She had a strong suspicion Fiona had provided the blind, rug and bean bags and was annoyed. It would be churlish to complain when she had just accepted Fiona's gift of Paul Evans's time, so she kept these thoughts to herself.

'Apart from the geese? Someone out rowing, or fishing. Maybe not now but when it's finished.' He looked out over the partially drained reservoir. Cottage roofs and chimneys jutted out of the water, resembling a flotilla of strange ships.

'Come and sit here with me.' Louise patted the mattress.

A knowing smile flickered across Richard's lips. He took off his boots and knelt alongside her. 'I know your plan.'

Louise wiggled up the bed, giggling, as he followed.

'I know this was a ploy to seduce me.' He straddled her, then pinned her arms above her head. 'You're a wicked woman. Okay. I surrender. You can have my body.' He let go of her arms and ripped off his shirt.

God, she had missed him. Missed this. He undid the buttons on her blouse and groaned with longing.

Louise slid out of her clothes, exposing full breasts, her nipples erect. Richard took one in his mouth, then the other, tugging gently. She undid his jeans, and he helped, his erection straining against the confines of clothes. They made love slowly, gently, exploring one another's bodies, with kisses, touch and tongue.

'Richard,' she whispered. He needed to use a condom. His eyes held hers as he entered her, and she cried out with the ecstasy of having him inside her. She locked her legs around him, rocking her hips, arching her back until they both came with gasps and sighs of pleasure.

'If people can see in, maybe we should have closed the blind,' Louise said.

'A bit late now.' Richard laughed as he dressed.

Louise reluctantly fished around the blankets to find her knickers and bra. It was too late to worry about the unprotected sex they'd just had.

'I would offer to make a cup of tea but it's a bit of a rigmarole using the camping stove. I usually bring a flask of coffee home from work. Orange juice is fine for me in the morning.'

'I know. I get it. The house isn't ready for me to move in, but hopefully it won't be long. I'll get my inheritance and then we can pay for the plumbing and electrics.' Louise grinned. 'We just made love for the first time in our new home.'

'I know. Wasn't it great?'

'Yes. Wonderful views of the reservoir,' Louise teased. 'And you were pretty good too.'

'We'll have it ready soon, I promise. Now, tell me this big news. Are you pregnant?'

'No.' Where had that come from? 'No. I wanted to tell you why the police brought me back in for questioning. I told you, I'm not ready to start a family. And I'm sorry but I might never be.'

He frowned. 'I know, you said that. I just thought. When you said you had something to tell me. Never mind.'

She hated the way the light went out of his eyes. 'Having a career is important to me Richard. The holiday village is your dream and I'm excited to be part of that, but there are other things I want to do, too.' Finish writing the novel she had started. Develop the community library service. Curate the museum barn. 'I feel like I'm making up for lost time. The years I wasted, believing I was responsible for Pa's accident.'

'I know.' He hugged her tight. 'I'm proud of you, Lou Lou. So, what is it you have to tell me?'

'Okay.' She took a deep breath and stepped back from him

so she could watch his face. 'They found something, Richard. It had been thrown into the reservoir. A murder weapon.'

His eyes widened. 'What? So, Eddie really was murdered? Bloody hell. How did that happen? I was with him up until the end. At least, I thought I was.'

Louise bit her lip. 'It was a shovel. Someone saw me throwing it into the reservoir.'

He frowned. 'What do you mean? Why would they say that?'

'Because I did. It was stupid. I wasn't thinking, just acted on instinct.' Richard stared at her in disbelief. Maybe waiting for her to say she was having him on. She continued. 'When I got swept away by the mudslide you and Eddie were fighting. I didn't know… I just thought…'

'You thought I killed him?' His jaw clenched.

'No. Yes.'

She could see the hurt in his eyes, and her heart contracted.

'How could you, Lou Lou?'

'I know. It was stupid. I've got to stop acting on impulse.' She tried to force a laugh, but it caught in her throat.

He shook his head. 'I feel as though I don't know you anymore. And you certainly don't know me if you thought I could murder your husband.'

'I didn't. Not really. You know me better than anyone. I'm sorry. I wish I could go back and do things differently, but I can't.' She wouldn't beg for his forgiveness. Their relationship had to be built on mutual trust and respect.

Richard rubbed his jaw. 'We were close as kids. Maybe I just clung onto a dream. First love and all that. But your time living with Eddie has changed you, Lou Lou.'

'Of course, it's changed me. You and I were apart for twenty years. We've both changed. But I've never stopped

The Canary Girl's Secret

loving you. We were, are, meant to be together. It's living apart that's causing the friction--'

'--No. It's your involvement with criminals like Pete Murray. When were you going to tell me you met up with him? Fliss told me when she invited us to Dion's gig at the Coach and Horses. As if we could be in the same room as him. The man who led Eddie back to you. Did he tell you to dispose of the shovel?'

Louise couldn't keep up with Richard's line of thought, putting two and two together and making five. 'I didn't tell you I met Pete because I didn't want you to know we met outside the police station. I was about to go in and own up to my stupidity in throwing away the shovel. So, now you know everything.'

'I don't want you seeing Pete Murray,' Richard said.

A surge of anger fuelled Louise before she had time to think. 'I will see who I want. When I want. Nobody, and certainly not my partner, is going to dictate how I live my life. I had enough of that from Eddie.'

'You've just proved my point. Living with Eddie, has changed you. You assume I'm like him. What about Big Jim? Have you been in contact with him since Eddie died?'

'No. Of course not.' She couldn't tell Richard that Big Jim was back in Yorkshire. Maybe Richard was right; her past was stalking her, and there was nowhere to hide.

'I'll drive you back to Bill and Esther's,' Richard said.

They drove in silence, as Louise was lost in thought. If Eddie was murdered, then Pete Murray might know something. Her mind kept replaying the night of the flood, looking for clues, because if there was no other suspect, the police might try to pin it on her, or worse, Richard.

When they pulled up outside the cottage, Richard said, 'I'm sorry we had a fight, Lou Lou.'

'Me too. And I'm really, really, sorry about, you know, the police and everything.' Louise knew what she had to do next. It would break her heart, but she had to protect Richard. 'I think we should spend some time apart.'

The colour drained from Richard's face. 'No. I love you, Lou Lou. I'm sorry I lost it back there.'

'I love you too. But I think we need some space. When we got together again everything happened so quickly. There's a lot going on for us both, right now. I hate having rows like that and I'm afraid with us living apart there will be more misunderstandings. It's too much pressure on our relationship. Let's just give it a few weeks. When the house is ready, I'll move back in and we'll start afresh.'

'Is that what you want?' Richard said.

No. Louise gave a silent scream. It was not what she wanted, but it was what she had to do to protect Richard. 'It won't be forever,' she replied. 'Anyway, you'll be busy making and selling tables, and working in the shop.' With Fiona, she thought.

'Can we write?' Richard said.

'Yes. I'd like that. We share the same PO Box. I'll look forward to checking my mail.'

They parted as friends, but Louise's heart was heavy. She prayed that she had done the right thing in letting him go.

20

SATURDAY JUNE 25TH 1966

'Are you sure Richard doesn't want to watch Dion's band tonight?' Esther said from her prone position on the couch.

Louise hadn't told Esther about her temporary break with Richard, or the reason he wanted nothing to do with Pete. 'No. Richard needs to get on with finishing our house, because if he doesn't, I'll be sharing my room here with your baby.'

'Suits me. You can do the night time feeds. I saw you borrowed Margaret Drabble's book, what did you think?'

'I read it from start to finish on my journey to and from London. It was strange because I experienced the exact same thing as Rosamund, the protagonist, did in the story.'

'You had sex on the train?'

'No. A woman asked me to hold her baby, just like the woman in the clinic asked Rosamund. And I felt it too. The heavy warmth. The snuffly breath and wide soft cheeks. The book wasn't what I expected. It was about Rosamund's love for her baby. It was funny too. The scene where she ran a hot bath and bought a bottle of gin. Her friends turn up unannounced. They drink the gin and the bath goes cold.'

Esther struggled up into a seated position. 'So, what are you saying? Holding that woman's baby has transformed you, that you might consider motherhood, after all?'

'No. It was just weird. I had those feelings – well observations – and then, a few pages on, so did Rosamund. I liked her character. She was intelligent, studying for a Phd, but naïve and unsure of herself. A real person.' Louise had made notes about the writing of character, for her own novel.

'So, definitely no to becoming pregnant?'

'Definitely no. I'm too old. Besides, you need me to take over as community librarian. I sent in my application this week.'

'Well done. They'll be biting your hand off. Now, much as I would love to spend the evening slothing, we need to get ready to go out. I'm looking forward to seeing Pete again.'

Louise wasn't in the mood to party. She hated herself for hurting Richard. The look on his face when they said goodbye was heart-breaking. But she needed to see Pete. If Eddie was murdered, then Big Jim would have a good idea who was responsible. She needed Big Jim on her side – his protection – if the police tried to pin it on her or Richard.

Dion's band was playing California Girls when Louise and Esther squeezed into the crowded bar. Fliss had promised to save a table for them in the back of the bar where the band was playing.

'Go and find Fliss. I'll get the drinks. Are you sure you want a ginger beer?' Louise said.

'Yes. It's good for my heartburn and nausea,' Esther replied.

'You're not a good advert for pregnancy.'

When Esther was out of earshot, Louise checked both bars looking for Pete. His motorbike was parked outside, and he wasn't sitting with Fliss. She had returned to the bar and was waiting to be served when he came up behind her and gave her shoulder a squeeze.

She turned. 'Pete, I need to talk to you in private. It's important.'

'Sure.' He frowned. 'Outside?'

They wove their way out of the bar. Groups of friends were seated at the outside tables or talked in clusters, enjoying the novelty of a warm summer evening.

'Have you seen my new bike?' Pete said.

Louise followed him across the car park to stand by his bike. It was quieter there.

'Okay. What's this about? You're frightening me.' Pete put one hand on the motorbike seat, seeming to draw comfort from this connection, or maybe imagining his getaway.

Louise bit her lower lip, unsure where to start. 'I'm guessing Fliss still doesn't know about your links to the Mob?'

'No. I told you, that's all in the past. You're not going to try and blackmail me?'

'Of course not. But I do have a favour to ask. It's important, Pete. You're the only one who can help me.'

The headlights of a car swung in an arc, illuminating them.

'Go on,' Pete said.

'The police suspect me of murdering Eddie. Someone knocked him out with a shovel before he either fell, or was pushed, into the reservoir. Do you know what happened that day?'

Pete shook his head, his eyes fixed on Louise. 'Go on.'

'You know I went to Beck's farm in search of Ma Beck's will? Once I found it, Richard and I fought our way back up onto firm ground. Eddie was waiting for us. I had a row with Eddie up there, on the road above Beck's farm.' Louise sighed. 'When I lost my footing with the mud slide, he was alive – fighting with Richard – but alive. They stopped fighting as soon as I fell. Richard drove away, so he could alert emergency services. There was a strong current and if I hadn't been a strong swimmer I could have got into difficulty. We thought that's what happened to Eddie – he fell in after me – but now the police think they've found a murder weapon. The shovel. It was on Beck's farm, which doesn't make any sense because Eddie wasn't down there. Which is why I'm asking. Do you know what happened?'

Pete covered his mouth. Then he sighed heavily. 'Even if I did know something, which I don't, I wouldn't say. I'm sorry Louise but I can't risk being drawn back into that world.'

'Neither can I, but we both know it has a habit of catching up with you. Okay, you don't know for sure but you must have some idea. The Bellamy Brothers men made several appearances under the guise of being building contractors. You and I both know they're villains. Could they have had another kind of contract? A directive from Big Jim? I know Eddie crossed him, and Big Jim isn't known for his forgiving nature.'

Paul gave a wry laugh. 'Sounds as though you've figured it out.'

'So, if they gave Eddie a reason to visit the farm house, he might have risked it.' Louise's mind was racing. Did Eddie know that she'd found Ma's will beneath the floorboards? Maybe he thought there was more treasure to be found. 'They could have lured him there to kill him,' Louise said.

'All I know for sure is – yes, you're right – Jim had a contract out on Eddie Boyd and the Bellamy Boys were somehow involved. That's all I know. But you can't use that information. If word gets back to my uncle that I've grassed him up he won't show any mercy. I told you he's evil. I'm his brother's son, but as I said, my dad died working for him. So, go figure.'

'Okay. But we have to think.'

'We?'

Louise peered into the dark to see his expression. He smiled. Pete was a good guy. He'd just got mixed up in the wrong crowd – the same as her. 'Big Jim has contacts everywhere. There'll be someone in the police force working with him or willing to take money, there always is. That's why he gets away with so much. If he doesn't want me to tell them what I know, he'd better get them off my back. Do you think you could get that message to him? Tell him I worked it out for myself, which I did. And in return, I'll keep your past from Fliss. Deal?' Louise said.

'I'm going to tell her soon, anyway. I love her, Louise. I don't want secrets between us. Just in my own time.'

'Please help me, Pete. I'm frightened I could get put away for this. Innocent people might end up in jail. And if Richard gets pulled into it, I'll never forgive myself.'

He stroked the engine cover of his bike. 'It's a Triumph. I bought her from a guy I met at Uni. He needed the cash to pay his rent.'

'I guess you're still living off money earned from crime. Minding me, for example.'

'Okay. Okay. You win. I'll talk to my uncle. But I can't promise anything. He might be happy for you to take the blame.'

That thought had occurred to Louise. But if he wanted to play dirty, she had heaps of information on him and the Mob. 'Just do your best. And thank you, Pete.'

'And then, will you finally forgive me?'

'Yes. Provided you treat Fliss right. And, you tell her about your connections before too long.'

'Deal.' Pete opened his arms. 'A hug to seal it?'

'A hug to seal it.' She was glad of his arms around her. It made her feel safe and grounded. She missed Richard so much it hurt.

As soon as they stepped inside, Fliss ran at them. 'Oh, thank God you're still here. It's Esther. You need to take her to the hospital. She had a stomach cramp and went to the toilet. I followed her in and waited outside. She was crying. Saying there was blood. Then shouting my baby. My baby.'

'Who's with her now?' I shouldn't have left Esther alone, Louise thought. How could she face Bill, if Esther lost their baby?

'Mary-Jane Williams. She's a nurse. Bill knows her from work,' Fliss said.

'Okay. Deep breath. We need to stay calm for Esther. Let's get her into the car. I'll drive.'

'We'll follow on my bike,' Pete said.

21

MONDAY JUNE 27TH 1966

'They're keeping her under observation,' Bill said when he arrived home from his visit to the hospital that afternoon. He hadn't been permitted to see Esther earlier that day when he finished his shift, so he returned during visiting hours.

'But the baby's alright?' Louise said.

'They think so. Thank God. But we're not out of the woods yet. She must have complete bed rest, which is why they're keeping her in.' Bill looked exhausted. He couldn't have slept properly since Friday night.

'What can I do to help?' Louise said.

'Nothing. I've told the library service she won't be at work for a while. Esther suggested you keep things ticking over with the mobile library but you'll have to talk to your boss about that. I'm going to get my head down for a while.'

It was awkward living in the cottage with Bill whilst Esther was in hospital. It didn't feel right, and Louise was afraid people might talk. The small rural community hadn't caught up with the liberated thinking of 1960s Londoners.

In Esther's absence, Louise had busied herself cataloguing books and tidying the shelves. Tomorrow, she was meeting Esther's boss, Diane Chippendale, at Harrogate library. They would have received her application by now. If she had to drive Mobi and manage alone, she would, but hopefully, there would be someone to help her.

A black Bentley had been on Louise's tail for some time as she drove Mini to Harrogate for the meeting. It was so close behind her now, Louise decided to pull over so it could pass. She signalled, slowed down, and stopped close to the verge. The Bentley followed, pulling in behind her. Police didn't drive fancy cars. Louise's heart thudded. She would keep her door locked. The driver got out of the Bentley. He opened the passenger door in the back. A chauffeur? Louise recognised the man's bulk as soon as he climbed out of the car. Big Jim.

She turned off her engine. Relieved it wasn't a rapist but nonetheless afraid, she got out to meet him.

'Good morning, Mrs Boyd,' Big Jim said. 'I understand you've something you want to discuss with me. Shall we conduct our business in my car? Less noise away from the traffic.'

A dark blue Hillman slowed down as it passed them. The driver turned his head and stared.

'In the car,' Big Jim said.

'I'd rather talk here, if you don't mind. I've a meeting in Harrogate and I don't want to be late.' He gave her a long, cool look, and Louise's stomach dipped. 'But of course, meeting with you is more important.'

'I'm glad you remembered that. Shall we?'

The chauffeur opened the door, and Louise climbed in alongside Big Jim.

'You asked a favour of me,' he said.

'Yes. If you don't mind. I know how influential you are and hoped you might be able to put in a good word for me.'

'Cover up for you, you mean?'

Louise felt heat rising as her blood boiled. 'No. I haven't committed a crime. It's a misunderstanding.'

'Last I heard, perverting the course of justice was a serious offence. Destroying evidence in a murder case. Dear, dear. Doesn't look good to me.'

'You know I didn't kill Eddie,' Louise said. The fact that they both knew who was responsible hung in the air unsaid.

'And, say I were to cover for you; what do you propose to do to repay your debt?'

Louise swallowed. 'I don't know.'

Big Jim gave this some thought. 'Okay. Here's the deal. I'll have a word in the right ear. Get you and your boyfriend, Richard Braithwaite off the hook. But you'll owe me.'

'How much? I've already given you anything I might have inherited from Eddie,' Louise said.

'You repaid part of his debt to me. Being the kind-hearted chap I am, I let you off paying the full amount. No. I'll decide how and when you're to repay me for the favour you ask'

Louise nodded. 'Yes, Mr Murray.'

She waited in her car until the Bentley had driven away. What had she done? If Richard found out, he would be furious. It would confirm everything he said. Living with Eddie had changed her; she was tainted by her connection to the Mob. Shaken by this encounter, Louise would have turned the car around and headed home, but Diane Chippendale was expecting her and Louise had to make a good impression.

. . .

Esther had spoken favourably about her boss, but Esther spoke well of everyone. Now, as Louise watched the older woman scrolling a microfiche, horn-rimmed glasses perched on her nose, she felt unsure of herself. Louise had left school early with few qualifications. Mrs Chippendale would think her uneducated and overambitious.

'Mrs Boyd?' Diane Chippendale looked up over her glasses.

'Yes. Well, Louise Pearson, if you don't mind. I prefer not to use my married name.' Louise extended her hand.

'Of course.' Diane stood up and shook Louise's hand. 'How's Esther? Resting I hope.'

Louise was on safe territory. She updated Diane on Esther's condition, explaining that she was on bed rest until further notice.

'So how do you feel about manning the community library single-handed?' Diane said.

'I'm willing to have a go. It's important to so many villagers: People who are housebound. Children. She smiled thinking of Janine and Dylan. In a rural community, the library service connects people. It's important to Esther that we keep it going and it's important to me.' Louise blushed.

'Well said. I've booked a table at The Walnut Tree. Mr Harris is joining us.' Diane packed away her papers. Louise was confused. Had Mrs Chippendale mistaken her for someone else? Did she know Louise was an unqualified library assistant?

'Mr Harris?'

'Indeed. He was impressed with your application for the Library Association Registration Exam sponsorship. Consider this an interview if you like. We might as well do it in a civilised way over a bite of lunch. Ready?'

The Walnut Tree was an elegant restaurant tucked into a side street off the Kings Road. Their table was at the back of the restaurant, where they would be undisturbed. Louise sat facing Mrs Chippendale and Mr Harris, a comfortable-looking man in corduroy trousers and a tweed jacket. She had a view of the bustling restaurant, whereas her interviewers had the advantage of no distractions, facing only Louise and the wall behind her.

'Tell me about yourself and why you've applied for a sponsorship with our library service,' Mr Harris said, as soon as introductions had been made.

Louise's mouth was dry. She sipped some water. 'I love books. From a very young age I was transported by the magic of stories…' Louise spoke fluently about her passion for books and commitment to the local community. The waiter arrived twice and was waved away.

When Louise finished her account of herself, conversation between the three of them flowed freely. The waiter hovered once again by their table, and Mr Harris said, 'I think we're ready to order.'

Relaxed now in their company, Louise chose cottage pie from the menu. Mr Harris, the same. Diane chose an omelette and chips.

'I'll get my assistant to draw up a contract for you, Louise. I was impressed with your application and even more so now we've met. The registration exam is just the first step. It will take many years of study before you qualify as a librarian but I see potential in you. It's a rewarding life for people like us, book lovers.'

She was going to train as a librarian. Louise could barely believe it. And tomorrow she would take Mobi out on the road, alone. Richard would be proud of her. So would Ma, Louise thought. It felt as though she had found her purpose in life. At last.

Diane was talking about her planned holiday to the Italian

lakes when Louise gazed past her, the other diners unseen as her mind dwelled on life as a librarian. She imagined herself gathering important research papers and books together for academics and historians. Louise's eyes settled on the neat arrangement of hair in a chignon––a blonde woman who was sipping white wine. It took a few seconds for the realisation to hit. Fiona. And opposite her, raising his glass in a toast, was Richard.

Louise took a gulp of water.

'I almost forgot,' Diane exclaimed. 'I found a reference to that relative of yours. The one Esther asked me to research.'

Louise immediately thought of her father. How did Diane Chippendale know Blake Sommerfeld?

'The St. Clairs. They were an important family in the nineteenth century. Miss St Clair, must be the unmarried daughter, Daisy. My goodness you come from pedigree stock.' Mrs Chippendale laughed and dabbed her mouth with a napkin. 'Daisy St. Clair was something of a philanthropist supporting the arts, and a leading figure in the suffragette movement. The Leeds librarian enjoyed researching your–– great aunt?'

'I don't think we're blood relatives just connected through friendships in the past.'

Fiona was standing up. If she visited the bathroom, she would pass by their table.

'I'll hand you the file of information my colleague found. Hopefully you'll be able to trace Daisy St Clair, if she's still alive, from the last known address.'

Richard stood up. They were leaving. Together. They had obviously driven to Harrogate to avoid being seen by locals.

'So, college starts in September,' Mr Harris said. 'As a trainee librarian your salary will remain the same but you'll have one day in college each week and assignments to complete at work. We'll find you placements across the service so you get varied experience.'

'I can't tell you how grateful I am. I won't let you down,' Louise said.

'Here's the file on the St Clairs,' Mrs Chippendale said, when they were outside the restaurant. There was no sign of Richard and Fiona. 'Let me know if you find your aunt Daisy. And if you have any questions whilst covering for Esther, just give me a call.'

They said their goodbyes and walked to their respective cars. Mrs Chippendale had a meeting in Leeds, so Louise had followed her to the restaurant in Mini.

Richard and Fiona worked together. They were work colleagues, and so it was entirely natural they might lunch together, especially if they were out that way on business, Louise told herself as she drove home, but deep down, she didn't believe it. Well, if something was developing between Richard and Fiona, she only had herself to blame. She couldn't get together with Richard until Big Jim was off the scene and both of their names cleared. What had she done in making a deal with the devil? The only thing she could do to protect Richard.

Louise switched on the radio. These Boots Are Made for Walking. Louise sang at the top of her voice. She was going to train as a librarian. And with Daisy St. Clair as a witness to Ma's burial, she would claim her inheritance. There would be enough money to finish their house and maybe build one cabin. It wasn't going to be easy, but nothing worthwhile ever was. Everything was going to work out. One day at a time, Ma whispered.

And now she had a file on Daisy St Clair. What a fabulous name. She couldn't wait to read about this illustrious figure. How were you connected to the St. Clairs, Ma?

22

JUNE 1916

She was to be married. Beth Hardy, the woman who swore she would never give up her independence to be a wife and mother. Mrs Beth Winterton. Wife of Lieutenant Winterton of the Royal Flying Corps. She'd told Rosie her news, and the girls in the factory, but had sworn them to secrecy. 'I'm telling you, because you're my closest and dearest friends, but it must go no further until my betrothed…' she had hugged herself, imagining Daniel, 'is ready to announce our engagement.'

'We could have a double wedding,' Connie said, when the girls were taking a break from the factory floor.

'Lieutenant Winterton – will you be Lady Winterton of some'at?' Iris paused, holding her cigarette away from her.

'No,' Beth laughed.

'Well, the Lieutenant and his wife-to-be will have a grander wedding than the likes of you Connie Drinkwater. They'll be lords and ladies of the manor and the like invited.'

'You couldn't be more wrong,' Beth said. 'Daniel doesn't have any family to speak of. A step mother he can't abide. His father died and he has no siblings. We haven't talked about the wedding but I'm sure it will be a quiet affair. I'd like to marry in the little church in Thorncrest. It's so pretty. And it was our outing to that valley that led to his proposal. I would love a double wedding, Connie if your family approve. I don't have much family left and so it would be good to share our joy with your loved ones.' Beth felt a wave of grief. They came like that, crashing over her when she thought she had adjusted to the loss of Fred and Archie.

'Maybe Geoffrey will propose and I can share your wedding,' Rosie said.

'Fine. Why don't you all have one big wedding celebration and I'll be a communal bridesmaid––the one with no beau.' Iris rolled her eyes.

'Ooh when you get married you can have all of your sisters as bridesmaids. They're so pretty,' Connie said. Iris's five sisters were, like Iris, blessed with halos of golden curls.

'Fat chance I'll find a husband with all our men at war.'

A piercing whistle told them their break was over.

Three long weeks passed before Beth got news of Daniel. He wrote a letter, which was delivered by Rosie.

Dearest Beth,

My darling girl. I have been fit for nothing since the glorious time we spent together in Thorncrest. Despite my dreamy demeanour, and general lack of attention for the everyday – or maybe because of that – Captain Palmer has informed me, I'm to be moved to special duties. No more patrolling the beautiful skies of Yorkshire, imaging you asleep in a house far below. I can't wait for the day when I can call you, my wife. When I am curled up next to you in bed.

There's a dance on Friday, week. I hope you can get time off work to be my guest. Captain Palmer has invited Rosie, so we will arrange a carriage for you . Every day apart from you feels like torture.

I hope Daisy has forgiven me. She said, do the right thing. The only thing in my world that feels right is being with you. Forever.

Love and kisses,

Daniel

Lieutenant D. Winterton, Royal Flying Corps.

Beth read the letter repeatedly until she knew the words by heart. How much longer could this war last? She longed for it to be over; for her and Daniel to marry. She didn't care where they lived, America or England, so long as they were together. It would be tough for her parents if she moved away. She was all they had left, but Beth couldn't think about that; Daniel's happiness came first. If Daniel needed to live in his homeland, then she would support him. Maybe her parents could relocate. Make a fresh start. Her mum had gone into a depression following the memorial service. Although Beth still felt her loss keenly, loving Daniel had eased some of her pain.

On the day of the party, Daisy put aside any misgivings and helped the girls to dress. She carried an armful of dresses into Beth's bedroom. 'I think we're a similar size. You're welcome to borrow anything you choose. The beaded, jade dress is gorgeous. And I have a feather creation for your hair. How are you going to style your hair? I should have asked Clara to stay on to help you.'

Beth laughed. 'I've never had a maid help me dress and I'm not going to start now. But thank you, Daisy. This is so kind of you. Would it be frowned upon if I wore my hair loose?' Beth was remembering the day at the waterfall. Daniel loved her hair; he would appreciate a natural look.

'Very bohemian. I approve. But, let's weave flowers into it. You'll look like a Rossetti painting.'

When Daisy had finished helping her to dress, bizarre when Daisy was of the gentry and Beth a former housemaid, they both stood back to admire her reflection in the long mirror. The jade dress was like a river with sunlight reflected off it; chiffon draped over sheer silk, it clung in all the right places, and flowed over her body, shimmering as it caught the light. Beth caught her breath. She looked incredible.

'Do you think Daniel will approve?' Beth grinned. She knew he would and expected Daisy to enthuse.

But her landlady frowned, then squeezed Beth's shoulder. 'You're a vision of beauty, darling.'

When the carriage arrived, Daisy saw them off like a proud mum. 'Are you sure Geoffrey has arranged for your carriage home? Have a wonderful time but don't consume too much alcohol as it will dull your senses and with no escort you need to be alert for your own protection. I'll leave the hallway lit for you. Have a wonderful time.'

'That was kind of Daisy, loaning her things,' Beth said as they pulled away from the house. Rosie had borrowed long gloves and a tiara. 'I don't know why she was against my courtship with Daniel but she seems to have come around.'

'I think Camille's sudden departure hit Daisy hard. Clara told me she left the country soon after delivering your bike,' Rosie said.

The note on violet paper. Beth had forgotten about it after the shock of her telegram. *Forgive me.* 'Does Clara know why Camille left and where she went?'

'No. But she hinted that there was more to Daisy and Camille's relationship than artist and patron, or artist and model.'

Beth remembered the painting of Daisy reclining nude she

The Canary Girl's Secret

and Rosie found in the salon the day she met Daisy. 'Oh. That would make sense. Poor Daisy. She's not been herself since the art auction. I selfishly thought it was all about me and Daniel but if she's missing Camille, maybe feeling abandoned and unloved it explains a lot.'

Through the window of their carriage, Beth saw the imposing stone buildings of Leeds had been replaced by rolling moors. She felt a flutter of excitement as she anticipated seeing Daniel again.

'I know Daniel is being moved from Yorkshire but he couldn't say much in his letter. Has Geoffrey told you anything?'

'Only what you know. He's going to be flying over German territory, taking photos or something,' Rosie said.

Beth gasped. 'No. I didn't know that. Why didn't you tell me?'

'Sorry. I thought you knew. He's not fighting or anything. Just reporting back on things. You know – taking photos. It can't be that dangerous, can it?'

'Yes. It's dangerous. His plane could be shot down. He could be taken prisoner. Why are they sending Daniel? It's not fair.' Beth put her head in her hands. Thank God, she would be seeing him soon. Maybe Rosie had got it wrong. Daniel would explain. Tell her she was worrying about nothing.

It was dark by the time they arrived in Ripon. Geoffrey was waiting for their carriage. He looked dashing in full dress uniform. Beth couldn't wait to see Daniel in his finery. Ladies in confections of lace, chiffon, and tulle, were being handed down from carriages; hair-combs and feathers bobbing. A few heads turned to appraise Beth's bohemian look. She grinned, anticipating Daniel's reaction. The only one that mattered. She searched behind Geoffrey but couldn't see him.

When Geoffrey paused from showering Rosie with

compliments and chaste kisses – –his lips on her gloved hand – he greeted Beth. 'I've ordered a magnum of champagne to celebrate our beautiful ladies.'

'Is Lieutenant Winterton waiting for us inside?' Beth said, still searching the faces of officers gathered at the front of the building.

'I'm sorry Miss Hardy, Lieutenant Winterton was called away earlier today. I'm sure he'll join us as soon as he can. Shall we?'

Beth frowned, reluctant to go in without Daniel. Rosie glared at her, and so Beth took one of Geoffrey's arms and Rosie the other.

As soon as they were seated, Beth turned to Geoffrey. 'Why have you sent Daniel on a dangerous mission? Why him?' She ignored warning looks from Rosie.

'My dear girl, I haven't sent Lieutenant Winterton anywhere.'

Beth sighed with relief.

'It was my superiors. One of the big chiefs requested Lieutenant Winterton. You ought to be proud of him. It's a great honour and one well deserved. Daniel Winterton is an excellent pilot and a respected officer. Ah, here are our dinner companions. Let me make some introductions.' Geoffrey stood up to greet two couples making their way to the table.

Second-Lieutenant Barclay and his wife, Emma, and Lieutenant Appleby and his sweetheart, Catherine, a shy girl who blushed every time she spoke, settled themselves at their table.

Beth tried to concentrate on what Emma Barclay was saying. Something about the scarcity of domestic staff now women were volunteering for the war effort. Beth was one of those women, not a lady of the Manor despite her get-up, but she was too distracted to offer this information. Where was Daniel?

The band struck up, Oh Johnny Medley. 'This was our first dance,' Rosie exclaimed, jumping to her feet. Geoffrey and Rosie took to the floor, followed by the other two couples. Emma had the grace to hesitate, not wanting to leave Beth alone at the table, but she waved them away. 'I'm fine. Daniel will be here any moment, I'm sure.'

But she wasn't. At nine-thirty a message was delivered to their table. The private handed it to Geoffrey, saluting as he did so. They all waited as Geoffrey opened the folded note and read it.

'I'm sorry, Beth.'

Beth swallowed hard. The room blurred. No. Not Daniel.

'Daniel's okay.' Geoffrey reassured. 'But I'm afraid it's not good news. He won't be joining us this evening. It's this photo-reconnaissance mission. We thought he wouldn't be moved for a few weeks but apparently, he was needed for training, and briefing. This is all hush hush but I'm telling you so you don't worry.' He spoke quietly, although they were alone at the table with Rosie.

'How can I not worry? He'll be flying over enemy territory.' Beth wiped away a tear.

Rosie put an arm around her. 'Maybe we should leave?'

'No. No. I'm sorry, spoiling the party. You're right, Captain Palmer. Daniel is alive and well. Thank you for sharing confidential information with me. I really appreciate your kindness. Now, take my beautiful friend onto the dance floor and show us how to dance. I remember your moves from the ball when the two of you met.'

As Beth watched them gliding across the dance floor in one another's arms, she sent up a prayer. 'Please God keep Daniel safe.'

23

AUGUST 1916

Daisy gave voice to the secret fear Beth had been holding close. They were alone in the kitchen, unpacking the evening's meal delivered by Mrs Kavanagh; fish and potato pie, and raisin pudding. Beth felt as though she were living on a diet of bread and potatoes; she longed for fresh fruit and vegetables, lean meat, and a fillet of cod, not the tiny scraps of fish hidden within the potato of Mrs K's pie.

'You could claim a bigger ration of dairy. It would do you good,' Daisy said.

Beth came out of the larder, where she had stored the pie for later. 'We get extra milk to stop us looking like canaries. I don't think it stretches to butter and cheese but I've a friend in the dairy. If we need more, I could have a quiet word.'

Daisy shook her head. 'I meant in your condition. The baby.'

Beth felt the blood rush from her head. She sat down. 'The baby?' But she knew. When the morning sickness started, and her nipples felt tender, she had counted the weeks. 'What makes you think…?'

'About twelve weeks?' Daisy asked.

Beth nodded. 'But I don't know that I am.'

'When did you last menstruate?'

Beth blushed. 'Before I went to the waterfall with Daniel.'

'I thought as much. Sorry, darling. You're pregnant. It's starting to show. And so, you need to eat a healthy diet. It's not a good idea to be working in the factory, either.'

'I have to work.' Nobody else knew. Not even Daniel. He said they were to marry. She would write to him. The next time he had leave, they would marry – before the baby was born. 'I need the money.' It wasn't just the money. She needed to be with her friends. To be occupied; to stop her mind wandering to a dark place.

'This dairy. Could you ask for a transfer?' Daisy sat down opposite Beth at the kitchen table.

'I couldn't tell anyone.' Beth put her head in her hands. To admit she had made love out of wedlock was shaming. Connie, Iris, and Rosie might understand, but Mr Hamilton? She cringed. And she didn't want John Beck to know.

'If you leave it with me, I'll use my influence to get you moved. I promise, nobody will know the reason. But you must look after this baby.'

Beth stroked her bump. Daniel's baby. She was carrying a little Daniel. 'I need to let Daniel know he's going to be a father but I don't know where to send a letter. I've not heard a word from him since he was sent away on this mission.'

Daisy looked at her thoughtfully, then turned her back to light the oven. When she straightened up and faced Beth, she said, 'I've a friend in the War Office. Write to Daniel and I'll see it reaches him.'

'Thank you, Daisy.' Beth wasted no time. She prayed that

Daniel would soon be home so they could marry. And in the meantime, working in the dairy would be fun. Although she would miss chatting with Iris and Connie.

Beth told Rosie her news that evening when they had gone upstairs to prepare for bed.

'I've something to tell you,' Beth said. She took Rosie's hand and led her into her bedroom. 'Sit down.'

Rosie sat alongside Beth on her bed. 'What is it? You're scaring me? Is it about Geoffrey? I knew he was too good to be true.' Rosie put her head in her hands. 'He's married, isn't he?'

Beth laughed. 'No, he's not. Geoffrey is perfect. Perfect for you. And I'm happy for you both. It's not that.' She stroked her belly. 'I'm pregnant.'

Rosie screamed, and Beth covered her ears.

'I don't want everyone to know. Daisy's pulling a few strings to get me a job in the dairy. We'll have to make up a story. I know – too much TNT. I'm sensitive to the chemical and need a break to try and get it out of my system.'

Rosie nodded. 'That would work. But soon it'll be obvious.'

'I've written to Daniel. As soon as he has leave, we'll get married. After that, I don't mind if people find out. My parents would be upset if they knew – but it won't be so bad if we have a date to wed.'

Early-morning milking was at six, and so Beth kept to the same hours and caught the train in with Rosie. She was grateful to have this time with her friend. Geoffrey had no news of Daniel but assured Beth, through Rosie, that Daniel was doing important work as squadron leader and his silence was no cause for concern. Rosie had agreed not to share Beth's news with Geoffrey, as Daniel had to hear first.

John Beck was delighted to have Beth working with him. On the first morning, he greeted her like a long-lost friend. 'I knew you'd find a way back to the cows. You're a natural dairy farmer like me.'

'I don't know about that. They're beautiful creatures but you'll have to teach me how to milk. I'm a complete novice.'

And so, John sat alongside Beth and instructed her in the art of milking. It was calming: the methodical squeeze and pull of her hands, a warm, musky scent from the cows, an occasional low as one of them objected to being moved.

'I think I saw your family farm,' Beth said.

Squeeze. Pull. She could hear milk hitting the pail as John worked beside her. 'Beck's Farm. When the war's over I'll buy some cows and get the dairy up and running again. My parents kept one, but she no longer produces milk. What were you doing out that way?'

'I grew up in Knaresborough. I had a friend, Mary Button. She lived in Thorncrest,' Beth said.

'The Buttons. I knew Simon. He would have gone to war. Sometimes I feel guilty that I'm not fighting.'

Beth's cow lowed and shifted position. She rubbed her flank. 'Okay, girl. I'll get better at this. Just be patient. You're doing an important job for the war effort John.'

'Your hands and arms will ache tonight but you'll find it easier over time.' He sighed. 'I'm a diabetic. I can manage it fine but it would be a risk out in the field. So, I'm doing what I know. Hardy. Hardy. Any relation to Fred Hardy?'

Beth stopped milking. Hearing his name as though he were still alive brought a wave of emotion. She could go days feeling relatively calm about her loss, and then a memory, or a word, would send her reeling. Breathe. Just breathe.

'Are you okay?' John said, without pausing in the steady rhythm of milk hitting pail.

Beth repositioned her hands. Squeeze. Pull. 'Sister. Fred and Archie. My brothers. Both dead.' Squeeze. Pull.'

Now John stopped. 'Oh God. I'm sorry Beth. So, sorry. Damn this bloody war.'

They worked in silence. The squish of milk, John's pail, then Beth's, counted the time. Eventually, when Beth felt as though her forearms were burning from exertion, John said. 'Let's take ten.'

They stepped out of the barn into the early morning sunshine. 'I told you. You're a natural,' John said.

'I'm not, but I'll learn.' Beth wondered whether to tell him the reason she had to work in the dairy before it became obvious.

'Knaresborough. Ivy Cottage?' John said.

'That's right.'

'I've been to your house. When I was a boy, I played with Fred and Archie. My parents know your parents. Fancy that.'

Beth gulped. She couldn't risk her parents finding out she was pregnant through the Becks. 'Small world,' she said.

The day passed quickly. She delivered several milk churns to the factory and managed to slip into the canteen when the girls were taking their break.

'Here she is, our lovely milkmaid,' Iris said when Beth plonked herself down at their table. 'How's life on the farm?'

'It's more tiring than you think. Honest to God, my arms are killing me. I'm going to look like Popeye. And I miss all of you. But I'm not sorry to get away from the noise of the machines.'

'You don't look yellow,' Connie peered at her with a knowing look. 'I've handled more TNT than you. Is there another reason for your transfer that you're not telling us?'

Beth couldn't stop the smile tugging at her lips. 'You know I would tell you, if I could.'

'Nuff, said.' Connie nodded.

Iris frowned, and then the penny dropped. 'Oh. Oh!'

'Daniel will be home on leave soon. So…' Beth widened her eyes, hoping to convey her meaning.

'We'll have to start planning our double wedding,' Connie laughed.

'Can I be your bridesmaid?' Rosie said.

'Enough,' Beth laughed. 'Tell me the news I'm missing from the factory floor.'

'Hamilton has been seen about town with the supervisor from room 42. You know, the one with a lazy eye,' Iris said.

'She doesn't have a lazy eye,' Rosie said. 'I think one eye is a bit smaller than the other.'

'I think it's attractive,' Connie said.

Beth smiled, listening to her friends. The war had brought hardship, but it had also brought her the friendship of these remarkable women, Daniel, the love of her life, and, she put a hand to her belly, the beautiful little soul nestled inside her womb.

Rosie saw the movement of Beth's hand and winked. 'Meet you usual time for the train home?'

24

SEPTEMBER 1916

It was an ordinary day. She had returned home from work with Rosie, marvelling at the change of season; how the air smelt different at the end of summer--a trace of wood smoke in the air, an earthy sweetness as though the last dregs of summer were being wrung out and hung to dry. The light was different too. The sun lower in the sky. A golden glow, old gold, mellowed with time, unlike the bright new shininess of spring. It had been these thoughts and that of her baby – his or her tiny features being formed, fingers and toes, a beating heart – protected in the warmth of her womb, that had accompanied her on the walk home.

'Ooh post,' Rosie said, swooping up a pile of mail from the letter tray in the hall. 'Daisy. Daisy. An invitation to a cocktail party. Why don't we get party invitations?'

Beth sat on the stairs and massaged her foot. They'd swelled up again. 'I need to find a more comfortable pair of shoes.'

'Oh.' Rosie froze, her mouth open.

'What is it?' Beth cocked her head. Their eyes met, and Beth saw her fear. 'Rosie?'

Rosie's hand was trembling when Beth reached her side. She clutched an envelope with the words, Zurück an Absender – Gefallen. Beneath was written their address.

'Can you read German?' Rosie said.

'No.' Beth took the envelope from her. It had a red-inked mark in Gothic script. She turned the letter over. It had been slit open and resealed with wax. 'We'd better wait for Daisy. It could be for her.'

'What do you think it is?' Rosie said.

In the pit of her stomach, Beth knew. She broke the seal and opened the envelope. Inside was her letter addressed to Lieutenant Winterton. A sickening scent of fire and engine oil; the paper scorched like lightly toasted bread. 'Oh Rosie,' Beth stumbled into a chair.

The front door opened. 'What a glorious day. September is my favourite month of the year,' Daisy trilled as she threw her hat at the hat stand. 'Missed.'

Her tone changed as she took in the scene before her. 'What is it?'

Rosie handed her the discarded envelope that had contained Beth's letter to Daniel.

'Oh darling. You shouldn't have opened this. Why didn't you wait for me? I'd have–'

'––What? What could you have done, Daisy?' Beth yelled. 'He's dead. That's what it says, isn't it? Dead. Dead. Dead.'

Daisy studied the envelope. 'It's been returned from Germany. Return to sender – deceased. This,' she traced a finger over the mark in red ink, 'is Swiss. It's come through the Red Cross repatriation service. Have you opened your letter, darling?'

Beth shook her head. She handed it to Daisy, unable to bear the truth.

Daisy opened it for her. Beth knew what was inside: her letter telling Daniel she was pregnant and her photograph – one taken in a studio to celebrate her sixteenth birthday. 'His body was found by the Germans,' Daisy said. 'The corner of your letter's been snipped; the mark of a German field censor.'

'I don't want my bloody letter returned. I want Daniel,' Beth shouted. 'I want Daniel.' Her voice broke as she fell into Rosie's arms with a juddery sob.

'Put her to bed, darling. I'll prepare a brandy and warm milk.'

Alone in her room, Beth stared up at the ceiling. He couldn't be dead. It wasn't possible. They were to be married. He said she could fly his biplane; travel with him to America. Before Daniel, she couldn't imagine loving a person so much that without them life had no meaning. 'I'm sorry,' she whispered to the foetus curled up in her womb. Daniel's unborn baby would never know his or her father. She ought to feel grateful that she carried a part of Daniel with her, but the reminder of what might have been was too painful. *Why couldn't I have died with him?* she thought.

Day turned to night, and Beth barely moved from her position on the bed. An untouched cup of milk stood on her bedside table, with a layer of skin where it had cooled. Someone knocked on the door – Daisy? Rosie? Footsteps coming and going. Then daylight flooded her room. Still, she lay. As though she were dead. Beth wished that she was.

. . .

Around the middle of the day, there was another knock. This time Daisy barged in uninvited. 'I'm sorry, darling, this can't go on. You've barely eaten in three days. In here, Clara.'

Clara entered with a jug of hot water. She put it on the washstand and backed out.

'Will you bathe yourself or do I need to supervise?' Daisy said.

Beth shook her head. 'Go away. Please let me be.'

'I'll leave, if you promise to get up and have a wash. You left your supper tray and breakfast. We can't afford to waste food. So, make yourself presentable and come down to lunch. I mean it, Beth. Losing Daniel like that was a tragedy. But we're at war. These things happen. Daniel was brave. Don't tarnish his memory by indulging in self-pity. I'll give you thirty minutes. If you're not down by then, I'll have to reconsider your lodging agreement. I provide room and board because you're working for the war effort. If you're going to take to your bed, it will have to be elsewhere. So, up!'

As the door banged shut behind Daisy, Beth sat up. How dare she? Self-pity? Beth felt as though her heart had been cut out. Just because there was no blood, it didn't mean she wasn't bleeding to death. Daisy had no idea what it felt like. This surge of anger propelled Beth to act. She threw off her clothes and scrubbed her skin with soap and water. When she reached her belly, her movement softened – gentle sweeps of the soap and rag around her bump. Twenty weeks. She wouldn't be able to hide her pregnancy much longer. *What am I going to do?* Her parents didn't know, and now, with no prospect of a wedding, she couldn't tell them.

'Miss St. Clair, asked me to check on you,' Clara said, entering the room. 'Do you need any help?'

'No.' Beth sighed. 'I'm coming down.'

The Canary Girl's Secret

When Beth entered the dining room, Rosie leapt to her feet. 'Oh Beth. I'm so sorry. Come here.'

Beth was afraid to move or speak in case she fell apart.

Rosie wrapped her arms around Beth and held her tight, stroking her hair. 'It's okay. I've got you. Hush.' She rocked Beth as though she were an infant, and Beth felt a wall within crumble. She let out a sob. It sounded like an animal in pain. 'There, now,' Rosie soothed.

Mrs Kavanagh had provided a vegetable pie with a little ham. Daisy was right; they could not afford to waste food, but Beth couldn't eat.

'You need to, for the baby,' Daisy said, serving her a small portion.

Beth loaded her fork and eyed it like medicine. She struggled to chew a mouthful but couldn't swallow. So, Beth sipped some water and toyed with the food on her plate. 'How was work this morning?' she said, trying to shift attention away from her.

'I'm in room forty-two for the next week, filling shells – well putting the fuses in. I don't mind it. It's quieter in there. Connie's doing the same shift so it's all about the wedding she's planning. Sorry, Beth.'

'It's okay. I'm happy for her. I suppose I'd better get back to work,' Beth said, throwing Daisy an apologetic look. Daisy was of the stiff-upper lip brigade, and Beth felt a little ashamed of her emotional collapse.

'Don't go back until you're ready,' Daisy said, surprising her. 'You are up and about, that's the main thing. We need to discuss how we manage your pregnancy now a marriage is not to be forthcoming.'

'I can't have a baby. My parents would be outraged if they knew I was pregnant. Nobody at work knows.'

'Well…' Rosie gave an apologetic look. 'Connie and Iris

might have guessed. I didn't say anything. But they know to keep quiet.'

'Okay. If you must go back, stay until we can't hide it. Then, you'll have your baby here or at the local hospital. I have several midwives amongst my contacts. You'll have to tell your family sooner or later, Beth,' Daisy said.

'No.' Beth spoke more firmly than she intended, but she was adamant her parents weren't to know. Daisy was right, they would have to eventually but not until she had a plan. 'Let's wait until the baby's born,' she said.

Returning to work was a good move. Beth felt the pain of losing Daniel acutely, but the routine of getting up early for milking, and the gentle rhythm of work distracted her, and for a few seconds each day her mind became still. In time, Daisy assured her, those seconds would become minutes, and eventually the minutes might amount to an hour. Beth couldn't imagine ever feeling happy again.

She had been back at work for two weeks. The regulation work smock had served Beth well in disguising her bump, but at twenty-one weeks pregnant, it was beginning to show. That morning, she had decided it was time to give notice. The plan was a story about her parents needing her support at home following the death of her brothers. She'd prepared John by mentioning her parents in conversation. They were indeed struggling, and if she were a better daughter, she might have done just that, but she wasn't. Beth hated herself for lying, for being a neglectful daughter, for not wanting to be a single mother, and for being furious with Daniel for dying.

'Could you carry a couple of pails over to the factory?' John said, when it was close to the end of her shift. 'You can drop them off and leave from there. It's about time now.'

'I wanted to talk to you about leaving altogether,' Beth said. She'd planned on having that conversation today but kept putting it off. For a man who had helped birth calves, she was amazed he hadn't guessed she was pregnant, but then he barely looked at her, concentrating his attention on his beloved cows.

'I thought as much,' John said. For a moment Beth thought he was going to say he knew, but then he added, 'I know your mam is struggling. They'll be glad to have you home.'

She would miss her friends. Their cheerful banter when she joined them in the cafeteria. Connie had planned her wedding down to the icing design on her wedding cake. The bottom tiers were to be made from cardboard, but the top tier would be elegant enough to grace the pages of a society magazine – at least in Connie's imagination. Iris entertained them with stories of her siblings, her squabbling sisters, and the little brother she adored. Halfway across the field, between the dairy and the factory the baby inside her moved.

'Oh,' Beth cried. It was the first time she had felt him or her. 'Daniel. Our baby moved.' She imagined his hand cupping her belly. It was real. She was having his baby. A tiny Daniel. *If it's a boy, I'll call him Daniel, and if it's a girl, Daniella. I'll tell her about her amazing father.* Beth quickened her pace, anxious to share the news with her friends. The pails were heavy, and she had to put them down to reposition her hold.

Bang. The sound was deafening. Beth cowered, afraid they were being bombed. Bang. The sky lit up. A blaze of red. The factory was on fire. Beth ran towards the fire, stumbling on grass tussocks. As she neared the building, Hamilton detached himself from a cluster of officials. He stepped into her path. 'You can't go in. Stay well back. There could be another explosion.'

'But. Rosie. Connie. That's room forty-two.' Beth looked

on in horror. Nobody could have survived that explosion. 'Please. I've got to get them out. You don't understand. They're all I've got.' She fought against Hamilton's restraint, thumping her fists on his chest.

'Fire and ambulance are coming. Here they are now. Get home lass. You'll only get in the way here and I believe you've an extra one to take care of.' He nodded at her knowingly.

'I can't. I have to find them. Rosie will be looking for me. We catch the train together.'

A Red Cross lady was holding her arm. 'Come along sweetheart. Let's get you away to safety. The emergency services will rescue your friend. How about a nice cup of sweet tea?'

There was nothing Beth could do. She sat shivering in the welfare room of the main factory. People came and went, updating them on progress. There were casualties. Some of them taken to hospital. Nobody could tell her whether Rosie and Connie had survived. Eventually, John Beck arrived, maybe summoned by Hamilton or just drawn to help when he saw the explosion. He travelled on the train with Beth and then insisted on walking her to the door of the house.

'We're not to tell anyone of this incident,' he said.

'Why? How are the girls' injuries going to be explained?' Beth said.

'Accident at work. Which it was. One of the shells exploded. Instructions are, no word of this can get out. Understand?'

Beth nodded. She just wanted him to leave so she could go inside and find Rosie. Her friend would have been looking for her at the station.

'I'll say goodbye then, lass. It was good working with you. Give my regards to Mr and Mrs Hardy.'

Rosie wasn't home. Beth sat in the front room watching

the road. Any minute now, Rosie will come up the front steps, she thought. But Rosie didn't come home.

The silence that followed was dreadful. By telling her to keep silent, John, on behalf of the management, had taken away her emotional support. The girls in the factory could talk to each other, but Beth wasn't going back. And who would she talk to? A letter from Hamilton informed her that Rosie, Connie, and Iris had all died in the explosion. Iris wasn't on the rota for that day but had stepped in as last-minute cover. Beth guessed it was so she could be with her friends – more time to chat and joke. Their smiling faces, the easy banter. It broke her heart to think of them. All dead.

First her brothers, then Daniel. When Beth thought she could bear no more pain – that her girlfriends would help get her through – they too were torn from her life. A cruel, cruel God. What had she done to deserve this suffering? Beth shut herself in her room. Curled up like the foetus inside her, she hid beneath the blanket on her bed. Daisy could knock on the door all she liked. She could throw her out on to the street; she really didn't care. It felt as though she were free falling into a dark abyss. If she lay very still, it would swallow her up and she wouldn't need to try any more. Just give in and let it sweep her away. Because there was nothing left to live for.

The baby kicked. 'I'm sorry,' she whispered.

25

SATURDAY 2ND JULY 1966

The next morning, Louise caught Bill as he was about to leave for the hospital. 'Will you be seeing Esther, today?' she asked.

Bill paused as he checked his pockets, then searched around for his keys.

'By the kettle,' Louise said. She was bursting with news and missed her friend and confidante.

'Thanks.' Bill pocketed his keys. 'Yes. I'll pop in first thing and then again at lunchtime. I'll probably stay with her when my shift ends.'

'Will you eat in the hospital canteen or shall I prepare something?' It was awkward, this forced domesticity without Esther as a buffer.

'No, I'll sort myself. But thanks.'

'Please tell Esther my meeting with her boss, Diane, went well. They're going to sponsor me to train as a librarian, well prepare me to train. And I've information on Daisy St Clair.' Bill's eyes had glazed over. He would be thinking about his schedule for the day and worrying about Esther and the baby.

'It's okay. Just say, Louise said thanks for everything. I'll visit her myself as soon as I can.'

'Got it,' Bill said, before heading out the door.

Alone in the kitchen, Louise couldn't settle. She tried reading Daisy St Clair's file again, her biography and address, looking for clues, but she couldn't concentrate. Why hadn't she just said hello when she saw Richard and Fiona in the Walnut Tree? There was no reason they shouldn't lunch together; they were work colleagues. And she reminded herself, it was her idea they had a break. It was time to get her life in order, or she was going to lose Richard.

First, a phone call to Aunt Emma. Richard was right to chastise her; she shouldn't have left London without saying goodbye to her mum and giving her the opportunity to explain herself. Her mum didn't have a phone, but Aunt Emma did. She picked up on the second ring.

'Hello, Aunt Emma. I'm sorry I haven't been in touch. How's Mum? Has she been discharged yet?'

'About time you called. Your mum was upset you took off without saying goodbye. I must say I was surprised you left without saying hello to me. Pearl said you had an emergency at home.'

It was true. If she had known Richard had been taken in for questioning, she would have left London immediately. So, Louise replied, 'There was an urgent matter. I'm afraid it's been taking up a lot of my time. But things are calming down here. How's Mum?'

'You know Pearl. She's not one to be held back. If the doctor hadn't agreed to her going home tomorrow, I reckon she would have walked out. I'm keeping her here with me until her arm's out of plaster.'

'That's kind of you, Aunty. Thank you. There's something I want to ask you.' Louise hesitated. Her absent father was a taboo subject. 'When I was in Mum's flat I found some unpacked boxes, books, toys that sort of thing. There was a letter tucked inside one of the encyclopaedias. It was from my father.' She waited for a reaction.

'Your father?'

'Yes. Blake Sommerfeld.'

A few seconds passed before Aunt Emma said. 'What makes you think this Blake Sommerfeld is your father?'

'Because the letter was addressed to my precious daughter. He wrote that he wanted to be part of my life. That my mum was to tell me about him when I was old enough to make my own decision about meeting him.' Now, she had said it. There was no turning back.

'In an encyclopaedia, you say? The old set that belonged to granny Ruby?'

'I guess so. I hadn't seen them before.'

'What was the date on that letter?'

'There wasn't one. He lives in Australia. At least he did when he wrote the letter. I've contacted him but I don't know if he's still alive. I want to meet him Aunty, but I don't want to upset Mum. Is there anything you can tell me about him?'

At the other end of the line, Emma exhaled a deep breath. 'Would you mind sharing his address with me?'

Louise didn't like to ask why. She hoped Aunt Emma wasn't going to try to settle a family vendetta. When she had relayed the information, Louise asked after her cousins, and the baby – Emma's grandchild. 'Please give my love to Mum. I didn't tell her about finding the letter but I will when I see her.'

'And when will that be?' Aunt Emma said.

'Soon. I promise. Thank you for looking after her. If I could take leave from work to care for her in London I would, but my boss is on sick leave, so I've got to hold the fort here.

I'm staying with friends whilst our house is being built.' Louise gave Aunt Emma, Bill and Esther's address and their phone number so her mum could contact her when she was out of hospital.

When Louise put the phone down, she felt as though one burden had lifted. Her aunt hadn't been horrified by Louise making contact with her father. So, he hadn't done anything terrible that would make him a threat to her. And her aunt was bound to tell her mother, so that would pave the way for what would be a difficult discussion. Now that she had got over the shock of discovering a father, her anger had dissipated. If she wanted Richard to forgive her for acting rashly and jumping to conclusions, maybe she should cut her mum a bit of slack. Besides, she was too happy and excited at the prospect of training as a librarian to hold a grudge.

Two more things to fix. Report to the police. She had tried to pervert the course of justice, and that was wrong, but she hadn't harmed Eddie. If Paul Evans hadn't told her to say 'no comment' to every question, she would have explained this.

She couldn't be beholden to Big Jim. He was a dangerous man. There would be no getting back with Richard until Big Jim was no longer a threat to either of them.

Before leaving for the police station, Louise penned a letter to Richard. He'd asked if they could write, and as she was the one who instigated their separation, she ought to be the first to do so. There was so much she wanted to tell him.

My darling Dicky, I miss you so much. I've exciting news. My application to train as a librarian has been accepted – well the first stage of the process. I'm going to be sponsored by the library service. And the other good news – –I've some information about Daisy St Clair. This is the woman who organised Ma's funeral. I'm sure she will be able to provide the evidence we need. The St. Clairs are an important family, so that might hold some weight with the Corporation.

You would have heard about Esther. Bill spends most evenings at her bedside.

We won't be apart forever. I'm just trying to sort my life out so I can be the friend you deserve. I love you and always will.

And then as a postscript a quote from Jane Eyre: *Life appears to me too short to be spent in nursing animosity or registering wrongs. Charlotte Brontë.*

Satisfied that it wasn't overly dramatic and clearly gave her intention for them to get back together soon, Louise sealed the envelope.

When Louise dropped by the post office to deliver her letter, the girl serving said. 'Do you want to take the one for you?'

Louise's heart skipped with joy. Richard had beaten her to it. 'Okay,' she said with a smile.

'Just a postcard.'

Louise's waited whilst the girl went out back. 'Here you go.'

It was a postcard of another reservoir in Yorkshire. Louise flipped it over.

Written in capitals with a red pen, it said:

Louise Boyd owes Jim Murphy.

And beneath. *You will honour your debt when I say so.*

Fear and fury fought within Louise. Thank God she found the postcard before Richard. This had to end. Trembling, Louise staggered from the shop.

'Your car keys,' the girl shouted after her.

'I have a confession to make,' Louise said to the officer on duty at the police station.

'Hello Louise,' he replied. 'How's Esther?'

'Fine, thank you. Can I see Detective Jenkins?'

'He's not in. I can leave a message.'

'There must be someone who can take down a statement from me. It's about a murder investigation.' Louise caught herself almost shouting. She was desperate to clear her name. To shake off her debt to Big Jim. 'Please. Just let me tell you.'

'Sorry. No can do. It has to be Detective Jenkins.'

'When's he due in?' Louise bit her nails. Big Jim had discovered her PO box, so he was bound to know where Richard lived and worked. She had to protect him.

'He's unlikely to be in today. Don't worry I'll leave a message.'

Paul Evans emerged from a back office, talking to a man. Louise shrunk back, hoping he wouldn't see her. Too late. He said goodbye to the man and turned. 'Louise. What are you doing here?'

'I was just after an update, on the case,' she lied. Paul would tell her to keep quiet, but she'd had enough of being told what to do. 'I need to know if I'm free to leave the country,' she improvised. It was partly true if she wanted to visit her dad in Australia.

He took her elbow and steered her out of the police station. Outside he said, 'So, where were you planning to go?'

It was none of his business. But Louise didn't want to alienate him, so she said, 'Nothing definite yet.'

'I'll make some enquiries for you. Richard Braithwaite's been cleared. Fiona asked me to get confirmation he was no longer of interest to the police before they went any further in agreeing a business partnership.'

Louise gulped. 'Simms Enterprise?'

'No. A holiday village. They hadn't bothered to tell him he

was off the hook so I expect it's the same for you. leave it with me.'

How could he? Yes, they needed the money, but this was their venture. Okay, she'd said, the holiday village is *your* dream, but to approach Fiona and accept her offer of investment was a betrayal. He should have spoken to her first. And yet, they weren't married; they weren't even business partners. To date, Louise hadn't invested any money in building their home or buying the land and materials for the holiday village. They had been waiting for her inheritance, and now, unless Daisy St. Clair could provide evidence that Elizabeth Beck was dead, it might never happen. No Richard. No. She had to visit Daisy St. Clair in Leeds before her life completely unravelled.

26

SATURDAY 9TH JULY 1966

Daisy St. Clair's secretary had agreed to Louise visiting Miss St. Clair in her townhouse. Now, as Louise checked the directions and made her way along the leafy avenue of grand houses, she felt unsure of herself. She hadn't given a reason for her visit and was surprised at the ease of access to what was a renowned public figure in the local area. Many of the houses had been converted into flats. Louise studied the front doors, where there were several names listed, and the windows; different blinds or curtains on each floor, with very different styles. Flower motifs on one window, floral curtains on the floor below.

A woman was watering pots of geraniums on the steps to her basement flat. She called up to Louise, 'Another beautiful day. Could do with a spot of rain.'

Louise stopped to admire the display of colour, blue salvia contrasting with the bright red geraniums. When they had finished discussing the merits of a container garden in a limited space, Louise asked, 'Have you lived here long?'

'All my life and my mum and dad before me. You're not from around here?'

'No, London but now I live in Thorncrest, not far from Harrogate.'

'I know it. Visiting friends?' The woman put down her watering can and stretched her back.

'Daisy St. Clair. She was a friend of my … grandmother, Elizabeth Beck.' It felt right describing Ma as her grandmother, although it wasn't true.

'A bit of a character, Miss St. Clair. But a good soul. Did a lot for the women around here. Funded a home for unmarried women and a refuge. I haven't seen her in a long while. She used to walk by in her velvet coat, and beautiful hats. A glamorous lady. Give her my regards. She won't know me but let her know she's not been forgotten.'

With an image of Daisy St. Clair now forming in her mind, Louise strode with purpose to number thirty-four. The front door was burgundy with a brass knocker and bell, which Louise rang and then waited. A young woman answered the door. Her secretary?

'Louise Pearson. I think Miss St. Clair is expecting me,' Louise said.

'Yes. We received your letter. I'm Eve, Miss St. Clair's assistant. Come in.' Someone was playing the piano with gusto. The smell of incense infused the house. 'Daisy's in the salon. She'll be glad of company.'

Louise followed Eve into a room crammed with furniture and objets d'art. Bronze figures, ornate clocks, a vase of peacock feathers, a marble bust, and stuffed birds in a glass case, all jumbled together fighting for space on tables, dressers or the floor. Louise stepped around a stuffed walrus, and the woman playing the piano changed to a slow, soft tempo.

'Sit,' Daisy said.

There wasn't an uncluttered chair in the room, so Louise perched on the edge of a chaise lounge where magazines and books had been stacked.

'I'll bring refreshment. What would you like? Tea, coffee, port, or a sherry?' Eve said.

'A cup of tea, please,' Louise replied, a little uncomfortable with being left alone with this formidable woman.

'A room or a patronage? If you're an artist…' she ran her fingers over the keys. 'I'll need to see your work. Have you brought a portfolio?'

'No, I haven't. I'm not an artist. I was just hoping you could tell me something about my dear friend, Elizabeth Beck.'

Daisy stopped playing abruptly. 'Beth,' she said the name almost as a sigh.

Louise waited for more. She hadn't heard Ma referred to as Beth, only Liz.

'If I could turn back the clock.' Daisy looked beyond Louise, as though watching a film replaying the past. 'I should never have sent her on that wretched bike. She was so young. Impressionable. No. Back before then. The day I met Camille. Oh, I was a fool. Love makes fools of us all.' Daisy shut her eyes tight, as though squeezing away painful memories.

Louise was unsure what to say, but she was saved from a response by Eve, who backed into the room carrying a tea tray. Eve balanced the tray on a glass case of stuffed birds – an impromptu table – and poured the tea. She tossed a china doll, trumpet, biscuit tin and oil lamp from a cane chair and sat down.

'You forgot the biscuits,' Daisy said.

When Eve left the room, Daisy poured a measure of whisky from a hip flask into her cup of tea. Then, she winked at Louise. 'When are you expecting?'

'Oh. I'm not,' Louise gave a half laugh.

'Are you sure about that? I'm rarely wrong.'

'Absolutely.' Except she wasn't. Her period was late, but Louise wasn't too concerned; it was the disruption in her cycle after coming off the pill for a few days.

Eve returned with a plate of assorted biscuits. She looked from Daisy to Beth and back again. 'If you both have everything you need, I'll get on with sorting your paperwork, Miss St. Clair. If you need anything ring for me,' she said.

Louise wondered whether Daisy had records about the funeral, maybe even a copy of Ma's death certificate. Eve would know. But Eve had gone.

'Why did you send Beth off on a bike?' Louise said, taking Daisy back to her recollection in the hope it would lead to some answers about Ma's life.

'I had to get a message to him. Camille. Oh, Camille. Forgive me, she wrote. I never saw her again.' Daisy's face crumbled as a tear slid slowly from one eye, settling in the crease of her wrinkled cheek.

'You arranged Beth's funeral,' Louise said.

Daisy opened her eyes. She looked startled, as though seeing Louise for the first time. 'Who said, I did?'

'I read it in the Parish records. That's why I'm here.'

'You won't get anything out of me. Trying to trick me into exposing my friends and associates. No, Camille. Not this time. Get out. Get out.' Daisy threw an ashtray across the room. It hit the teapot and sent the tray crashing to the floor. Louise jumped up as hot water scalded her shin.

'What's going on?' Eve hurried into the room. She gathered up the broken teapot and milk jug, returning them to the tray.

'I'm sorry,' Louise said. 'I think I stirred up memories.'

'It's okay. I shouldn't have left you. I thought it was a good day. But…' Eve shrugged. 'I'm going to show Louise out. Don't move from your chair. I'll be back in a minute to clear this up.'

At the door, Louise asked Eve about Ma's funeral.

'I don't know. Sorry. I've only been working for Miss St. Clair for the past year. Her memory's going and she gets confused. Some days she's better than others. I don't think you'll find any answers here. It's best not to remind her about the past as she becomes distressed and it's not good for her.' Eve's message was clear. Don't bother Miss St. Clair again. So, that was the end of that line of investigation. And Louise was no closer to proving Ma had died.

'Esther. You're home.' Louise was thrilled to see her friend. 'I've missed you. Are you okay?' Please don't let anything have happened to the baby, Louise thought, crossing the room to hug her.

'We're both fine – me and the baby that is. Bill too. But how are you? Bill tells me you've been working long hours. I hope it's not been too much covering for me.'

Bill made them a pot of tea, and they took it into the garden to sit on the patio. The little cottage garden was bursting with colour and birdsong. Hollyhocks, delphiniums, and phlox providing a haven for bees. The intoxicating scent of an old rose, which tumbled over a neighbouring wall. Beyond the garden, they could see the grounds of Simms Manor. Louise tried to keep her mind off Richard and Fiona, but it was hard; all she could think of was the two of them together. Bouncer padded out after them and settled himself at Esther's feet.

'Bill said you went to Leeds in search of the mysterious Miss St Clair,' Esther said.

Louise told her about the visit. 'So, I can say goodbye to receiving any money from Beck's farm.'

Esther batted a fly away from the sugar bowl. 'You can't

give up. There must be someone else who was at her funeral. I mean where else could she be if not buried in Thorncrest?'

'I know.' Louise felt incredibly weary. 'I can't rest until I know what happened to her.'

'You just missed Richard.'

Louise's heart jolted. 'Was he calling on me, or Bill?'

Esther laughed. 'Both I should think. He had lunch with us. Just sandwiches and soup. Bill spoke to him more than me. I had a lie down upstairs and they came out here to share a beer or two. He was disappointed to have missed you. I think he would have hung on until you came home if Fiona hadn't called him away.'

Louise bristled. 'What do you mean, called him away? I didn't think he worked for her on Saturday afternoons.'

'She saw his car and knocked on the door. They left together. '

Of course they did, Louise thought. It was her own fault for pushing him away. Richard's visit would have been a response to her letter, but she had left it before discovering Big Jim's postcard. Now more than ever, she had to put some distance between her and Richard.

'It must be hard for you living apart,' Esther said.

'I'll move out before your baby's born,' Louise replied.

'You'll have to, as you're sleeping in what will soon become the nursery.'

Louise realised with a shock that she had perhaps outstayed her welcome. Esther and Bill had expected her to be back living with Richard soon. Maybe Esther was thinking, with no inheritance, it would be an age before they could afford plumbing and electricity. It was true. She would have to make other arrangements, as living with Richard was beginning to feel like an impossible dream. But how could she live in Thorncrest without him? It would destroy her to see

Richard and Fiona living together in the house he had built for her, developing the holiday village. She wanted Richard to be happy, but that didn't mean she had to witness it.

'You look tired,' Esther said.

'I am.' Louise yawned. She felt heavy, as though dragging herself through treacle. It was a struggle to keep her eyes open. 'Work's been busy. Fun. I love driving Mobi, who would have thought? And you know I love finding the perfect read for our customers, but I'm tired.'

'And the journey to Leeds. Why don't you go and have a lie down? We thought we'd buy fish and chips for supper tonight. Cod okay for you?'

'Yes please.' Louise's response was automatic. An afternoon nap was beckoning. 'But I'll share a few chips. Not very hungry.'

Nauseas was how she felt. Not surprising given all the stress of that day. At least Esther and her baby were well. And she had a dream job. If she left Thorncrest, she could say goodbye to training as a librarian. Tears hummed in her temples. A lump in her throat. 'Don't let me sleep for too long.'

27

TUESDAY 12TH JULY 1966

Louise was parked outside the Coach and Horses. They always had a lot of punters at this stop; with it being a Tuesday, avid readers had finished their books over the weekend, and the pub took advantage of the library visit by inviting villagers to buy a coffee. An elderly gentleman was discussing the technique for carp fishing – Louise had found him a book on freshwater fishing – when PC Williams mounted the library steps.

'Hello young, Percy,' the older man said. 'How's Stan, your dad?'

'He's well thank you, Mr Douglas.' PC Williams looked unsure of himself, as if shrinking in size.

'I taught young Percy. Seems like the other day, but look at him now. A policeman. Your dad must be proud of you. Taught him too.' Mr Douglas patted PC Williams on the back. 'Here to find a book? This young lady will help you. And if you don't see what you want, she'll order it.'

PC Williams straightened his spine and coughed. 'I'm here on business, but I can wait.'

'Oh. Right you are. I'll get out of your way. I expect you want to impart information to be distributed through the library round. It's an important community service.'

Louise and PC Williams avoided eye contact and remained silent until Mr Douglas took the hint and left with a cheery goodbye.

'I visited the police station last week but there was nobody there to take my statement. Is that why you're here?'

'Possibly. DC Jenkins wants to meet with you. When would be convenient?'

'Now's good. I usually take a lunch break around now. My next stop's at three. Admin work keeps me busy until then. So, if it's convenient to DC Jenkins.'

They arranged for Louise to make her own way to the police station. She parked Mobi outside the cottage and went inside to tell Esther.

'Can I come with you? Not into the police station just into the village. I'm going crazy cooped up indoors all day every day,' Esther said, already on her feet.

'I don't know. Bill said you have to rest.' Louise frowned.

'I won't do anything strenuous. A little stroll. Maybe sit on a bench so I can watch the world go by. I'm bound to see people I know. Have a chat. Believe me, I won't do anything to risk my pregnancy. This little one in here is precious. You have no idea, Louise. We've been trying for a baby for years. I thought it was never going to happen.' Esther's eyes brimmed with tears. 'Sorry. A bit over emotional.'

'Okay. But try and stay seated rather than going for a walk.' Louise had thought Esther's pregnancy was unplanned, that maybe, like her, she put career first. If Esther lost her baby, and Louise was responsible in any way, she would never forgive herself.

She drove to the police station as though carrying trays of eggs. Esther laughed, 'I won't break if you go over a pothole.'

When Esther was safely seated on a bench by the village green, Louise prepared herself for the interview with DC Jenkins. She had arranged it herself, so there was nothing to fear. PC Williams was behind the front desk.

'I'll take you straight through,' he said.

DC Jenkins was waiting in an interview room. Another police officer, a young man in plain clothes, sat in the corner of the room, maybe to observe or take notes. Louise had hoped this interview would be informal.

'I wanted to give a statement,' she said, suddenly nervous. 'I know you're busy, so if you'd like me to just write it down?' Why hadn't she asked Paul Evans to accompany her?

DC Jenkins gave her a long, cold stare, and Louise squirmed in her seat. Eventually he said, 'What were you doing with James Murray on the morning of Saturday 27th July?'

It took a couple of heart-beats for Louise to realise he was talking about Big-Jim. The day he followed her in his Bentley. She cleared her throat. 'Um. Well. Nothing really. Mr Murray knew my husband. He must have recognised my car, as he followed me on the A59.' Louise remembered the Hillman, which slowed down whilst the driver turned to stare.

'Your husband. The deceased, Eddie Boyd?'

'That's right.' Louise's throat was dry. She looked around for a jug of water, but there was none.

'How long have you known James Murray? And why was he following your car?'

The policeman in the corner looked expectantly at Louise, his pen poised at the ready. Why should she cover for Big Jim? She had asked to make a statement to clear her name and break any ties with him. Now was her chance. But years of conditioning and a fear of Big Jim made her freeze. 'May I have a glass of water?' she asked.

DC Jenkins shook his head. 'Later. This is important.'

'Okay.' Louise took a deep breath. 'James Murray – Big Jim – was our landlord when we lived in London. My husband Eddie worked for him.'

'We know the nature of your husband's work, Mrs Boyd,' DC Jenkins said meaningfully. 'What I want to know is your role in this business. So, I repeat. Why was James Murray following your car?'

It was time for her to come clean. 'I did something stupid. Very stupid. That's why I wanted to give a statement.' She told him how she had disposed of the shovel. 'But I didn't kill my husband and neither did Richard Braithwaite.' Why had she mentioned his name? Think before you speak, Louise.

'I'm waiting for an answer to my question,' DC Jenkins said.

'Oh. Well. I was afraid I might be wrongly accused of harming Eddie. Richard and I last saw him at the top of the hill. I have no idea why, or if, he returned to the farmhouse. I'd asked Big Jim to help clear my name because if there was any foul play, Big Jim would have known what happened.'

DC Jenkins nodded his head. 'Do you know what he was doing in Yorkshire?'

'It may have had something to do with a contact in Harrogate. My husband Eddie was involved in some business at a club there just before he died.'

The young policeman was scribbling furiously in his notepad. He looked up when DC Jenkins said, 'A jug of water please.'

'I didn't know. When I married Eddie Boyd, I didn't know…' How much should she convey?

'That he was a gangster? A low-life?' DC Jenkins said.

The Canary Girl's Secret

'I thought he was a philanthropist. Kind. And he was mostly. Just a …'

'Thief?'

The policemen returned with a glass of water, and Louise took a gulp. 'Am I still a suspect?' she said.

DC Jenkins raised his eyebrows. 'A suspect? For what, exactly?'

'I didn't kill Eddie Boyd. I'm sorry, I shouldn't have thrown the shovel into the reservoir.'

'No. You tried to destroy evidence and pervert the course of justice. But you've redeemed yourself by admitting to this crime. And you've been helpful in another investigation concerning James Murray.' DC Jenkins stood up.

'So, if I wanted to leave the country, I would be free to do so?'

DC Jenkins frowned. 'We wouldn't have reason to stop you. Thank you for your time, Mrs Boyd.'

Out in the fresh air, Louise took deep breaths. She looked over at Esther; her face tilted to the sun as she leaned back on the bench. Her question hadn't been hypothetical. Every cell in her body told her to run. Get as far away from Thorncrest, from England, as possible. Big Jim would find out about her interview with DC Jenkins. Louise replayed it in her head. She hadn't ratted on him – not exactly. But he wouldn't see it like that. If Big Jim thought she had broken his confidence, he would make her pay. With her life? Possibly. She wrapped her arms across her chest. There was nowhere to hide. Australia. It was an idea that kept nudging her. Go and find your father. She'd heard about the one-pound pom scheme. It would mean getting an application approved before anyone discovered she was pregnant.

Louise stepped back into the shade as she watched her friend. Esther wanted a baby more than anything else in the world. How would she feel if she lost her baby and Louise – she couldn't ignore the possibility, no, the certainty, any longer – was pregnant? Pregnant. Louise covered her face with her hands. Richard's child. The thought filled her with joy, wonder and absolute terror. She couldn't have this baby, but neither could she harm it, or give it away. In the past few days, she had become protective of the tiny embryo growing inside her, talking to it in her head, feeling an incredible love for this unformed being. But she couldn't tell Richard. He would do the right thing, he always did, but this wasn't just about them. They had to protect the baby. If she stayed in England, it would put Richard and the baby at risk of retribution. He could have a better life with Fiona. She had to be selfless and move aside for Richard to live a better life than the one he would have with her.

Louise watched as a woman with a Yorkshire terrier talked to Esther. She would miss her friends and Yorkshire. The woman and dog ambled up the lane, and Esther arched her back. Louise hurried over. 'Okay. I've finished here.'

'Good. Shall we have a spot of lunch?' Esther said.

'Might as well.' Louise wouldn't be able to concentrate on admin work. Leaving Thorncrest, her friends, Richard, and her dream job, would break her heart. If she allowed her mind to dwell on this, she would lose her nerve, but staying in Thorncrest wasn't an option.

28

APRIL 1918

Beth hugged her arms across her chest and closed her eyes. A robin trilled. His insistence a reminder of life. It felt as though all was lost. The death of her brothers, her friends, and Daniel. Thousands of men killed at war and now the Spanish flu devastating communities. And yet she was alive, and the robin sang. His answer came from the other side of the graveyard. A female robin returning his call? Mum and Dad were still alive. She was alive. And somewhere, baby Daniella would be kicking her little legs. Maybe teething. She could think of her baby now without her breasts filling with milk. She hadn't told her parents. In the days after Daniella's birth, Daisy had tried to persuade her. 'You need to go home. Let your mother care for you both.' But Beth was adamant. She would carry this burden alone.

'You were not a burden, my little rosebud. I was just so tired. I couldn't care for you,' Beth said in her head. She often had these conversations with her daughter. Imagined her developing, becoming a little person. She would be fourteen months old today.

Daisy had found a home for Daniella. Adopted by a woman who had miscarried three pregnancies. The woman, Ruby, said Beth's baby was a precious pearl. A gift to her from heaven. Daisy had made all the arrangements through her connections. At the time, Beth hadn't wanted to know. All she could remember about that time was a feeling of being buried alive. She had fallen into a deep hole, and the ground closed up around her. A vague memory of the baby being held at her nipple. Its angry cry as she turned away. It was like a rat clawing and sucking at her breast. Shame and guilt swept over her. How could she have been so callous and uncaring? Poor little Daniella. The tiny babe created by her and Daniel, made from love. 'If you are looking down on me Daniel, forgive me.'

She opened her eyes. Bluebells and tiny white anemones grew between the gravestones. A weak sun warmed her face. A chorus of starlings, heralding spring. Since moving back to Knaresborough, she often came here. The valley of Thorncrest held happy memories of the perfect day and night she spent with Daniel.

A footstep crunched on gravel, and Beth let out a cry of surprise.

'I'm sorry. I didn't mean to disturb you.' A young man stood on the path leading from the church.

'It's okay. I was lost in thought and you startled me.' Beth was getting good at compartmentalising. Storing away her grief and pain so she could function. There was a time when living seemed impossible; she just wanted to follow Daniel, Rosie and her friends.

'Beth Hardy?' The man said. His voice was familiar.

'Yes.' She walked towards him. 'John. John Beck. How lovely to see you.' She meant it. His smiling face reminded her of happier times. And he was the one person she could talk to about what happened at the factory that day.

'I'm here to put flowers on the graves of my Ma and Pa but if you're in no hurry would you like to come back with me to see our farm?'

'Do you have cows?'

'We do.' John laughed.

Beth heard the cows before they reached the wide gates to Beck's farm. They spoke little on the journey. With her bike in the cart, alongside a few empty milk pails, Beth sat beside John as he guided the Shire horses home. His voice was tender as he coaxed them. The sway of the cart, the earthy scents of horse sweat and bluebell sap – John had picked a bunch of bluebells for his kitchen table and Beth clutched the sticky stems in her hands – held her to the earth, and stopped her mind from straying to dark places.

'Good girl. Nearly there.' He murmured, and for a moment Beth thought he was talking to her.

'They're fine horses,' she said.

'They should be enjoying retirement but better this than going to war. If they had been fitter and younger, they would have been requisitioned by the army. We don't need two but with them being old ladies its kinder letting them share the load. Bessie and Martha.' John kept his eyes on the road. This was the most he had said since they set off. 'Here we are,' he said, as the horses slowed at the top of the hill. Beck's farm.'

As soon as she set foot inside the gates of Beck's farm, Beth felt at home. The beautiful old farmhouse seemed to open its arms to her. Sunlight winked off its windows. The weathered walls — holders of a hundred happy memories – she could feel it in her bones. They settled Bessie and Martha in one of the barns. A cow lowed. Then another joined in.

'Can we say hello to the cows,' Beth said.

'Best not. They need to be milked. I can do it later. You'll be wanting a cup of tea.'

'Who helps you milk?' Beth said.

'It's just me. But I only have four cows. They're not a lot of work. In the day we had a thriving dairy. My mam made cheese and milk for market. I'm just glad to have cows back on the farm.'

'Come on. Remember, you taught me how to milk.' Doing was what she wanted. Not talking. They would talk eventually about the explosion but not now.

'If you're sure?'

Milking the cows, preparing vegetable beds and sowing carrot seeds kept Beth busy throughout April. In May, she planted turnips and seeds. The best part of each day was the journey to and from Beck's farm. John arrived with a horse and cart to collect her when he had finished early morning milking. They would both face forward, absorbing the smells and sounds of nature, as the world transformed with the advent of spring. Each would share a thought.

'When the sky lit up. I couldn't believe it. Gone. They must have died instantly.' Lacy flowers on the hawthorn – Connie's wedding dress. Was her fiancé still alive? Maybe they were together in heaven. A blackbird sings and swoops. She's spotted a worm.

Clop-clop. Clop-clop. 'We were all called in the next day. Reminded of the official secrets act we all signed. I don't know how they stopped relatives working it out. Too many workers had accidental deaths at work,' John said. Baby lambs skipping in a field. Her own baby, Daniella. Daniel's baby.

Clop-clop. Clop-clop. 'I couldn't go back. It was my last day, anyway. But it felt as though I never said goodbye. I kept expecting Rosie to come home.' Bluebells threaded through a wood. Rosie's indigo-blue hat.

They didn't exchange many words, but they didn't need to. They had shared a devastating experience. One they would never forget. But on those early morning journeys, Beth felt as though she was letting go, putting each painful thought to rest. She hadn't told John about her pregnancy, that she had a daughter. One day. When the time was right.

It had started as a working arrangement. John needed help on the farm, and Beth needed the diversion. In June, when he could afford to pay her, Beth insisted they use the money to buy some chickens. 'We can sell eggs as well as milk,' she said.

In August, John asked her to marry him. It was a pragmatic proposal. Living together on the farm made more sense. Beth didn't need to give it much thought. They had always got on; John was a kind and decent man. There was no courtship – no romantic love, but they had a strong bond and shared a passion for farming.

It was as though she were a different person to the young woman who moved to Leeds at the start of the war determined to live her life the way she chose, seeking independence and adventure. Now, all Beth wanted was solitude and certainty. She loved how the farm connected her to the land, the enforced routine of milking, feeding the chickens, planting and harvesting vegetables. They both worked hard, coming together in the evening to sit by the fire. John would light his pipe, and Beth would busy herself with sewing and darning. They acquired a sheepdog, the runt of a litter, in exchange for a pail of milk and called him Shadow, as he kept close to Beth, maybe sensing her need for comfort.

They made love for the first time on the day they got married. It was a quiet affair – the wedding, which took place in Thorncrest church, and the act of making love. John was shy, an inexperienced lover, and Beth found herself taking the lead, hungry now for sex, to obliterate the memories. Her passion was the expression of anger, a release of pent-up stress. Her orgasm, a letting-go. If John was surprised by her abandon, he didn't say so. They carried on by day as they always had, each of them busy with daily tasks, evenings spent by the fire.

At night, under the cover of darkness, their interaction changed, charged with passion, it was as though they became different people. They never spoke about sex, even when the gas lamp was extinguished for the night.

One evening as they sat by the fire, John mentioned their apparent infertility. 'I don't mind us not having children,' he said.

Beth hadn't given it much thought. They'd been married for almost a year, and at first, she had expected to fall pregnant, had tried to prepare herself mentally, afraid of the inevitable guilt about the baby she gave away. Daniella. She hadn't yet told John. Not because she was being deceitful, although in a way she was by omitting to tell him about Daniel, but she needed to try to start anew. Conversations about life before the explosion were too painful. She watched John now, trying to read him. Everything he said and did seemed to be focused on making her happy, or at least content.

'It's surprising that I've not yet conceived,' Beth said.

'Not really. It's the cordite you handled in Barnbow that's to blame. But if you want a family, we could consider adoption.'

'No. Unless you want a family, John. I'm happy to be just the two of us.' Shadow whined and rubbed his nose against Beth's stockinged toe. 'And you, boy.'

'Me too.' John lit his pipe, and the subject was closed.

Beth thought she might still become pregnant in time, but it never happened. If she told John that she had conceived in the past, he would blame himself for being infertile. It was best to let him think it was her history of working with cordite.

29

SATURDAY 16TH JULY 1966

It was ridiculous, she was only popping into her local post office to collect her mail, but finding Big Jim's postcard on her last visit made her jittery. Louise parked around the corner and hurried to the door, wearing sunglasses and a headscarf.

'Anything for me today?' she asked Bert, the postmaster, who also served as garage pump attendant, and local taxi service.

'No. I don't think so, lass. One for Mr Braithwaite, if you want to take that one?'

Louise hesitated. She didn't want the village to know about their separation. He hadn't told Esther and Bill, and neither had she. They would have to soon. Louise pushed down the lump in her throat that had a habit of forming whenever she thought of Richard.

'A bill, I expect,' she said, forcing a half-laugh. 'He won't be in a hurry for that one.'

'No. It was something from the District Council. It'll be about that holiday village of yours. How's it going? Will it be built in time for my grandkids to visit me from down South?' He laughed. 'Baby's due next month so you've got time. At least until he or she is four. I'm hoping it'll be a little boy. I'll take him fishing.'

'I'll let Richard pick that one up. He'll be excited to receive it, and I may not see him for a while. We're both busy, so keep missing each other.'

'And I wondered...' Maybe she should have visited another post office out of area.

'Yes?'

'Do you have any information about the Assisted Passage Migration Scheme to Australia? I thought I would carry a few leaflets on the mobile library. There's a directive to promote it, apparently.'

'Is that so? Yes. I should have something about that. Hold on.' He disappeared into the back of the shop. The bell sounded, and Louise froze, afraid to look around.

'Hi.' It was Pete.

Louise's chest tightened. She steadied herself with a hand on the post office counter. It's just Pete, she tried to calm herself, but his presence triggered memories of the day Eddie found her.

'Here they are,' Bert said, returning from the back room.

'Thank you.' Louise grabbed the leaflets. 'Bye, Pete.'

Back in the car, Louise took deep breaths. She flicked through the leaflets. Australia. Build your children's future. Ten pounds can take you to Australia.

A loud rap on the passenger window. Louise jumped, throwing the leaflets across the front seat. Pete peered in. He signalled for her to wind down the window.

'Glad I caught you.' He shifted his weight from foot to foot. Then he looked up and down the road.

'Do you want to get in to talk?' Louise said.

Pete nodded. Louise cleared the seat of leaflets, and he climbed in beside her. 'Have you seen my uncle?'

Blood rushed to her head. 'Why do you ask?'

'He tracked me down. Visited Fliss's flat when I was out and left a message.'

Don't let him harm Fliss. This was why her friend shouldn't get involved with Pete. Why Richard was better off without her. 'Did he tell her anything?' Louise said.

'Of course not. He was charm personified. Fliss has been asking why we don't invite him to supper. He asked me to meet him at a club in Harrogate.'

'Okay.' Louise didn't want to hear anymore. 'And are you?'

'No. Did he contact you?'

She explained how Big Jim had followed her car and made a deal with her. 'But I've not heard from him since.' She didn't mention her visit to the police station.

'I'm going to tell Fliss everything. I can't ask her to be my wife if there are secrets between us.'

Louise gasped. 'You're going to propose?'

Pete grinned. 'I am. If she's willing after I've told her about my dodgy past. So, keep it quiet. We might beat you to the altar.'

When Pete left her, Louise sat for a few minutes trying to calm herself. If – no when – Big Jim heard about her chat with DC Jenkins, he would come after her. A mysterious car accident. A house fire. He wouldn't care who else got hurt. Louise clutched her belly. The only place she might be safe from him and his henchmen was on the other side of the world. Why didn't her father respond? If he didn't write soon, she would have to take her chance and surprise him.

She was trying to give Esther and Bill some time alone in the cottage and so she drove to the museum barn.

'Where are you, Ma?' Louise addressed Ma's empty

armchair. What was her life like before she married John Beck and moved to the farmhouse? Beth Hardy, Daisy had called Ma. Hardy wasn't a name, she had investigated. Maybe there was something in the parish records about the Hardy family.

Three hours later, Louise had found the names Frederick and Archibald Hardy listed as soldiers who died at war in a book of remembrance for Armistice Day. Faded black and white photographs of their young faces were included alongside fourteen others. Louise remembered them in silence. Ma's beloved brothers. She thought Ma had been an only child, as there had been no talk of living relatives. Her stomach rumbled. Why hadn't she packed a lunch? It was two-fifteen. With no particular plan other than finding something to eat, Louise returned to her car. Bill was at home today, and she wanted to give them time alone. If they had still been together, she would have spent the day with Richard, at least the afternoon. What was he doing now? Working on their house. Louise corrected herself. His house. Maybe Richard and Fiona's, one day. They had received planning permission for the holiday village, but there was still a period of consultation on the number of cabins, access, and any amenities offered. The letter would be an update of this process. How optimistic they had been, imagining a little glade of timber cabins, a village store – a mini Braithwaite's in memory of Richard's mother and brother. They dreamt of creating a lake and planting trees. Maybe this vision would become a reality, but it would never be hers – hers and Richard's.

As Louise started the engine, she remembered Ma's ledger was still on the back seat of her car. Lunch could wait a few minutes longer; best put it back now. It was a kerfuffle unlocking the padlock and pulling back the bolts of the barn, but she had time to kill and nowhere to go.

The ledger had been in a packing box, but now, as the

The Canary Girl's Secret

tableau of Ma and Pa's living room came to life, Louise looked for a fitting home. Ma would have written the entries sitting at Pa's desk. She'd always thought of it as Pa's desk, but now, Louise realised, it was probably used more by Ma. She thought she knew her beloved guardian, but it was a fantasy. They had lived together for two to three years, and she had been a child. Somewhere among the possessions collected over her lifetime there must be a clue to Ma's mysterious past. Louise couldn't believe she would fake her death, knowing it would hurt her loved ones. She had friends, people who cared about her. Louise sighed. There wasn't a clue. She'd been through everything.

Louise returned the ledger to its rightful home in the bureau. She rolled back the desk lid to display tiny drawers and pigeonholes, a hidden inkwell, and a green leather writing surface. As a child, she'd longed to own something so grand. Except then, she'd imagined using the drawers and pigeonholes as rooms and dormitories for tiny dolls, the desk their school. Louise opened the ledger to a page that would interest visitors to the museum barn, instructions on how to make butter, and placed it on the leather inset. Then, she positioned the inkwell as though the writer had momentarily left their task. She needed a pen. Louise opened a drawer underneath the desk's top. Empty. She wasn't surprised as she had emptied and packed away the contents herself. But there must be a pen somewhere. An old-fashioned ink pen. She ran her fingers around the back, hoping to find one lodged against the side of the drawer. Ah, what was that? Her finger explored a metal protrusion. A clip? Louise peered in, but it was too dark and too far back to see properly. There was one on the other side too. She fiddled with them and click; the bottom of the drawer came loose. A false bottom. Why had she not known this as a child? The bureau became even more magical. It was wasted on a grown-up. Then, remembering her mission, Louise's heart quickened. If Ma had a secret, this was where she would hide it. A torch. She needed a torch. There might be one in the glove compartment of her car. They used torches when living in the caravan, but she was too impatient to look. At first, she thought it was empty and felt a pang of disappointment. But when she traced her fingers around the newly exposed section, she discovered something taped to the underside of the drawer. It could be a price tag or manufacturer's guarantee. She tried to keep her expectations low as her fingers impatiently tugged at the tape.

It was a piece of yellowed paper neatly folded to the size of a matchbox. Louise held her breath as she unfolded it. Inside, written in a familiar hand, was an address: Beetabon Ranch, Dubbo, NSW, Australia. Louise gasped. This had been written by her father. She had read and reread his letter so many times; there was no mistaking his handwriting. Why did Ma have his address? How did she even know Louise's father, when Louise hadn't known of his existence herself? Her mum had questions to answer. There was so much Louise didn't know. It was as though her whole life had been a lie.

When Richard came up behind her, Louise was still holding the paper. Her eyes blurred with unshed tears. 'I thought I'd find you here,' he said.

Louise showed him the note. 'It's my father's address. Hidden in Ma's bureau. Both Ma and my mum have been keeping secrets from me.' Her stomach rumbled.

'Come on.' Richard took her hand to pull her from the armchair. 'Say goodbye to Ma and Pa. I'll buy us lunch at the Coach and Horses.'

30

SATURDAY 16TH JULY 1966

'You've got to talk to your mum,' Richard said, when they were seated at a table in the pub.

'I know. There's a lot of things I need to sort out in my life. How did Ma know my father? It just doesn't make any sense. And she went to some trouble to hide his address.'

'It was clever of you to find it. But I can't think why Ma Beck would have his address,' Richard said.

'I know. It feels as though my whole life has been a lie.'

Richard reached across the table to take her hand. 'I've never lied to you,' he said. 'You and me. We're real. I said some mean things. I'm sorry.'

Louise wanted to ask him about Fiona, why they were lunching in Harrogate, and the business partnership Paul Evans had mentioned. It was no doubt innocent, but there was the potential for something more to develop between Richard and Fiona. If she loved Richard, and she did with all her heart, she had to let him go. She extracted her hand from his. 'A lot of what you said was true. I have changed, living in London, mixing with celebrities. To be honest coming back here feels a bit stifling.' Louise turned her head, unable to meet his eyes.

'Oh.' It seemed Richard was lost for words. The 'Oh,' a sound of shock, as though she had stuck a knife in him, and in a way she had.

'But now, I've got the opportunity to train as a librarian, my life is opening up. You should ask Fiona if her family would like to invest in your holiday village. I was hoping my visit to Daisy St Clair would result in evidence of Ma's passing, but the poor woman is losing her mind. So that was a dead end.' She was rambling. Throwing everything at him. 'You've a solid business plan. You and Fiona make a great team, professionally and...' Louise couldn't finish the sentence. She had to sacrifice her future with Richard, but it was too much, imagining Richard and Fiona together. 'Anyway, I was considering a trip to Australia to meet my dad. Not getting the inheritance, us taking a break, maybe it's done us both a favour.' She took a deep breath. Her hands were shaking.

'Two Ploughman's,' the publican said, as he set down their plates. Slabs of cheddar cheese served with pickled onions, chutney, and crusty bread. They both stared at their plates.

'Do you think this was ever a lunch enjoyed by ploughmen?' Richard said, his voice hoarse.

Louise pressed her lips together, willing her tears not to fall. 'Maybe,' she whispered. When she met his gaze, there was only love in his eyes.

'It's hungry work farming,' Louise said. 'Remember when we had a few days off school to help with haymaking?'

'You left your lunch on the wagon and forgot to wear a hat,' Richard said.

'You shared your paste sandwich with me and took off your shirt.'

Richard screwed up his face. 'Took off my shirt?'

'Yes. I remember feeling awkward because I couldn't take my eyes off your gorgeousness but I wasn't meant to feel like that because you were Dicky, my best friend.'

'I never knew that.' Richard gave a sad smile.

'We were very young,' Louise said, as she chased a pickle around her plate.

'I was in love with you,' Richard said.

'I know. First love. But we're adults now…' Louise trailed off. She felt spent, unable to keep up the pretence any longer.

'I understand,' Richard said. 'I always knew you would do great things. I don't want to tie you down. Now you've got this opportunity. You have to fly. Be everything I've always known you could be.' He too, was setting her free.

'We'll always be friends,' Louise said.

Richard nodded. He put his knife and fork together. Neither of them had eaten more than a couple of bites. Louise couldn't swallow the food stuck in her throat.

'There's a lot of cheese,' Richard said.

'Can you imagine having a portion like this during the war? Heaven knows how many ration points this would have cost,' Louise replied.

They gave up on lunch and walked to their cars. Louise couldn't remember ever feeling this sad. Not even when Pa died, and she was sent back to London.

That afternoon as she rinsed their tea things, Louise said, 'When you need me to move out Esther, just say so. I'll look for a room to rent. They might let me have one at High House. One of the dormitories used by contractors working on the reservoir. Remember, I slept on a bunk bed opposite Fliss. It was okay.'

'I promised Richard you would be safely returned to him.'

'What am I? A package put in storage?' Louise snapped. 'Sorry. I'm just a bit tired.'

'It's no wonder, covering for me. Come and sit down. Leave the washing up to Bill.'

'Nearly done. Besides, if I sit, I'll drop off to sleep and I need to re-cover some of the books which are falling apart. They're in Mobi. I'll go and get them.'

'Sit,' Esther said.

Louise sighed and gave in. 'Okay, but if I drop off to sleep, I'll blame you.'

'There's no need for you to move out until the baby comes. It will sleep in a carrycot in our room for the first few weeks, so Bill can work on the nursery then. To be honest, we don't want to prepare more than we have to, until the baby's actually here.' Esther bit her lower lip.

Louise covered Esther's hand with hers. 'It's going to be okay.'

Esther nodded but Louise could see the anxiety in her eyes. 'Now, what about you? Why are you so tired? Is your room comfortable, not too warm? Is it noisy, facing the road?'

'No. It's very comfortable. Perfect temperature and peaceful. Baby Esther is going to be very happy in her nursery. Or baby Bill. I don't know why I can't sleep. Lots on my mind.' Louise had told Esther about finding her father's address in Ma's bureau, but she hadn't mentioned anything else: her encounter with Big Jim, her missed period, her conversation with Richard. Bill and Esther would find out soon enough that she had split up with Richard, but Louise couldn't face Esther's scrutiny; she would crack under pressure. Nobody must find out about her deal with Big Jim. When he found out she had gone to the police, he would exact his revenge.

'Well, don't worry about the course. You'll find the entry exams a doddle,' Esther said. 'And I heard through Fiona, your house will soon be ready. She says Richard has arranged for the plumbing and electrics to be installed, but you'll already know that. When are you going to talk to your mum?'

Louise had given this a lot of thought. It would be best to meet her mother face to face, but finding the time to travel to London was a challenge. Maybe she could combine the visit with one to the Australian embassy in London. She was still waiting for the application forms to arrive in the post, but a face-to-face meeting would be helpful to plead her case. She didn't have a professional qualification to offer, and the medical might reveal her pregnancy, so there was not much in her favour, apart from a father who was a resident of Australia. That's if he were alive. Weeks had passed with no reply to her letter.

'I'll telephone her; try to arrange a meeting.' Louise yawned. 'And now I'm going to fetch those library books before I've run out of energy or will.'

On Tuesday morning, Louise took Mobi out on the regular round. She'd planned on phoning her mum on Sunday, but early that morning a car crashed into Bill and Esther's front wall, knocking it down. The driver didn't stop to explain himself. There was an almighty crash, then the car reversed and sped away.

'Drunken driver,' Bill had said.

Removing bricks from the flower beds, and listening to Bill's rant about careless drivers had absorbed her time, and attention. So, another couple of days passed without Louise making the call. I will definitely call her this evening as soon as I get home, Louise said to herself as she manoeuvred Mobi around a sharp bend. Below her, the valley was now drained of water. The reservoir had battered the remains of cottages and the old mill. It was a pity the Corporation had prevented access to the valley; she would have loved to walk amongst the remains, remembering the days that she and Richard had played in the Mill house and fished for sticklebacks. The view from their new home – Richard's new home – would be interesting. She hoped he couldn't see the remains of Braithwaite's grocery store or Thorncrest church. They would be pulled down soon, as would Beck's farm, but the inevitability didn't make it any easier.

A deer stepped into her path, and Louise slammed a foot on the brake pedal. Concentrate. If she wasn't careful, she and Mobi would be joining the graveyard of cottages below. 'Where did you come from?' Louise and the deer surveyed one another before it leapt away, disappearing from sight as it descended the valley.

Louise took a deep breath and restarted the van. Pewstone. She hoped Susan Jeffries would visit with her gorgeous grandchildren. Was she becoming just a teeny bit maternal?

'You will be an advanced reader,' she said to the little bean in her womb. 'By the time you go to school, you'll already be reading.' Where would that school be? Australia? Would her child have an Australian accent?

It was going to be hard leaving Thorncrest and her job. At this time of year, Yorkshire was stunning. Oxeye daisies smiled their yellow centres from a grassy verge. A light breeze from her open window carried the distinctive cry of a curlew, Koo loo. Then, the answering call of its mate, like a distant echo. Woodlands dotted with purple foxgloves. The moors, now vibrant shades of green. Farmland and cute stone cottages. She loved Yorkshire all year round, but it was spectacular in the summer.

Welcome to Pewstone. Louise slowed down and prepared to pull into the layby. She had a copy of Stig of the Dump for

Janine and Dylan. In her head, Louise had made an inventory of the books she would introduce to her child. A smile tugged at her cheeks. You, my secret little bean, are the only good thing in my life right now. Because she was about to lose everything else.

Susan and the children did not arrive until it was time for Louise to leave, and then, Susan came alone. Louise was in the driver's seat when Susan approached her window. Louise wound it down.

'No Janine and Dylan, today? If you wait a moment, I'll climb into the library and find the books I saved for them.'

'No. Don't worry. They've enough reading for now. I wanted to catch you because I've got something for you.' Susan looked pleased with herself.

'Okay. Hold on.' Louise climbed out of Mobi.

Susan was fishing in her shopping basket for something. 'Ah. Here it is. I put it in an envelope to keep it clean. Jane says you can keep it. You know Jane Biggs? They have a farm on the road to Pewstone. You probably passed it.' Susan handed a brown envelope to Louise.

Mystified, Louise opened it and pulled out a black and white photograph. Four young men carried a coffin on their shoulders as mourners looked on.

'One of those boys is Neil Biggs, her son. Jane and Gerald went to Ma Beck's funeral and she took that photo. Jane says you can keep it, as you were asking about the funeral. Anyway, I rushed over here to catch you. Can't stop as I've got to collect Dylan from a party.'

'That's so kind of you, Susan. And Jane. Please thank her. It means a lot to me. I just wish I could have been there.'

Louise slipped the envelope into her bag to study later. She had lost a few minutes and would have to hurry to her next stop.

When Louise finished her round, she returned Mobi to the cottage. But she could not park as a van was parked outside. Emblazoned on the side were the words Bellamy Brothers Builders. Esther was handing a mug of tea to a builder, George Bellamy, the man Louise suspected of killing Eddie. His presence there was a clear warning: we know where you are and what you've done. The car crashing into their wall was no accident.

'Kettle's just boiled, Louise,' Esther said. 'Stop and have a break before you get back to work.'

George Bellamy held Louise's gaze. 'Alright?' he said.

'I won't stop for tea,' Louise said. 'I'll leave Mobi on the lane and take Mini. I need to pop in to High House.'

She had to move out of the cottage as soon as possible. Esther, Bill and their baby weren't safe as long as she lived there.

31

TUESDAY 19TH JULY 1966

Fliss was behind the reception desk when Louise arrived at High House. Her face was downcast, the sparkle that usually fizzed from her, absent.

'Oh. It's you,' she said.

Pete must have told her. Was she wrong to have kept his secret? 'Hi Fliss. I was hoping to see Mr Formoy, but if you have a moment, can we talk?'

'Mr Formoy's out. He's visiting Richard, as it happens. I thought you would know that.' She frowned.

'No.' Louise sighed. She was going to have to tell their friends soon. 'What's he doing… never mind.' It was none of her business why Formoy was visiting Richard. 'I wanted to ask Mr Formoy if I could rent a room or even a bunk bed here in High House. Just until I've a more permanent home. That's if the rooms and dorms are still available. I don't suppose they're used much by contractors now the project's almost complete.'

'We've a few contractors staying. In fact, now it might get busy again. It depends on how much manpower we can recruit locally to clear the valley. Then it will need re-flooding. But I'm sure there'll be a bed available if you don't mind slumming it in the women's dorm. Not many female contractors so you'll probably have it to yourself as you did before.' Fliss's face had softened.

'Good. So, while I'm waiting for Formoy, how about a catch-up over coffee?'

'Okay. Take a seat and I'll prepare a pot.' Still a little formal, but understandable if Pete had told her about his past.

'Do you have any contractors from Bellamy Brothers working on the reservoir?' Louise said casually when they were sitting down with mugs of coffee.

'No. I don't think so.' Fliss checked her records. 'Why? Is there anything else I ought to know. Apart from the fact you and Pete were members of a London gang. Criminals.'

'I was married to a man who worked in casinos and yes, he was a criminal. He fixed games for a fee. Hustled. Eddie the Rick. I didn't know this when I married him. When I came to Thorncrest I was running away from him and my life as part of that world.'

'And Pete followed you.'

'Yes. He did. I didn't know, until Eddie found me, that it was Pete who'd given me away.'

'But you forgave him? Why? And why didn't you tell me, your best friend, that my boyfriend was a gangster?' Fliss's hand jolted, splashing coffee over the room bookings page.

'Pete, a bit like me, was dragged into that world. He would have told you, his dad died when he was young and his dad's brother Big Jim found Pete work. At first you don't know what's going on. Gangsters aren't like the baddies on the TV with scary music warning you. Eddie was charming. I wouldn't have married him if I hadn't thought him kind and generous – a good man. Pete isn't like them, Fliss. He's one of the good guys; I promise you. When he realised what he'd got into he got out. I didn't know you two were going to get involved. And when I did, it was too late to warn you. Besides, it's in his past. I've forgiven him as I've forgiven myself. We did what we had to do at that time.' She hoped her words would be enough.

Fliss busied herself wiping up the spilt coffee, her mane of red hair covering her face.

'Well. He's told me now.'

'And?' Louise said.

'I told him I would have to think things through.'

'Well, I might as well tell you, Richard and I have split up. I didn't know Formoy was paying him a visit. Does he want Richard to help with cutting trees in the valley?'

'You can't have. You two are perfect together,' Fliss exclaimed.

'I know. It's complicated. Please don't tell anyone. At least not yet.' Louise regretted sharing her news. It made it feel real, and she wasn't ready yet.

'So, you don't know? Formoy's meeting Richard about the land he's put on the market. I was surprised because of your plans, but it makes sense now,' Fliss said. 'Oh, here's Mr Formoy now.'

As soon as Louise had finished talking to Formoy, she set off in search of Richard, hoping she would catch him at the house. Formoy had generously offered Louise the use of her old room on the first floor at a very reasonable rate. She suspected he felt guilty about the loss of her inheritance.

She couldn't bear the thought of Richard selling their land. He would be throwing away everything, and he was doing this because of her. Oh Richard. There had to be another way. His land rover was outside the house when she drew up.

Standing on the land she had helped Richard purchase,

with expectations of a future together, Louise crumbled inside. It was no longer her home. If she wanted to keep Richard safe, she had to pretend she didn't care. That she didn't ache with love and longing. This was the first time after their breakup. It would get easier. Louise gathered herself, drawing on the acting abilities she had honed whilst working for Big Jim. She could do this.

The thrum of an electric saw died. Louise tentatively entered the house and found Richard in the kitchen measuring a piece of wood, a pencil clamped between his teeth, a look of concentration on his face.

'Richard?'

His body jerked in surprise and then, on seeing her, flinched. 'Did you want to collect your things?'

Louise hadn't thought about that. It felt so final. 'Yes. Best get them out of your way. If you have a visitor…' She was thinking of Fiona.

Richard frowned. 'I wasn't expecting you. If you don't mind coming back another time, I'll have them packed and ready.'

'Okay,' Louise said.

He waited.

'Fliss told me you––'

'I picked up my mail––'

They spoke at once.

'You first,' Richard said.

'You've put your land back on the market,' Louise said. She tried to stop staring at his bare chest, her eyes tracing his biceps, pectoral muscle, a tiny bead of sweat glistening on his clavicle.

Richard nodded. 'Yes. I got a letter from the District Council confirming I could sell it as a development plot.

You've been in a few times picking up mail, I hear. Anything interesting?'

Louise met his quizzical gaze. 'No,' she said a little too quickly. 'Don't worry, I'm changing my postal address to High House, as I'm moving out of Esther and Bill's cottage.'

A silence heavy with all that was unsaid fell between them.

'Okay, I'd better be going,' Louise said. She had failed in her plan to stop him selling the land, but it was too hard being with Richard and yet not being with him.

'Why don't you sit outside and I'll get us both a cold drink. I could do with a break. Beer?'

'Orange squash or water, please,' Louise said.

Outside, Louise found a bench seat and table. Richard's work. She stroked the smooth timber, still picturing the contours of his body. *You were conceived in this house, little bean*, she thought.

'Here you go.' Richard had put on a shirt. He handed her a glass of squash. 'The view of the reservoir is interesting rather than picturesque but it will be great once it's re-flooded.'

'Do you have to sell the land, Richard? Couldn't you ask the Simms to invest in the holiday village?'

'Why would I do that?' Richard said.

'Before I came back into your life ruining everything you and Fiona were happy together. She's a good business woman and her family are keen to invest in lucrative projects. This is your dream, Richard. You can't give up on it so easily. There must be a way.'

Richard took a few sips of his beer. He pointed out a bird with a long crest; it reminded Louise of the hats she displayed in the museum barn. 'A lapwing,' he said.

The bird picked its way between rubble, stopping every now and again to dip its beak into the mud for food.

'There is a way. I have a plan,' Richard said.

'Oh, does that mean you won't sell the land?'

'Not all of it. I've taken out a loan against the house to pay for plumbing and electricity. We won't sell all the land, just a small parcel to help get the holiday village started.'

'We. You mean you and Fiona?' Louise said. She kept her eyes on the lapwing. A flash of green and purple as the sun reflected off its plumage.

'You really think Fiona and I should get back together?' Richard said.

'Yes. I do. Why not? You would be perfect together.'

'Oh. I'm glad you said that.' Richard concentrated on drinking his beer. Louise watched the lapwing fly away. 'So, you'd be happy to hear we're getting married?'

Louise spun to face him, knocking over her glass of squash. 'When? How? Why?'

Richard wiped his mouth with his sleeve. Then, he stood up and turned away from her. 'As you say, it makes sense. We're already working together in the shop. And Fiona's excited about the holiday village.'

He was returning to the house. She ought to be pleased for him. It was what she wanted. Louise ran after him.

'When?'

'When did I ask her or when are we getting married?'

'Both. Either.' Louise tried hard to control her emotions, to stop herself from holding him. Telling him, *No, I love you*.

'Fiona wants to keep the engagement a secret. Promise me you won't say a word to anyone?'

Louise nodded mutely.

32

WEDNESDAY 20TH JULY 1966

Nursing a broken heart, Louise had taken the brown envelope with the photo to bed with her. She'd been saving it for a quiet moment, imagining that the image could transport her to that time, so she could pay her respects to the woman who had loved and cherished her. Her mum had that opportunity, and she barely knew Ma.

She kissed the brown envelope, sending her thanks to Jane and Susan. The photograph was in pristine condition. The black and white images clear. There was Thorncrest Church, just as she remembered it. So sad, it was about to be pulled down.

'I should have been there,' she said out loud, taking in each of the mourners. There was Daisy St. Clair, looking like a film star. Louise wished she had met Daisy then; she was quite a character. Louise studied each face, hoping to find a familiar one. The young men — farmers who had carried the coffin. A woman stood alone, away from the other mourners. Louise narrowed her eyes to see better. For a moment she thought it looked like her mum. Her palms pulsed as she took a closer look. It was her mum. She was wearing her best coat. The dark green one. No, it couldn't be. Louise jumped out of bed, but there was nothing she could do at that time of night. It was too late to phone her aunt's house.

All night she had tossed and turned. Angry. Frustrated. And very, very sad. I will be a better mother to you, little bean. I promise.

By morning, Louise was exhausted, and to make things worse, she experienced her first bout of morning sickness, as though the little babe within was complaining at her lack of sleep.

'You can't go in to work today,' Esther said, when she found Louise in the kitchen drinking hot water with milk.

'I have to. I got behind with admin yesterday, after visiting Formoy at High House.'

'There's no hurry for you to move out. Stay home today and I'll help with the admin. I need something to keep my mind occupied. You don't have any library stops.'

Louise felt another wave coming and rushed to the bathroom to throw up. Her body and brain felt wrung out. Utterly spent. Downstairs, she heard Esther talking on the phone.

Her face splashed with water, Louise returned to the kitchen.

'I phoned Diane and explained. She said, take as long as you like. But when you're feeling up to it, she would like to meet with you to talk through your work schedule from mid-August. It sounds as though a lot of thought has gone into your at work training. I almost envy you starting at the beginning. I loved training as a librarian.'

Louise covered her face with her hands. She would have to tell Diane and Esther that she wouldn't be accepting the training and sponsorship. But not yet. It was a dream come

The Canary Girl's Secret

true; how could she walk away from what felt like the opportunity of a lifetime?

'Go to bed, sweetheart. You're very pale,' Esther said.

It was one-thirty when Louise awoke, feeling thirsty; her head muggy. She had to phone her aunt. Bill was at work, and Esther would be having her nap about this time. Louise peeked around Esther's door to make sure. She was propped up with pillows, a look of serenity on her sleeping face. Louise tip-toed away.

Before dialling her aunt's number, Louise took a few deep breaths. She would try to keep calm, coax out the truth. Her aunt answered on the second ring.

'Louise. How wonderful to hear from you. I told Pearl you would phone as soon as she was home. Well, your mum is doing nicely. She has an appointment to go back to the orthopaedic department at the hospital tomorrow. They said something about occupational therapy.' Then, her aunt lowered her voice. 'I didn't tell her about the letter you found. As far as your mother is concerned you left in a hurry to deal with an emergency to do with the reservoir. You know her heart is weak. We don't want her to have another stroke. So, don't say anything to upset her. Understand?'

Louise let out her breath in frustration. 'Well, I have found something else that needs explaining. Maybe you can answer this one. What was my mum doing at Elizabeth Beck's funeral? She didn't tell me Ma had died. I had no idea they were in contact. Why didn't she tell me?' Louise realised that she had been shouting.

'Louise,' her aunt said firmly. 'I don't want you talking to your mother whilst you are like this. I don't think you realise how unwell she's been. I'll tell Pearl that you rang when she was getting dressed. It takes her an age to put her clothes on, of a morning. And that you'll phone again. So, I'll give her your love. Okay? And Louise. Make sure you do call again. And don't upset her. You hear me?'

Chastised, Louise hung up. Her aunt had a point. She'd neglected her mother. The phone call was long overdue. It was just that her mother made it so hard to love her. She did love her mum; they had once been very close, but anger and resentment got in the way.

Esther joined her in the living room. 'I heard you on the phone. Is everything okay?'

'Yes. I'm sorry I should have asked before using your phone. I'll leave some money for my call.'

'Don't be ridiculous. Unless you were calling Australia?' Esther laughed then looked serious. 'Were you?'

'No. I was phoning my mum. Well, my aunt. I didn't get to talk to mum. There's something I want to show you. Wait there.'

Louise returned with the photograph. 'This is a photograph of Elizabeth Beck's funeral, and that woman,' she stabbed the photo, 'is my mother. My mum went to Ma's funeral and didn't tell me she had died. So, what do you make of that?'

Esther took the photograph from her. 'Are you sure it's your mum?'

Louise nodded. 'Absolutely.'

'Then, there will be an explanation. You know the church couldn't have arranged a funeral without a death certificate. This photograph might be enough to convince the Corporation of Elizabeth Beck's passing.'

Louise sighed. 'Maybe. But what's the point? I don't have the energy to fight anymore.'

'And that's because you aren't well. Go back to bed. I

brought in the cataloguing and orders whilst you slept. It's good to be working again.'

Louise reluctantly agreed. Her head hurt from dehydration, and she couldn't keep down any food. 'Have the builders finished working here? Bellamy Brothers,' she said.

'Yes. Did a good job on the wall. We didn't even call them. They heard about the accident and just knocked on the door. Maybe the drunk driver had a guilty conscience.'

'Maybe.' Louise said. 'I've arranged to move into High House this week. I'll miss you but it's for the best. You and Bill can start decorating the nursery.'

And I can start planning another new life, Louise thought.

33

THURSDAY 28TH JULY 1966

'Would a photograph of Elizabeth Beck's funeral convince the Corporation that she died?' Louise asked Formoy as she struggled with a box of books and stationery.

'Let me help you with that,' he said, offering up his forearms as a landing place for the box.

'You would be here all morning. This is just the first box. Thanks for letting me rent my old room.'

'Well, I do have a ten-o-clock meeting. The photograph.' He tilted his head to one side, as he did when delivering bad news. 'Not really. We would need the death certificate. It's not just that the coffin was empty, it was full of sandbags. As though it had been weighted to make it seem a body was within. It's a mystery. Why would someone fake their funeral? I don't mean to upset you, but you need to know the seriousness of this and why the Corporation can't accept your claim.'

His words took her breath away. 'Sandbags? You mean it was a fake funeral?'

'Yes. I'm sorry to break the news like that. But that's why the Corporation is unlikely to release an inheritance to you.'

'So, Elizabeth Beck is still alive? In which case Beck's farm belongs to her.' Louise was angry on Ma's behalf. And for herself. She was sick and tired of being deceived.

'Ye-es.' Formoy drew out the word. 'But there's a section in the Bill that says the Corporation will take ownership of dwellings if a compulsory purchase order can't be delivered to the home owner. I'm sorry, Miss Pearson. But you can stay here as long as you need to.'

'Thank you.' Louise stooped to pick up the box she had put down on hearing this news. 'I'll finish unloading this lot, then I'm off myself for a meeting in Harrogate. I know you did what you could for me and I appreciate it.'

En route to Harrogate library, Louise popped into the post office to pick up her post –an application pack from the Australian embassy – and arranged to have her mail redirected to High House.

'Back working for the Corporation?' Bert said.

'No. Just staying there until things get straightened out.'

Louise was saved from further interrogation by Kaye White, who came bustling in the door, her arms loaded with brown paper packages. 'Ooh, it's going to be another warm one. Sad to see our little village being pulled down.'

'So sad,' Louise said, as she made a hasty exit.

The village exposed by the drained reservoir was not the village of her childhood. In just a few months, the flow of water had softened walls, coating them in weed, swept away the tumbled stones, and flattened fences. It was in limbo. A bit like her life. A life with Richard and their baby, the perfect home they had planned and built, an exciting business venture, a career as a librarian – all of it a pretence. Like the

The Canary Girl's Secret

abandoned village, each element of her life was being dismantled. The truth hidden from those she loved.

If I don't tell Richard he's going to be a father, I'll be as bad as my mother, Louise said to the babe in her womb. But if she told him, he would do the right thing, as Richard always did. Why was he marrying Fiona? If she knew he loved her, she would be glad for him, but Louise didn't – couldn't – believe that was true. And how could he give up his dream? From when he was a boy, Richard had dreamt of building a village. Louise regretted saying that it wasn't her dream. She had given the impression that she didn't share his passion, and she did; it was just that she had dreams of her own as well. And look how that had gone. The opportunity to train as a librarian had been given to her, and she was about to throw it all away. She would have to tell Diane Chippendale when they met in just thirty-minutes time. Louise gasped when she realised the time. So long as there wasn't a herd of cows crossing the road, she would just about make it.

Diane took Louise through to the staff room for their meeting. 'Interrupt us if you need anything, Sally.' Diane introduced them. 'You'll be working with Louise when she starts her training programme next month,' she said.

Louise blushed, knowing she should explain now. Instead, she gave a warm smile. 'I'm looking forward to working with you.'

It didn't take long for Diane to get down to business; she was well prepared with a folder of papers and a stack of books.

'I've gathered together some essential reading so you can get started ahead of the course.' Diane took her through the chosen books: The Public Library System of Great Britain by Lionel McColvin, Library Classification and Cataloguing by A.C. Foskett, Introduction to the Use of Library Resources by

Geoffrey Carnall. 'They might sound a bit dry, but believe me they will be a constant source of reference in your first year.' There were more, and Louise took the stack of library books from her. 'You can have these on loan for a few months, but I recommend you invest in buying one or two.

'Now your placements. I've drawn up a schedule of activity to give you a range of experience. Most of the work will be here in Harrogate but I've also scheduled some time shadowing a school's librarian, a few weeks in Leeds University library, and some museum work.'

Louise had to close her mouth. This was even more spectacular than she could have imagined. 'You've arranged all of this for me?"

'It was a pleasure. It took me back to my training. I got quite excited and envious of you discovering this incredible world of knowledge. It opens up the world to you.'

They spoke about the museum barn Louise was curating in Thorncrest and how it could be linked to the Yorkshire Archaeology and History Society. 'I'm sure you could get funding for your museum. Your work in setting it up will really help with your training. Oh, another thing. How would you feel about facilitating an after-school reading club here in Harrogate? Sally would help until you felt confident working alone.'

Louise left with her arms full of books and papers, her head buzzing with ideas and her heart full of anticipation and joy. Wait. She wasn't going to do this. In her car was the application pack for emigration. So why did she feel like skipping and dancing? If she weren't loaded down with books and extremely unfit, she would run across the moors throwing her arms wide like Julie Andrews in The Sound of Music.

As she drove home, Louise came down from her high. Why did this amazing opportunity have to come now, when she had no choice but to say no? Even if she didn't emigrate, she couldn't work once she had the baby. Part of her wanted to pretend that she wasn't pregnant, that she didn't have to go back on the run from Big Jim and the Mob, that Richard wasn't going to marry Fiona, but she had to face reality. The life she desperately wanted would always be out of reach. *It's not that I don't want you, little bean. I guess I just want too much.* Was she greedy? Selfish? Probably. Maybe that's why she was being punished. One more week and then she would tell Esther and Diane that she couldn't take up the new position. And when would she tell Richard? Her timing had to be right; too late for him to do anything stupid like propose. Maybe just before she was due to leave for Australia. Tonight, she would complete the application form. Then there would be no turning back.

34

TUESDAY 9TH AUGUST 1966

'Post for you,' Fliss said when Louise stopped by the front desk.

An advantage of living at High House was the staff restaurant. She had just enjoyed one of Peggy's cooked breakfasts. Tuesday was an admin day, and she intended to make some headway with her studies. An inner voice kept trying to remind her that she wasn't going to do the course, but her heart refused to listen. Every day she put it off until the next.

'At least I don't get any bills whilst I'm living here,' she said, reaching for the mail.

'No. And this one looks interesting,' Fliss said, waving it just out of reach.

'How so?'

'Airmail.'

'Gimme,' Louise shrieked. 'I've been waiting for that one.'

Fliss grinned and handed it over. 'Australia?'

Louise nodded. It had to be from her father. She would

wait until she was alone before opening it. 'How are you and Pete?' She asked, diverting Fliss's attention.

Fliss gave a dreamy smile. 'Back together. I can't help it, Lou. I love him.'

'I'm glad. He really is a good guy, despite his past. Just keep away from his uncle.'

'Well, that's the thing.' Fliss leant in and lowered her voice. 'He's in hiding – Pete's uncle. Apparently, he's a wanted man.'

'So, where's he hiding?' Louise asked. She didn't want to know as long as he was far away from her.

'Nobody knows, but Pete thinks he's fled the country. His network has gone underground. Honestly, the less I know the better. I'm just glad he's not around to bother Pete.'

'Amen to that. I'm going to hunker down in my room. Do a bit of reading. Can I get you a coffee?'

'Call that a job? Reading in your room?' Fliss rolled her eyes. 'If you can wait for a coffee, I'll bring you one up when I make Mr Formoy's mid-morning.

'Another reason I love living here. Thank you.' Louise blew her friend a kiss and hurried upstairs to read her letter.

Dear Louise,

Thank you for your letter. I am sorry it has taken me so long to reply. It did of course take me by surprise, and I needed time to think through my response.

Oh no. He didn't want to see her. He had a new family. She was a guilty secret. Maybe she shouldn't have written. Louise resisted scanning down the page. Deep breath.

I think it's best we meet in person to talk this through. I have a story to impart. One that should have been told to the people that matter, many years ago. This letter should arrive before me. At least I hope it does, as I am booked into the Coach and Horses from Friday, 12th August. Ask for me at reception. I'll stay for as long as I need to, so contact me there as soon as you are available.

Kind regards
Geoffrey Sommerfeld.

Louise read and reread the letter. Did it sound a little cold? Maybe he was just being guarded until they met in person. Then she drew a deep breath. Her father was coming to Thorncrest. Her dad. She jumped up and down, the excitement too much to contain. At least now she could talk to him about emigrating. It would help her application to the Australian embassy. There was no way she could settle down to work. Louise had to share her news with someone. Richard had always been the person she would go to with news, good or bad. He would be delighted for her, but she had to learn how to live without him. Fliss was of course curious and had asked about the letter when she delivered Louise's coffee, but until Louise met her father and heard what he had to say, she felt it best to keep quiet. Esther knew she had written, and a visit to her boss – albeit a boss on early maternity leave – felt like a legitimate reason to abandon the work she had planned.

Esther was delighted to see Louise. 'I've missed you. Come in and tell me your news. I'm climbing the walls sitting around here doing nothing.'

Louise told her about the work programme Diane had put together and asked a few work-related questions. It was almost a work meeting until Louise could stand the suspense no longer. 'I've got a letter from my father.'

'Why didn't you say so straight away. Come on. Tell me everything. Have you got step brothers and sisters?'

Louise showed Esther the letter. 'What do you think it means?'

Esther threw up her hands. 'I don't know but you'll soon find out. That's just three days away. Oh my God, Louise. You're going to meet your father.'

'I know.' Louise squealed and did a little jig. 'I won't sleep until I've seen him. I wonder what he looks like. Whether I have his features.'

'Oh, I gave your Aunt Emma your phone number at High House,' Esther said. 'I hope that's okay?'

Louise felt guilty. She hadn't tried to talk to her mum since the last aborted attempt. Now, with her father visiting, she wanted to avoid her mum for a few more days. And that wasn't the only thing she felt guilty about.

'Esther,' she said uncertainly.

Esther picked up on the tone in Louise's voice and turned from straightening a pile of Bill's motorbike magazines. 'Out with it. You've broken one of my mother's porcelain cups? You want to move back in because its unbearable staying at High House what with the cooked breakfasts and being waited on by Fliss?' Esther laughed.

Louise sighed. It wasn't going to be easy. 'Okay. Here's the thing. With my dad coming over to visit I've been thinking. We've a lot of catching up to do. He must be in his fifties now, maybe older. You've heard of the One Pound Pom thing, well ten pound nowadays? I was thinking, I might emigrate to Australia.'

As this information landed, Esther seemed stunned. She felt for the arm of a chair and sat down. 'Oof. Wow. I wasn't prepared for that.'

'No.' Louise said, her voice almost a whisper.

'Is Richard up for that? I knew he was selling some land but I didn't realise the two of you were emigrating.'

'Not Richard. Just me. That's the other thing. We've split up.'

'No. Not you and Richard. I don't believe it. You've just had a row. It's because of the pressure you've both been under. You'll sort it out.'

'We didn't have a disagreement. Just different expectations of our relationship.'

'The baby thing?'

For a second, Louise thought Esther knew, then she realised. 'Richard wanted a family and I wasn't ready. That and… I don't know.' Esther obviously didn't know about Richard and Fiona, and she had been sworn to secrecy.

'Okay. But what about your training? You'll wait until after your library registration exam? It's not ideal. Diane will be disappointed. She thought you would go all the way and qualify as a chartered librarian. Have you told her?'

'I'll be disappointed too,' Louise said. Then the tears came, as thick and fast as the water that would fill the reservoir.

'Oh, my love.' Esther put an arm around her. 'Hey, you don't have to choose. Your dad or career.'

'But I do.' Louise hiccupped. Only it was *a family* or a career, and she wanted both.

'Don't do anything drastic. Just wait until you've met your father. He might be dreadful. Come on, meeting your father is good news. Don't think beyond that. One day at a time.'

Louise smiled. Esther sounded like Ma. She did have a habit of letting her imagination run ahead of her instead of letting life play itself out. 'Thank you,' she sniffed.

'Better?'

'Better.'

'Well, that was a bit more dramatic than breaking my mum's heirloom tea set, which frankly, I'd be glad to see the back of.'

35

THURSDAY 11TH AUGUST 1966

When Louise returned from her library round, Fliss was excited to see her. 'You've got a visitor. Not here. At the Coach and Horses. I received a call about an hour ago. One of their guests wanted to meet with you, and they knew to phone here. Either that, or follow the mobile library. I said I'd let you know as soon as you returned. Who is it? They didn't say. Do you know?'

'Oh, my God. I wasn't expecting him until tomorrow. Did they tell you anything? When he arrived? What shall I wear? Look at me.' Louise held out her trembling hands.

'A he? Do you know who it is, this mysterious man?'

'I can't tell you just yet, but I will. I promise. I'd better tidy myself up.' Louise took the stairs two at a time.

Her father would have jet lag. He must have got muddled with the date of arrival because of the time change. Maybe in Australia it was already tomorrow. Contacting Louise was the first thing he had done on arrival. It had to be. He must be as desperate to meet her as she was to meet him. What if she didn't live up to his expectations? Louise took a long, hard look at herself in the mirror. Thirty-four-years-old. Unmarried. Uneducated. And poor. Not exactly the daughter he dreamt of meeting. She put on her favourite dress, a Mary Quant polka dot, and brushed her hair. Touched up her lipstick and eye-liner. Presentable. 'We're going to meet your grandpa, Little Bean.'

The pub was closed to the public as it was late afternoon. Louise tried the doors, but they were locked, and so she tried the off-sales. The bell rang as she stepped inside, summoning the landlady from inside the pub.

'Hi Nancy,' Louise said. 'You phoned High House to say a guest was looking for me. I came as soon as I heard.'

'You'd better come on in. I'll open the door out front.'

Louise's knees felt like jelly. She had tried to imagine what her father might look like. His letters gave little away. He sounded intelligent. Cultured. He lived on a ranch. A farmer? Had he come alone or with his wife – her stepmother?

'Go through to the guests' lounge and I'll send a message that you're here,' Nancy said.

Louise sat in an armchair facing the door. She tugged her skirt to try to cover more of her legs. A longer skirt or trousers would have been better. The door opened, and Louise's heart leapt in anticipation.

'Mum? What are you doing here?'

Her mother stood in the doorway looking pale and a little afraid. 'Louise. I had to see you. Emma told me about the photograph. I knew you wouldn't talk to me. Please let me explain.'

'You shouldn't have come here, Mum.' Louise kept looking around her mum, expecting her father to appear. Then she took in her mother's frailty, her arm in a sling, her shoulders slumped. 'I'm sorry. Of course, I'm pleased to see you. Yes. I'm furious with you but thank you for coming.' Louise opened her arms to her mum.

Nancy poked her head around the door. 'Can I get you a pot of tea and some sandwiches?'

'Yes please,' her mum said. 'Thank you, Nancy dear.'

Her mum sat in a chair opposite the one Louise had been occupying. She looked comfortable and quite at home, although it seemed a bit surreal to Louise. Her brain had not caught up as she still expected her father to walk in.

'Your Aunt Emma told me you found a photograph of Elizabeth Beck's funeral.'

Louise nodded. 'How could you, Mum? You know how much Ma meant to me. It was bad enough sending back her letters but you didn't even tell me that she'd died.'

'No. I'm sorry, darling. You have every right to be angry.'

'Not angry. Furious.'

'I thought, if I stayed at your local inn, I could say my piece and if you didn't want to see me again, fine. But I've got to explain.'

'Well, you couldn't have stayed with me, anyway. I'm back at High House renting a room.'

'How's Dicky?'

'Richard. That's another story,' Louise said.

Her mum nodded. 'Let's wait for our tea to arrive and then I'll explain everything. Then, if you want to, you can tell me about Richard and what's happened in your life since we last met.'

On cue, Nancy backed into the room with a tea trolley. 'Cheese and pickle, ham, and paste sandwiches, some fondant fancies, and a bit of Battenberg. Let me know if you want more hot water. Sugar and milk, there. You know where to find me Pearl, if you need anything.'

'With your feet up, I hope. We'll be fine. Don't you worry about us. Thank you, Nancy. It's as good as a tea at the Ritz.'

Louise had forgotten how warm and charming her mum could be. In her younger days, she was considered the life and soul of a party. 'I'll pour,' Louise said.

'I'm just going to tell it like it is. Okay. Here goes.' Her mum didn't wait for Louise to hand her a cup of tea and a plate. She launched straight into her confession.

'I didn't know anything about Elizabeth Beck when she contacted me in 1942 through the Women's Voluntary Service. I thought she'd heard about your unhappy experience when you were first evacuated. I couldn't forgive myself sending you to that dreadful couple; drunks the pair of them. They should have vetted the people offering their homes to vulnerable children. Anyway, I thought that was why I was paid a visit. We were living with Emma and her boys at that time if you remember? So, when we were offered a place for you on a farm in Yorkshire, I thought it was because I'd kept you home against war office advice. Your cousins weren't evacuated so I didn't see why you should have to go. At first, I said no. Then the woman came back and asked if I would be willing to meet with Elizabeth Beck, the woman who had invited you to stay on the farm. I thought it odd. Then I decided they were going out of their way to reassure me this placement was safe. So, I agreed to meet.

'I met Mrs Beck in the community hall of the church. I remember there was a jumble sale the next day and a few ladies were sorting through the donations, old clothes, toys, that sort of thing. It was busy with people talking to one another across the room. We sat in a corner and I felt awkward, her travelling all the way from Yorkshire when I already knew I was going to say, no.

'That's when she told me. "I'm your mother," she said.'

Louise gasped. 'Ma Beck was your mother? My grandmother?'

'Yes, darling. I was as surprised as you. I didn't know then that I'd been adopted. Mrs Beck called me Daniella, apparently after my father, Daniel Winterton. He died in the first world war. A pilot.'

Louise couldn't take it all in. 'Hold on, Mum. If she was your mother, why didn't you tell me? Why do you refer to her as Mrs Beck?'

Her mum took a sip of tea. 'It explained why my mother – the woman I thought to be my mum treated me differently to Emma, her real daughter. But this woman, Elizabeth Beck seemed cold. She told me her husband, John Beck, wasn't to know the truth, that she had given birth to me before marrying him. "I'm not asking you to forgive me for giving you away," she said. "I was an unmarried mother. I'd lost the love of my life, my brothers, and three of my best friends through war. I was in no fit state to be a mother. And you've had a good upbringing with a woman who desperately wanted you," she said, without waiting for me to confirm or deny this fact. It was a lie. Ruby Pearson desperately wanted Emma – her own daughter. Once she gave birth, I was no longer needed or wanted.'

Louise covered her mouth, dismayed at the cruelty of the woman she had believed to be her grandmother, Ruby Pearson. 'So why did she invite me to stay with her and Pa on Beck's farm?'

'Although it was too late for her to build a relationship with me, Elizabeth wanted to know her granddaughter. So, she suggested an evacuation to the farm. John Beck wasn't to know the truth, so you couldn't either.'

Louise sighed. 'I thought of her as my grandmother. I was close to her. I loved Ma.'

'I know you did, love. I'm sorry I spoilt that. I was jealous. I didn't understand why she couldn't love me as well.' A tear glistened on her mum's cheek.

Louise put down her cup and saucer to kneel at her mum's feet. 'It was mean. She should have mothered you.'

Her mum laughed. 'I was a bit too old to be mothered. I probably came across as self-assured and strong. The truth was, I felt like an abandoned child. Unloved and unwanted. I'd just found my birth mother and all she was interested in was her granddaughter.'

'So, why did you agree to my evacuation?'

'That's what my sister, Emma, said. She didn't know I was adopted, but when I told her, she said it made sense. Our mum was no longer alive. Emma and I just had one another. She told me to say no. To stay living with her and the boys. We had a row. I thought she was jealous my mum had come looking for me. Emma said it wasn't fair to you, sending you off again when I knew hardly anything about Mr and Mrs Beck. "She doesn't deserve to have a relationship with Louise," Emma said.

'She was right, but I hoped it would lead to a way in for me. That eventually, Elizabeth would acknowledge me as her daughter. But it never happened. You and she became close. I felt shut out. That's why I send back her letters.'

'Oh mum,' Louise said. 'I had no idea. I remember you and Aunt Emma having an argument just before I was sent away. Do you really think Pa never knew?'

'He didn't. Elizabeth Beck was good at keeping secrets.'

Louise didn't feel the time was right to tell her mum Elizabeth Beck had faked her funeral. 'How did you hear about her funeral?'

'An invitation was sent in the post, care of your Aunt Emma. I had no contact with Elizabeth Beck from the day you arrived back in London. At first, I wasn't going to go. She was a stranger to me. I'd long since given up wanting her to recognise me as her daughter, to show me a fraction of the love she had heaped upon you, her granddaughter. I decided I must be unlovable. Joe left me. And you.'

Louise threw her arms around her mother. 'I'm sorry. You are lovable. I love you.'

'Ouch. My arm.' Her mum flinched, and Louise pulled away.

'Sorry. Sorry. I've been a rubbish daughter. I'm so glad you came here to see me. It's more than I deserve.' It was Louise's turn to cry.

'No love. It's not. Let's try and be kinder to one another. No more secrets.'

'But I've got so many. Too many,' Louise wailed.

'You always were a secretive girl,' her mum said fondly. 'Too many books. You lived most of the time in your head, creating imaginary worlds.'

Louise knew her mum's reflecting was a tactic to give her time to recover and compose herself, not that she had to put on a brave face with Mum. Her mum loved her, whatever she did or said. Right now, Louise felt undeserving of that unconditional love.

'I don't want to keep secrets but sometimes it's necessary to protect those we love,' Louise said.

'I know. You can tell me anything you want. I won't judge.'

She couldn't tell her mum she was meeting her biological father here, maybe in this very room, tomorrow. Hopefully, by then her mother would be safely back in London. It would create another rift between them, and Louise realised she needed her mum in her life, even more than a father.

As Louise was weighing up what she could divulge, her mum said, 'Tell me about Richard. I've heard so much about him over the years, I really hope to meet him, now I've travelled to Yorkshire.'

'Richard.' His name brought fresh tears. 'Oh God. I love him so much Mum.'

'There now. Don't cry. Whatever's happened between you can be fixed if you love one another. I'm no expert in love. Never managed to keep a man. Not that I would have wanted the time wasters that I dated, your father included. I'll tell you about him. But first, Richard.'

Louise sighed. 'We were happy. Very happy. Maybe we went too quickly – living together, planning a business. I forget we've only really known each other as adults since I moved back here last year.'

'You were close as children.'

'Teenagers. But even then, it was only two or three years. But we were inseparable. In the twenty years we were apart, I missed him so much. I know it sounds as though I'm being fanciful. Romantic. But I honestly feel as though he's part of me. That we belong together. I can't imagine life without him. I don't want to.'

'So, what's the problem?' her mum said, helping herself to a couple of sandwiches.

'He's getting married to Fiona Simms, daughter of the business tycoon. You've heard of Simms Building Society?'

'I think they're bigger here in the North than down South. This doesn't sound like the young man you've told me about. He wouldn't marry a woman for money or connections. You always gave the impression he was a man of principle.'

'He is. That's one of the things I love about him. Richard and Fiona are business partners. They spend a lot of time together. She wants a family and I told Richard that I didn't.

And although he wouldn't marry for money, I can see he would be better off with her financially. That's another thing I didn't tell you, Ma Beck's will's invalid as we couldn't find her death certificate.'

'Bloody bureaucracy. I'll talk to them. Tell them I watched her coffin go in the ground. What a nonsense.'

Louise hadn't touched her tea, and now it was cold. The room felt hot and stuffy. 'Do you mind if I open a window?'

'No love. It's good to be in the countryside. The moors are magnificent. I can see why you love it here.'

Louise looked out of the open window to the dappled light of a crab apple tree. She wanted to tell her mum everything, but it was time she grew-up. Aunt Emma had warned her not to upset Mum whilst she was fragile.

'I've got tomorrow off work,' she said, turning back into the room. 'I can take you out in my little car.'

'That would be lovely, darling. But come and sit down. What I want to know is why you and Richard broke up in the first place.'

Louise sank heavily into her chair. 'We had a disagreement. I gave the impression I didn't share his dream of building a holiday village, but I do. I just meant there were things I wanted to do as well. Like training as a librarian. And mum? I've got sponsorship. I'm going to become a chartered librarian – eventually.'

Her mum thumped the table with one hand. 'That's my girl. I knew you'd be something grand with that brain of yours. Eddie spoilt you. Stopped you from being your own person. Don't let anyone or anything hold you back. You only have one life and believe me it flashes by far too quickly.'

Louise leant forward in her seat. 'But if we started a family, I wouldn't be able to have a career. I didn't have sponsorship when I told Richard, but I knew I didn't want to give everything up to be a mother. Then, our caravan flooded and we agreed to live apart until the house was ready. In that time, Richard and Fiona were thrown together and Richard and I drifted apart.' Breathless, Louise stopped before she said more than she ought to, the bit about the shovel and Big Jim.

'Have they announced their engagement?'

'No,' Louise said.

'Then you need to fight for him. If he's the man you make him out to be, he'll want you to fulfil your dreams; to train as a librarian. Don't you dare give up on him because you think you're not good enough.'

Louise had forgotten this version of her mum, the one who marched into her infant school to have words with a teacher who wrongly accused Louise of marking the desk with her crayon.

'I love him. I don't want to give him up, but why do woman have to choose between a career or family? It's not fair.'

'Times are changing. If you don't want to have children then don't. We didn't have a choice in my day. I wouldn't have changed having you for the world. But you live in a different time with this contraceptive pill––'

'––I'm pregnant,' Louise said.

'What?' Tea spilled from her mum's cup. 'And the father?'

'Oh, it's Richard.'

'Thank God for that. Does he know?'

Louise shook her head sadly. 'I can't tell him. He would do what he thought was the right thing. I want this baby and Richard, but not like this. And I don't want to give up the opportunity to train as a librarian. My life's a mess.'

Her mum laughed. 'Oh darling. You have got yourself in a pickle. You never do things by halves. I'm going to be a grandma. Your Aunt Emma told me to visit you this weekend. She was insistent. In fact, I can't return until Wednesday next week as the boiler's being serviced or something. So, we can unravel this muddle together.'

Thanks, Aunt Emma, Louise thought. How was she going to keep her mum and dad apart when he arrived the following day?

36

AUGUST 1924

Beth was collecting eggs when she sensed his presence – a shadow in the doorway glimpsed from the corner of her eye. John was on a neighbouring farm, assisting with the harvest, and so she was alone. Her first instinct was a fox. The thought of a fox creeping into the chicken-coup had kept her awake at night in the early days, but the ever-present threat chilled her. These hens were her babies. Crouched in the straw, Beth froze and listened. A cluck. Henrietta flapped her wings. Feathers swirled in the sunlight. All was still. Her imagination. She arranged the eggs in her basket, marvelling over their perfection and thanked the hens.

Life on the farm was good. Hard work but peaceful. And John was a kind, thoughtful husband. Beth felt safe and cherished. The trauma she experienced during the war would always be a part of her, a scar on her heart, a hole in her soul, but milking the cows, making cheese, collecting eggs – the gentle rhythm of each day – held her together.

As she crossed the yard, Shadow started barking. 'What is

it girl?' she called, still afraid of a fox lurking. Beth quickened her pace, her eyes searching the hawthorn bush, which seemed to be the focus of Shadow's agitation. 'Come on. Let's go inside and find you a treat.' She caught the dog's collar and steered her inside.

Shadow was happily gnawing on a lamb bone when there was a knock at the door. They rarely had unannounced visitors. It could be the pedlar selling haberdashery, or a gypsy wanting eggs and milk. Beth didn't want to meet with either and so she shrank away from the window where she might be spotted. A face peered in. Beth shrieked, and Shadow went crazy, her bone forgotten. Grabbing a broom to use as a weapon, Beth flung open the door.

'I'm sorry to disturb you,' the man said.

She couldn't make out his features as he wore a wide-brimmed hat, but there was something familiar about his voice. It made her stomach flip. 'We've no work to offer or provisions. You'd best be off.'

'I understand,' the man spoke softly. 'I didn't mean to scare you. I was looking for an old friend of mine, Beth Hardy.'

Her knees gave way, and she clung to the doorpost. This was too cruel. 'Who are you? What are you doing here?' she cried out in anguish.

'Beth. I'm sorry. It's me, Daniel.'

'Go away. He's dead,' she shouted. Shadow barked furiously.

The man removed his hat. It was Daniel. Those eyes – as blue as the summer sky.

'How can you be here?' she whispered before sliding down the doorpost to land in a heap.

Daniel crouched down and steadied her. 'Can I get you a glass of water? Help you inside?'

Beth allowed him to half-carry her into the kitchen and

settle her into a chair at the table. He filled two glasses with water at the tap and then filled Shadow's bowl with water. 'There you are girl,' he said to the dog.

She watched him, unbelieving. It must be a dream. Daniel died almost nine years ago. Someone playing a cruel trick on her? His voice, the way he moved was Daniel. But it couldn't be.

'I'm so sorry for everything I put you through, Beth,' he said. 'I didn't know you were pregnant. Not until I read a dispatch on the discovery of my dead body. There was a letter from you. It said you were expecting our child.'

Beth shook her head, trying to make sense of his words. 'Your dead body.'

'I know.' He covered his face with his hand. 'I'd better explain from the beginning. When are you expecting John home?'

Beth went cold. How did he know about John? 'My husband, John Beck?' she said, a warning tone in her voice. If this man was an imposter, he needed to know she was no walkover. But despite its seeming impossible, she knew it was Daniel. Her body had reacted to his presence before her brain could compute. Nobody else in this world or the next could make her feel that way.

'I made sure he was out before I called. Harvesting will take a few hours?'

'Yes,' Beth sighed. She didn't want to spend any more time with Daniel; she wanted it to be a dream so she could go back to a quiet and gentle life, but neither could she send him away. He had opened up a gaping wound. She hated him for tearing her apart, both then and now. 'What do you want? Why have you come back?'

'I came back to meet my daughter. Pearl.'

Beth went cold. 'Who told you?'

'Daisy. When I found out about your letter – which incidentally I never received, I came back to England. I'm staying with Daisy, who sends her regards and deepest apologies for all we have put you through. Look, can we go someplace else to talk? I'm afraid of being disturbed. This is top secret stuff. I know, come and have a ride on my plane. I've got the use of a biplane whilst I'm here in England. I know how much you love to fly.'

'Loved. That was a different woman – a girl. I'm not the same person, Daniel. You destroyed me.' She took him in, her Daniel. She hated him and loved him. 'Okay, I'll go with you, but understand I'm married to an honest and loyal man. I wouldn't hurt or deceive John for the world. Without John I wouldn't have survived. Did Daisy tell you I lost my friends: Rosie, Connie and Iris? They died in an explosion at the factory. It was too much after losing you, and my brothers. Except I didn't lose you, did I? You deserted me. Let me believe you were dead.' Anger surged through Beth, singeing her palms, burning her throat. God help her, she could kill him herself with her bare hands.

'I know. I know,' Daniel held up his hands as if in surrender. 'My darling, I would have done anything to change the course of my destiny. I tried. That day we made love I had a plan to make everything right. Please let me explain. Beth, Daisy and I are – were – secret agents.'

Beth gave a hollow laugh, then realised he was serious or had lost his mind. 'No. I don't understand.'

'Let's get out of here before we're interrupted and I'll tell you everything. I'm breaking my oath but I owe it to you.'

37

12TH AUGUST 1966

Louise had stayed the night at the Coach and Horses after collecting a few things from High House. The inn's restaurant was small and cosy, and as they were the only guests breakfasting, Nancy made a fuss of them.

'As you're special guests, I've given you the last of my homemade marmalade. I'll fetch you another pot of coffee and more toast. Sit as long as you like, although it's a beautiful day out there. The moors are looking glorious. Take your mum to the waterfall, Louise. I wish I could go with you.'

'So, what have we got planned for the day?' her mum said, helping herself to a spoonful of marmalade. 'This does look gorgeous. I remember you bringing home treats from the farm when you were evacuated. The Christmas you came home with a bag stuffed with cheese, eggs, and a Christmas pudding made by your grandma if I remember right.'

'My grandma.' Louise sighed. 'I wish I'd known at the time. I wanted Ma and Pa to be my grandparents. It felt lonely growing up just the two of us. I know we had Aunt Emma and her boys but,' Louise wrinkled her nose, 'I kind of felt like an outsider. That we weren't really wanted.'

'Emma was – *no is* – a good sister. That little house was cramped with two adults and four children. Your uncle was at war but when he returned, he needed some space. And I always gave Emma a hard time. It wasn't her fault mum treated us differently.'

Louise had given her father's visit a lot of thought. At first, she planned on keeping it a secret in the hope that she could keep her parents apart. But the last few weeks had taught her, it wasn't good to keep secrets. His letter was on her lap beneath the table. She curled her fingers around it.

'Mum. Before we go out, there's something important I've got to tell you.'

'I can't think of anything more shocking than the news you're pregnant, so hit me with it.' Her mum laughed and buttered another slice of toast.

'The reason I left London in a hurry, wasn't because Richard had been taken in for questioning about Eddie's accident. That did happen but I found out when I got back.'

Her mum stopped what she was doing and gave Louise her full attention. It was as though she was preparing herself for disappointment, and Louise felt bad about the unhappiness she had caused.

'I found this letter inside an encyclopaedia in your flat. I was looking in a cupboard for a bag to pack your overnight things. It just fell out.'

Her mum frowned as Louise passed the letter across the table. She opened it slowly, and Louise held her breath as she watched her mum's eyes slide back and forth across the page. Then, her face paled, and Louise felt dreadful. Aunt Emma had warned her not to distress Mum.

The Canary Girl's Secret

'Excuse me.' Her mum didn't make eye contact as she rushed from the room.

In the silence that followed, Louise regarded the half-eaten toast and marmalade that her mum had been enjoying seconds before. It was as though Louise had flung a grenade across the table, destroying the peaceful morning. Why did she always do that? Act without thinking? If her mum had another stroke on account of this news, she would never forgive herself. And she hadn't even mentioned that her father was expected at the hotel sometime today. If only she knew what time he was due to arrive. Five minutes passed. Nancy came to clear away breakfast.

'I don't think we've finished,' Louise said.

Another five minutes passed, and Louise became anxious. Just as she stood to go and find her mother, Pearl returned to the dining room, clutching a handkerchief. Her eyes red and swollen.

'Tell me exactly where you found this letter,' she said.

Louise explained.

Her mum listened, then said, 'In the box of books Emma packed up from Mum's house, when she died. I haven't looked at them, just stored them away with the other stuff. I didn't want anything from her, but Emma insisted I take something, so I said the books, because I thought you might like them, being a bookworm. Then, I forgot about them.' She gave a heavy sigh. 'I think I met him.'

'My father?' Louise said.

'My father,' her mum replied. 'I was about eight. Mum had taken Emma to the circus without me. She said it was because I'd been naughty, but I can't remember doing anything wrong. I was home alone, hanging around outside our house. We lived on a cul-de-sac, and all the kids played in the street. Looking back, I expect Mum had asked one of the neighbours to keep an eye on me. I was miserable, feeling sorry for myself, sitting on the garden wall, when a motorbike pulled up outside our house. The Donoghue twins held up their game of cricket to gawp and Maisie's game of Jacks paused as she too watched the man who dismounted and looked around him.

"24 Lark Terrace?" he said.

I nodded. He had a funny accent. I'd not met an American before. The other kids wandered over, so I wasn't alone, but it was our house he wanted.

"Mum's out," I said.

"And that would be Ruby Pearson?"

I nodded again. He didn't look like someone my mum would know. He was glamorous. I didn't know that word then, just knew he was different. A person who attracted attention.

"Is Mr Pearson home?"

"No, sir." I called him Sir because that's what we called teachers at school.

"Who's taking care of you?"

I didn't reply because I didn't know the right answer. I didn't want to get my mum in trouble.

"Where's Mrs Pearson?"

"She's taken my sister to the circus, sir."

The man crouched down so that his face was level with mine. "Is your name Pearl?"

I nodded.

"Well Pearl, I came here to meet you, but I can't do that without Mr or Mrs Pearson being home."

"But you already have. Met me. Because you're there and I'm here."

He grinned. "Indeed, I have. You remind me of your mother. I really hope we will meet again. I'm going to leave a letter for your parents. You're a very special girl, Pearl. Never forget that. Always know you are loved."

They were odd words from a stranger, but they made me feel warm inside. I'd been feeling neglected, punished; ashamed for not being good enough. I never forgot him, the stranger with eyes the colour of my favourite blue marble. He must have left that letter for me.'

'And your mum never gave it to you?'

'No.' Pearl wiped away a tear.

Louise's heart went out to her mother, but it meant she wasn't about to meet her father, and the disappointment was crushing. 'You said you'd tell me about my father.'

'I'm sorry, darling. There's nothing I would like more than to tell you that you too have a father who wants to be part of your life. He was a married man. I didn't know he was married at the time. He was my boss, older than me. I was naïve. Stupid. When he found out I was pregnant he wanted nothing more to do with me. Threatened to accuse me of stealing from him if I told anyone he was the father. He was a powerful man and I was nothing. A silly girl flattered by his attention, impressed by his power, and desperate to be loved. I'm not sorry. Having you was the best thing in my life. There's no way I would regret that. I'm just sorry I've been such a useless mother.'

They sat in silence for a while. Then Louise squeezed her mum's hand. 'Come on. Let's get out into the sunshine. I'll drive you around our fabulous countryside.'

'Can I meet, Richard?' Her mum said.

'If you promise not to tell him I'm pregnant,' Louise frowned.

'Okay, but you'll need to tell him sooner or later. Don't deprive your child of a father. We both know how that feels.'

'If that man isn't my father,' Louise said, as the penny dropped. 'Who did I write to? Because he's on his way here from Australia.'

38

FRIDAY 12TH AUGUST 1966

There was so much Louise wanted to show her mother: Mobi, her little library van, the half-drained reservoir with their submerged village emerging like a spectre, the moors – of course, the moors – in all their summer glory, and her friends. She wanted Mum to meet Esther and Bill, and Richard. But how could her heart cope with seeing the two people she loved most meeting for the first time? It should have been a joyful occasion introducing her to the man with whom she once wanted to share her life.

The tour around the valley and moors took them to the plot of land where Richard had built their house. It was as though Mini Mouse had a mind of her own, because Louise had tried to resist the pull of this place she held dear. It represented all that she had lost.

'It's a big plot,' her mum said when Louise pulled up alongside the expanse of land.

'Can you see that timber house?' Louise leaned across to point through the trees. 'Richard built that. He's a talented carpenter. Did I tell you it was his dream since childhood to build a village? We planned the whole thing. Little holiday cabins. A man-made lake, eventually, but that was in our ten-year plan. A shop to sell essentials. Dairy produce from neighbouring farms. I wanted city kids to experience country life as I did when I lived here as an evacuee.'

'An ambitious plan,' Pearl said.

'I know. We were living in a dreamworld. Meeting Richard again after those years living with Eddie, I really believed anything was possible. Even with my inheritance it would have been a challenge. And now...' Louise shrugged her shoulders. 'Anyway, Fiona Simm's family have plenty of money. Hopefully, he won't have to sell off any of the land. Where to next?'

'Not so fast. Drive in. Let me take a proper look,' Pearl said, leaning forward in her seat as she took everything in.

Louise hesitated. Richard would be at work. 'Okay. You'll be able to see the wreck of a caravan we were living in when I came to visit you in hospital.'

Mini bumped over the uneven ground as Louise swung through the gateway. The house looked magnificent. Its windows winking as they reflected the sun.

'It's a fine house. You're right. Your Richard is a talented craftsman. How many cabins did you envisage?'

'Five there,' Louise pointed to a place beyond the wooded copse. 'Then another four here. They would eventually look out onto the lake. A couple over there. And another five dotted around that area, between the trees. The shop would be in that vicinity too.'

'That's sixteen,' her mum said.

'Yes. It would have been incredible.'

Her mum had wandered over to the house, and Louise reluctantly followed, afraid of being discovered. Pearl disappeared from view, and Louise hoped she wasn't peering in through the windows.

The reservoir looked peaceful, as though it was gently bathing the cottages. A mother lovingly lapping water to clear away soap suds. A curlew's plaintive cry sounded like her heart breaking. Voices. Mum was talking to someone. Richard. Louise turned, ready to run, but she couldn't leave without her mum. Richard and Pearl came around the side of the house.

'Lou Lou.' Richard brushed his hands on his shorts. Sawdust danced in the sunlight. 'You brought your mum to meet me. I've been wanting to meet you, Pearl for an age. Can I call you Pearl?'

Her mum giggled girlishly. 'Only if I can call you Dicky.'

'Oh no! Only you and Louise know me by that name. But I'll allow you to. It's what my mam called me.' He smiled, and Louise's heart contracted with love.

'Did Fiona tell you I'd be home?' Richard said.

Louise nodded, afraid to talk in case she cried.

'I've packed up your things in boxes. I'll help you load them into your car.'

'Okay. Thank you,' Louise croaked.

'That can wait. I'd love to see around your house. Louise tells me you're a talented carpenter. I can hardly believe you built this house with your two hands.' Pearl took hold of Richard's hands and gave them a squeeze. 'And look how strong you are.'

Louise cringed with embarrassment. She just wanted to escape and have a good cry.

Richard beamed at her mum. 'Come inside and I'll show you around Pearl.'

Her mum glanced over her shoulder at Louise and winked as they followed Richard into the house. It smelt of baked pine. The kitchen was fully fitted, showcasing Richard's carpentry with handmade units.

'Oh, this is beautiful,' her mum said, running her hand reverently over a work surface. You made this? It's the most beautiful kitchen I've ever set eyes on. Why aren't you working full-time doing this?'

'Maybe one day. Come on, I'll show you the rest of the house.'

Louise left Richard to do a guided tour. Soon, it would be full of Fiona's frippery. Furniture and heirlooms transported from Simms Manor. She sat at the kitchen table; polished oak with natural edges, the different hues of grain a tribute to the wonder of nature. Her eyes strayed to an open letter. It had the Corporation logo. She twisted her head to read without touching. A generous offer. The words stood out on the page. A figure with several zeros.

'You've made a dream home. Perfect for raising a family,' her mum said.

Louise's eyes flew from the letter to Richard, and she went a deep crimson. 'Yes. You've done an excellent job, Richard,' she stuttered. How could he sell his land to the Corporation?

'Lou Lou there's something I need to tell you,' Richard said, an urgency in his voice.

'It's okay, Richard. I know.' Louise shrugged as if it didn't mean anything.

'You do?' A frown creased his forehead.

Louise nodded at the post on the kitchen table as Richard turned to kiss her mum goodbye.

'Well, I can see why you fell for him,' her mum said, when they were safely back in the car. 'Handsome. Talented. And such good manners. You can't let him go without a fight.'

'I'm not going to start scheming. It's too late. Richard and Fiona are getting married. I came between them once and

I'm not going to do it again. I had my chance and I screwed it up.'

'We'll see,' her mum said. 'Where to now?'

'Esther and Bill? I lived with them for a while. Esther is my boss. I'm covering for her whilst she's on maternity leave.'

'She's got a baby?'

'No. Expecting but she had a bit of a scare and is taking things easy until after the birth. Incidentally, Esther doesn't know I'm pregnant.'

As they drove the familiar route from Richard's house to Esther's, Louise asked. 'How did you cope being a single mum? I mean when I was first born.' Some conversations were easier to have whilst driving. It gave time to think and reflect as she focused on the road.

'Well, as you might guess, my mum wasn't too pleased. Said, that she'd not expected anything else from me, being the wayward one. But, credit to her, she wouldn't hear of us putting you up for adoption. Ironic now I know I was adopted. We seem to follow a pattern the women in this family. Elizabeth, me, and now you. Mum helped me in the early days. I think she liked getting her hands on another female baby to mould. I didn't turn out the way she wanted.'

Louise indicated and turned off the roundabout. 'How old was I when you moved out?'

Her mum was quiet as she gave this some thought. 'I left and then returned a couple of times. It was harder than I thought, I won't lie. We didn't have welfare benefits in those days like you do now. And there was a terrible stigma around being a single mum – a fallen woman. If not for my mum, I would have been sent to the workhouse.'

Louise gasped. 'Surely not.'

'Oh yes. The Poor Law was still in place, workhouse and all. Things changed after the second world war. Lady Hannah was my saviour. I don't know how my mum knew a woman like that but apparently, she did. Anyway, Lady Hannah gave me a job as a maid and allowed me to have you live with me. The other servants all helped care for you whilst I was working.'

'I don't remember,' Louise said, amazed this was the first time she was hearing about her early years.

'We weren't there long. As soon as you started to walk, we had to move. It would have been too much for the other staff. A baby in a crib was fine. I fed you and changed you. They just kept an eye on you.'

Louise slowed the car as they approached a couple of riders on horseback. 'And then?'

'Someone, kindly found me a room to rent. Mum told me about it. And I got work in a jam factory. Just enough money to pay my rent with a bit left over for food. We survived. As soon as Emma got married and left home, she came to my rescue, bless her. I don't know what I would have done without her.'

They overtook the horse riders. 'That's where Fiona lives,' Louise said, pointing to the grand entrance of Simms Manor. 'Fiona has a riding stable as well as her other business interests.'

'How the other half live, eh? Life would be very different for you as a single mum, Louise. I'd be here to help for a start.'

'I know. Thank you, Mum. We're here. This is Esther and Bill's place. Stay in the car whilst I check if it's alright for us to visit.'

'Please don't put the poor girl to any trouble.'

Esther was delighted to have company. She came out of the cottage to greet Pearl at the car. 'I've been dying to meet you. Come in!'

Bill was home having worked an early shift, and her mum

made eyes at him as he examined her slightly swollen fingers, asked about her dizzy spells, and generally made a fuss of her.

'You shouldn't be tearing across the country so soon after your discharge from hospital. I hope Louise is taking good care of you,' he said. 'Homemade lemonade or a brew? Esther's taken a liking for my lemonade so I make up a jug and keep it in the fridge.'

They decided on lemonade and took themselves out to the pretty cottage garden where they say under the shade of an apple tree. Louise and Bill lounged on a blanket, whilst Pearl and Esther occupied the two garden chairs.

Esther told Pearl about her pregnancy, whilst Pearl made sympathetic noises and offered suggestions for combating heartburn; drinking raw potato juice or baking soda dissolved in water.

'Oh, I almost forgot to tell you,' Esther exclaimed as she struggled out of her chair.

'Stay there. I'll get it,' Bill said.

'Louise's invitation from Fiona. It's on the dresser. Fiona's having a garden party next weekend. I hope you'll still be here, Pearl. I'm sure Fiona would love to meet you. We are all so excited you made the journey here. Did you come to support Louise when she meets her dad today? When's he arriving?'

Louise shook her head slowly at Esther. Just as well she'd told her mum everything because Esther would have blown it.

Esther clapped a hand over her mouth. 'Sorry. I assumed that's why you were here.'

Bill arrived back clutching an embossed cream envelope. 'What did I miss?' he looked from one startled face to the other.

'It's okay,' Louise sighed. 'Mum knows. But apparently, it's not my dad. We think our visitor might be mum's father. It's complicated.'

They had just recovered from Esther's faux pas when she made another. 'Thank goodness. Sorry but I'm relieved. It means you won't go off travelling across the world. We need you here as our future librarian.'

Pearl gave Louise an amused and knowing look. She'd been rumbled. It seemed she wasn't going anywhere. And now they were expected to go to a party where Fiona and Richard would no doubt announce their engagement.

'On that note,' Louise said, clambering to her feet, 'We'd better get back to the Coach and Horses so we can prepare to meet the mysterious Geoffrey Sommerfeld.'

'Ooh, I wish I could be a fly on the wall,' Esther said.

39

FRIDAY 12TH AUGUST 1966

Their visitor had checked into the hotel and left a message at reception. Please join me for a drink in the guests' lounge at seven this evening. Geoffrey Sommerfeld.

'Mr Sommerfeld is having a lie down. Fancy flying from halfway across the world to visit our little village. I told him the guest lounge would be quieter than the public bar. No-one will disturb you there. He's booked a table for dinner at eight,' Nancy said.

'You'd better change the booking to three people,' Louise said. 'He was only expecting me.'

'No.' Nancy consulted her book. 'Four people booked in the name of Sommerfeld.'

Louise and Pearl exchanged puzzled looks. 'Okay. Thank you, Nancy.'

In Pearl's room, Louise helped her mother change into an attractive shift dress, silver grey with tiny yellow and lilac flowers.

'This sling comes off in two weeks,' Pearl said. 'It'll be a relief. When I have full use of that arm again.'

'I'll go back to London with you. I should have cared for you in your flat. I'm sorry I deserted you when you needed me,' Louise said.

'Nonsense. You've got to work. I'm proud of you driving that library van and managing the service. They obviously think a lot of you. No. I'm okay living with Emma. She's a good sister. The best. The plumbing should be sorted by the time I return. But I'll be fine living on my own.'

Louise realised with a pang how much she was going to miss her mum. 'I wish I could afford a house so you could live with me here in Yorkshire.'

'That would be grand. But whatever happens, love; I'll be here to help when that baby's born. Even if I have to share one of them bunk beds with you.'

'Let's hope it doesn't come to that,' Louise laughed. The truth was, she didn't know what she was going to do or where she would live. 'But I will have to tell Diane Chippendale that I'm pregnant. Just not yet. I'm not telling a soul until I'm twelve weeks.'

'And when you do,' her mum said, with a grave nod of her head, 'You'll tell Dicky first.'

'Please stay until after Fiona's party. I can't face it alone,' Louise said, zipping up her mother's dress.

Her mum kissed her cheek. 'You're never alone. I'm always here. Okay. I'll stay until after the party. I want to meet this, Fiona.'

At six-fifty-five, when they had talked through every possible scenario, wondering who exactly they would meet, why he had booked a table for four, and what to do if he was an absolute nightmare and they wanted to skip dinner, Louise said, 'Ready?' and they made their way

The Canary Girl's Secret

down the creaky staircase, through reception to the guest lounge.

He was waiting for them in a high-backed armchair, his back to the door.

'Mr Sommerfeld?' Louise said.

He was younger than her mum. Louise's heart sank; she had made a dreadful mistake. Invited a complete stranger to travel thousands of miles on a wild-goose chase. She reached for her mum's hand and squeezed it. This would be a blow to her. Another disappointment.

He invited them to sit down. 'I requested a pot of tea, because I understand that's what you drink over here, and a decanter of whisky because I think I'm going to need a drink. If you would like something else, I'll order it now before we get down to business.'

'Tea's fine,' Pearl said.

'This is my mother, Pearl Pearson, and I'm Louise. I wrote to you but I think I might have got my wires crossed. Unless, you are my father?' As this realisation hit her, she whipped around to check with her mum.

Pearl shook her head.

'Then who are you? A solicitor?' Louise said.

Geoffrey poured himself a whisky and took a slug before replying. 'I'm your brother, Pearl. I'm sorry to tell you our father Blake Sommerfeld died in 1956. He asked me to find you and explain why he had to leave your mother when she was with child. It's a shocking story. Unbelievable. If I didn't know my father to be an honest man, I wouldn't have believed it myself. Are you sure you don't want a tipple of this?'

'Maybe after you've told his story,' Pearl said.

'Okay. I'll tell you in my dad's words. He wrote it down. But this is top secret. You mustn't share it with anyone. Not even your nearest and dearest.'

They nodded, intrigued, and Geoffrey unfolded a wad of paper. The same handwriting Louise remembered from the letter she had found. Slanting and loopy.

'Meeting Beth Hardy was the best thing that ever happened to me and the worst. I want to curse the day we met, but I wouldn't give up the precious days we spent together for the world. Maybe that's the price we had to pay; Beth more than me. If you are reading this, I have died – for real this time. I was sworn to secrecy, but I owe this to our daughter, Daniella. You were made from love, angel. I'm sorry we couldn't claim you as our own. So, here is my story. I hope you can forgive me.

I was a volunteer pilot with the Lafayette Escadrille when our plane came down near Zürich. My co-pilot was badly injured, but I got off lightly with smoke inhalation and a couple of broken ribs. We were taken to a Red Cross hospital in Switzerland, and that's when it all began. It was 1914. We knew of the trouble between Austria and Serbia, but war hadn't been declared. Beds at the hospital weren't in demand at that time, so I stayed until I'd fully recovered. Looking back, I realise they were preparing the hospital for war casualties, with Switzerland being neutral territory. There was a doctor who took an interest in me. He checked my lung capacity every few days and would stop to talk about bi-planes. He was fascinated by my stories of barnstorming with my pa in Ohio. At least, that's what I thought. We were on a first-name basis, me and Doctor Charles. I think I might have invited him to go up in my plane when I was discharged.

One evening Charles said to me, 'How would you like to assist with important war work?'

The Canary Girl's Secret

'What war?' I said. I thought he was joking. A trick he was going to play on the nurses. Daisy St. Clair was one of those nurses. She was a looker, and I'd noticed the flirtation between the two of them. But then he became serious.

'You would get paid a considerable sum. All you would need to do is pass on information. Flight paths used by French and British pilots. If you joined the Flying Corps, you could be invaluable. Think about it.' I didn't ask who I would be helping because I knew. Germany. The USA was neutral at that time, but there was no way I would spy for the Germans. I realised then he'd been playing me.

I planned on reporting Charles to my superior and asked the hospital administrator if I could be discharged. I didn't want to see doctor Charles again.

'I hear you've requested a discharge from hospital,' Daisy said the day after I made my request. Thankfully, I hadn't seen Charles since he made his offer, and I couldn't get away fast enough.

That's when Daisy told me she was working for a contact in British Intelligence. They had sent her to the hospital to observe and report back on Dr Charles. 'I know he's been talking to you,' she said. 'You must tell me everything he said before you leave here. He's a dangerous man. A German spy.'

I told her what he had asked of me. And that's when it began. Our plan was to feed false information to the Germans. I became a double agent working for MI5. I told Dr Charles I accepted his offer and later I enrolled with the Royal Flying Corps.

All was going well. Daisy fed me information, which I passed to my German contact. Planned military attacks that never took place, and some real information so I didn't arouse suspicion. But they must have suspected something as Camille

Beaufont was sent to spy on Daisy and me. Poor Daisy, Camille was her first true love. She was besotted with the woman. Love makes us do foolish things. I'm evidence of that. Maybe Daisy let her guard down. Or Camille was too clever for us. We had no idea she was on to us until the painting went missing. Mother and Child. Daisy hid a message for me in the back of the canvas. Camille disappeared the day after the art auction where the painting was stolen.

Camille was a German spy, and she had enough evidence to expose me. Daisy was safe as long as she stayed in England, but I wasn't. British Intelligence couldn't risk my being captured and tortured for information.

We were being watched. So, Daisy sent me messages using Beth. It was wrong. So wrong. Beth had no idea. First, a watercolour painting with the message written in invisible ink and hidden between the paper and backing board; then, in a loaf of bread, the message hidden in a hollowed-out section. Why Beth? If it had been anyone else but her…I fell in love. Totally, helplessly, in love.

I tried to ignore the messages. A command to meet with Daisy's contact. A staged plane crash with a burnt corpse. It had to look as though Daniel Winterton had died. But I wasn't ready to die. I couldn't – wouldn't – leave Beth.

In the end, I had no choice. I was kidnapped by MI5 and smuggled out of the country. A new life and identity as Blake Sommerfeld. As far away from England as possible. Australia. I didn't know Beth was pregnant, until years later.

I met Daniella when she was a child, but it wasn't fair to tell her who I was without her adopted mom's permission, so I left a letter to be passed on when she was older, but maybe it never reached her. Her name is now Pearl. Pearl Pearson, unless she has married. If you can find her, Geoffrey, please share my story. I can't make up for my wrongs. All I can say is, I'm sorry, Daniella. I loved you and your mother more than words can say.'

Geoffrey looked up from reading the letter, tears in his eyes. 'I'm sorry I didn't find you sooner.'

Louise hugged Pearl. 'Oh Mum. At least you know that he loved you.'

'I'll have that tipple now,' Pearl said.

Geoffrey poured, and she knocked back a healthy measure of whisky. 'I've so many questions. Did our dad have a good life in Australia? Did you know of his past?'

Geoffrey smiled. 'He married my mother in 1926. A year later, I was born. Yes, he had a good life. He owned an airfield and took tourists on scenic rides in his bi-plane, gave lessons in aerobatic manoeuvres. I suspect he continued working for Intelligence Services. He could be very evasive when questioned about where he'd been. My mum knew not to ask questions and would head me off if I kept pushing him on something he didn't want to discuss. He was easy going. A wonderful father. I'm sorry you didn't get to spend any time with him, Pearl.'

'Did your mother know about me?' Pearl asked.

'I honestly don't know. She had already died when I found out. She was only forty-four. Younger than Dad.'

'I'm sorry we found the letter too late,' Louise said.

Pearl nodded. 'But at least he visited me as a child. He was kind. And he had the most beautiful blue eyes.'

Geoffrey agreed. 'He was a good-looking man our dad.'

'Poor Ma. She thought he died. It must have broken her heart,' Louise said.

'Well, she found out eventually,' Geoffrey said. He topped up his glass and Pearl's. Louise shook her head when he offered the decanter.

'Beth Hardy's ashes were buried in the same plot as our father. I was absent the last five years of his life, living in Perth, which is some distance from his ranch in New South Wales. I know Dad would have loved me to take over the business, to learn to fly, but I've always been scared of heights.

'He was independent. After mum died, he carried on flying. Our dad was brave, and strong. He seemed indestructible to me. A force of nature. It didn't worry me that he lived alone. And then, in March 1956, I got a telegram asking me to come home. He had contracted septicaemia. It started as pneumonia. It was on his death bed he told me about you, Pearl. He asked me to find you and share his story. He also told me where to find Beth Hardy's ashes and gave instructions for them to be buried with him.'

Louise covered her mouth. It was so tragic. 'That's why Ma's body wasn't in her coffin. The one that was buried in Thorncrest Church graveyard.'

The three of them sat in silence, processing what was an incredible story.

'Thank you for coming all of this way to tell me,' Pearl said.

'It's the least I could do. Besides you're my sister.'

'I've got a brother,' Pearl said with a little sob.

'And on that note, I think we'd better join your sister in the dining room, it's gone eight.' Geoffrey stood up.

'I've a sister too?' Pearl looked around as if hoping said sister would walk in.

'Yes. It was your sister Emma who contacted me. I'd received Louise's letter and didn't know what to make of it. A PO box. No address. A young woman claiming to be my sister. I thought it was a scam. Someone after an inheritance. Then

Emma wrote to me explaining who she was and how you had been adopted. I stayed with her when I first arrived in England, and we travelled together to Yorkshire.'

'You mean Emma sent me here knowing you would join us?' Pearl said.

'Exactly so.' He grinned. 'Let's go and find her.'

40

SATURDAY 20TH AUGUST 1966

Aunt Emma and Geoffrey stayed on a few more days at the Coach and Horses. They kept Pearl entertained during the week whilst Louise was working. The story Geoffrey shared was staggering. When she thought of Ma – her grandmother – as a young woman believing the man she hoped to marry, the father of her child, was dead, it shamed Louise for thinking herself hard done by.

'As soon as that sling comes off and you're feeling up to it, I'd like you to visit me in Australia, Pearl,' Geoffrey had said. 'I'll show you around the ranch, and take you to the cemetery where your parents are buried. I've lived there the past ten years, since dad died. But it's too big for me. I'd given up hope of ever finding you. So, Louise's letter was well timed.'

It was no surprise to Louise that the sun shone brightly on the day of Fiona's garden party. Everything worked out perfectly for that woman. Not that Louise wished her any ill, but it would be good if a little of her lucky charm rubbed off on her. They are going to announce their engagement. Louise could think of nothing else. Somehow, she would need to be out of sight, behind a tree, or in the kitchen, anywhere but in full view of Richard when this happened. He must not see her face. She must not cry. It was good Mum was going to be there.

'You look gorgeous,' Pearl said, greeting her in reception. Louise was wearing a pale lemon shift dress with a matching jacket. She'd fallen in love with it on a shopping trip to Busby's and this was the first opportunity to wear it. Her hair was pinned in a neat chignon. 'Jackie Kennedy. That's who you put me in mind of. Will I do? I only packed one good dress but your friends haven't seen this one, only my brother and sister. I love saying that. My brother.'

'You look fabulous, Mum. But don't worry. All eyes will be on Fiona. I hope Richard doesn't mind her inviting me. You'd think he would have mentioned it himself when we saw him. Unless he doesn't want me there,' Louise said.

'I'm not missing this party. And don't worry, sweetheart. You'll outshine Fiona. Nobody but nobody could look more beautiful than you.'

'I think you might be a bit biased, but thanks Mum. I couldn't have gone alone. We'll wait until after the announcement and then, when it seems as though a reasonable amount of time has passed––five minutes? Okay twenty. Thirty. Really? Then we'll leave.'

'This business about there being an announcement is all in your head, darling. The invitation just says a garden party. Esther didn't say there was a special reason for the gathering. Posh toffs just like getting people together to show off their house and garden. There's bound to be champagne. I for one am going to enjoy myself. Shame, I've only one functioning arm. If there's to be food I'll not manage with a plate and glass.'

'I'm impressed you can do so much for yourself. I thought

The Canary Girl's Secret

you would need help getting dressed. When you get back from your trip to Australia, I want to find a way for us to live closer together, mum. Do you think you could get a council flat transfer to Yorkshire?'

'I doubt it. But don't worry, love. We'll find a way. Now paste on that smile. By the looks of all these cars, we've arrived at Simms Manor.'

'Don't call it that,' Louise hissed. 'It's my silly joke name.'

Esther and Fliss were seated on the patio, Fliss with a glass of Pimms, and Esther with homemade lemonade as Bill had prepared and carried over a pitcher. 'It's the sweet-sour flavour that I crave,' Esther said. 'This baby's going to have lemonade running through its veins.'

A girl Louise recognised as the one working in Braithwaite's grocery last year offered a tray of filled glasses to Louise. 'Champagne, Pimms or white wine?' she asked.

'I'll have a glass of Bill's lemonade?' Louise said. She'd love a glass of Pimms, but would the embryo she imagined curled up in her womb? It would only be a collection of tiny cells, but Louise was forming an attachment to her little bean.

'Your mum's great,' Esther said. They looked over to where Pearl was chatting with Fiona and Richard. Louise dreaded to think what she might be saying.

When Louise received her lemonade, she made her excuses and wandered over to rescue her mum, or more to the point, to rescue Richard. They were discussing Pearl's trip to Australia.

'I've never travelled further than Yorkshire,' Pearl said. 'I'm excited but a bit scared, not knowing what to expect. Funny how life can suddenly change. You think you know what's going to happen next year, and the next, then suddenly wham, everything's thrown up in the air. Life's full of surprises.' She winked at Louise. Subtle mum.

'Did you say hello to Paul Evans?' Richard said.

'No. I'll go over,' Louise said.

Paul was deep in conversation with Pete Murray. Louise wanted to know what they were talking about as it might affect her.

'I'll look after Pearl,' Richard said.

There was nothing Louise could do to manage damage limitation. But she gave her mum a warning look before picking her way across the immaculate lawn in her kitten-heeled shoes. The two men watched her advance with welcoming smiles.

'They've arrested George Bellamy as a prime suspect for the murder of Edward Boyd,' Paul said.

'Oh, thank God,' Louise exclaimed. 'And Big Jim?' She looked to Pete for an update, but Paul responded.

'James Murphy is a wanted man for a lot more than the murder of one man. He's the Mob Boss of a notorious London gang. Nasty piece of work. George Bellamy and his brother Charlie worked for him and it seems so did Edward Boyd, but you would know that, Louise – Mrs Boyd,' he said, shaking his head at her.

'Okay. I should have told you. Sorry. But I was afraid. I guessed Big Jim had something to do with Eddie's murder and I told the police.'

'You did what?' Pete said, astounded.

'I know. I've been terrified of retribution.'

'Well, fear no more. They've caught up with Big Jim and he'll be going away for a long time. Oh. Excuse me. I'm needed.' He left Pete and Louise to stride across the lawn back to the house.

'I admire your pluck,' Pete said. 'You're braver than me. Oh, looks like Fiona's father's about to make a speech.'

Louise's heart sank. Why hadn't she stayed close to her mum? Or ran into the kitchen. It was too late to hide now.

Fiona's father was a stout man, dressed in a tailored jacket despite the heat of the day. He clinked the side of a champagne flute with a pastry fork. Voices quietened as though a breeze had rippled across the lawn silencing them all.

'Family. Friends. Ladies and gentleman.'

Louise looked around her, wondering if some of their guests were in fact lords and ladies. Fiona was behind her dad to his left, looking bashful, but she couldn't see Richard.

'It is a great pleasure to see you all here in our home. My wife and I – Mrs Simms stepped forward to stand alongside her husband – are, as you all know, proud of our beautiful daughter Fiona.'

Louise let out an audible sigh. A couple of heads turned, and she covered her mouth. Oops.

'Fiona has everything we could want in a daughter. Intelligence. The renowned Simms business acumen.' A few laughs, from his business associates, Louise suspected. 'Wisdom and grace.' He looked fondly at Fiona.

'Thank you, Daddy.' She bestowed a radiant smile upon her father and their guests.

'Only a very special man would be worthy of my daughter's hand in marriage.'

A few gasps were heard from the audience. There were murmurs as news travelled ahead of the announcement. Louise searched for a tree, a bush, anywhere she could hide and sob uncontrollably without being heard.

'So, when this fine and upstanding gentleman approached me…'

Louise wanted to cover her ears and eyes. Instead, she crouched down as if to fasten the false buckle on her shoe. At least she wouldn't have to see Richard gazing at Fiona to cheers of congratulations. Could they leave now? Everyone was clapping and whooping.

'Thank you, George. I am honoured to be welcomed into your family. And I am the happiest man on this earth, now Fiona has agreed to be my wife. To Fiona.'

That wasn't Richard's voice.

'Found what you were looking for?' a voice said from behind.

Louise stumbled to her feet as Paul Evans kissed Fiona, to a cacophony of wolf-whistles and cheers.

'Richard. I thought…'

'I know. I'm sorry.' He flinched as if expecting her to throw a punch.

'How could you?' she yelled. A few heads turned. A shush from someone.

Richard signalled for her to follow him away from the crowd.

'Why did you tell me you and Fiona were getting married?' Louise snarled.

'Because you kept badgering me to get back with Fiona. I knew why. When I picked up my mail from the post office, there was a postcard from your friend, Big Jim.'

Louise gasped. 'Another one?'

'Apparently. The girl who handed it to me and said, "Are these clues? A game?" She told me you'd received one too.'

'What did it say?' Louise said.

'A damaged wall is nothing. I know what you did. The postcard was a photo of a pig,' Richard said.

'A pig. A reference to my meeting with DCI Jenkins? Or to me squealing? I helped them with their enquiries. They've arrested him and most of his network,' Louise said.

'That was a brave thing to do,' Richard replied. 'I hate that you've been going through all of this alone. I was shocked when I found the postcard, but relieved too. When you told me it was over between us, I wanted to die. Honestly, a life without you was more than I could bear.'

'I'm sorry, Richard. I had to protect you from Big Jim.'

'When I found the postcard, I understood. But you shouldn't have lied to me. We've got to trust one another.'

'And you should have told me, instead of pretending you'd asked Fiona to marry you.' Louise was still angry.

'I know. I'm sorry. I tried to tell you when you visited with Pearl but you said you knew.'

'I thought you meant about accepting the offer from the Corporation.'

'I'd never do that,' Richard said. 'But we do have to sell the land. All of it.'

Louise sighed. 'At least we have the house and each other.'

Richard pulled her to him and held her tight. 'I don't want to live another day without you. We've wasted too much of our lives apart.'

'Do you think we could sneak away now?' Louise said.

'What about Pearl?'

Louise had momentarily forgotten her poor mum. 'I'll go and get her. She won't mind leaving early.'

Her mum was chatting with Esther and Fliss on the patio. Louise watched from a distance; her mum was waving her free arm in gestures as the other two women laughed. It was good to see her so relaxed and happy. She really did thrive better in company.

Esther noticed Louise first. 'I'm pleased to see you and Richard are friends again. The sooner you two marry, the quieter everyone's lives will be,' Esther said.

Richard crept up behind Louise. 'I'd marry her tomorrow.' He hugged her from behind. 'We were thinking of leaving.

Lou Lou hasn't seen the units I've been making for the bedroom. A fitted wardrobe along one wall.'

'Really? You want to show Louise your bedroom. I've heard that one before,' Fliss giggled.

'Go. I'll stay here with Esther and Fliss,' Pearl said.

'I'll take your mum back with me to the cottage,' Esther said. 'Bill can run her back to the inn later.'

Her mum shooed them away.

As they entered the house – *their house* – Louise felt the stress of the past few weeks lift. 'Did you mean what you said about wanting to marry me?' she said, as they stepped over the threshold.

Richard led her into the front room, overlooking the reservoir and went down on one knee. 'Louise Pearson, will you marry me?'

'Yes,' she said. Now was the time to tell him.

'I know I said I didn't want to start a family yet,' she said, when Richard was back on his feet. 'And I still feel it isn't ideal. But things have changed.'

Richard led her to a deep, comfortably cushioned sofa. She slipped off her kitten heels and curled her feet up beneath her. 'I may have changed my mind.'

He kissed her gently. 'There's no rush.'

'No? Try telling our little bean that. I'm pregnant, Richard. And I'm really happy about it.'

He jumped off the sofa. 'Oh my God. Why didn't you say sooner? When? How?'

Louise laughed. 'How did I get pregnant? The usual way.' She explained how she had left her pills behind when she went to London. 'Now are you going to show me the bedroom?'

41

SEPTEMBER 1966

Derelict cottages and the tumbled walls of the mill were the backdrop to their wedding party – like spectral guests, Louise had reflected – rather than the picturesque view of the reservoir they would have enjoyed had they waited a year.

'I'm not risking it,' Richard had said, and Esther agreed.

'I couldn't stand the stress of you two mis-communicating again.' Esther was seven months into her pregnancy and, according to her last hospital check, was in excellent health.

'Mrs Braithwaite, a glass of champagne?' Richard joined Louise as she looked across the valley.

She took the proffered flute and clinked glasses with him. A few sips wouldn't hurt the baby. 'I know the valley has to be cleared but it's sad. So many happy memories of our childhood playing amongst the ruins.'

'A fresh start. New memories to make.' He raised his glass. 'Shall we go and join our guests?'

They had been arriving in various cars from the registry office. Fliss and Pete had stayed behind to prepare for the party. Richard took Louise's hand, and they wandered across the grass towards the glade where they had once planned to build a cluster of cabins. The sun glowed a mellow gold, as if wringing out the last of summer as autumn prepared her grand entry. Richard gasped and stopped in his tracks. A deer watched them from the shadow of a chestnut tree, then disappeared.

Louise let out her breath. 'That's the first deer I've spotted. Do you think it's a sign?'

Richard kissed her. 'I don't know but I've got everything right here and now that I'll ever want.'

'Are you sure? This land has been sold with planning permission. I feel as though you've had to give up on your dream,' Louise said.

'I have you. We have our little bean. I hope we find a name or we'll end up calling the poor child Bean. And somehow, we'll manage child care so you can complete your training.'

They had discussed various options: her mum moving to Thorncrest, although that was dependent on her getting a council flat transfer; Esther and Louise doing a job share and childcare share between them, but caring for one baby was scary enough, two would be terrifying; Richard giving up work, but Louise didn't earn nearly enough to make that viable.

'Oh look,' Louise exclaimed. Lanterns had been hung in the trees, creating what looked like a fairy grotto.

Fliss stepped forward to greet them, placing a crown of woven flowers on Louise's head. 'Fiona bought the plants and flowers,' she gestured to the overflowing tubs planted with miniature rose bushes, lilies, and the smiling daisy-like Cosmos amongst other plants, and table arrangements that matched Louise's crown, freesias, and lily of the valley.

Louise searched the happy, upturned faces of family and

The Canary Girl's Secret

friends, to thank Fiona. Then, Fiona stepped forward. 'Come here.' She gave Louise a hug.

Everyone cheered. Festivities had officially begun. Bill circled their guests, topping up champagne glasses. Everyone had contributed dishes of food, which Fliss and Pete had laid out on covered trestle-tables adorned with Fiona's table decorations, lit candles, and origami woodland creatures, created by Esther. Louise's heart was full to bursting.

When they had feasted, sitting around the table, and Richard had given a speech, followed by Bill as his best man, and then her mum, and finally Louise, her mum passed Louise and Richard an envelope. 'This is your wedding present from me.'

'You shouldn't have, Mum. Having you here at our wedding is enough. I wish you could live closer.'

Her mum smiled and winked. 'Be careful what you wish for.'

Dion started to play his acoustic guitar. Then a flute sounded from behind the trees, and one of Dion's fellow band members emerged. A harmonica. Then a trumpet. The musicians appeared like the deer. Soon the party was in full swing, with everyone dancing among the trees. Louise thought she couldn't be happier.

'Shall we see what Mum has given us?' she asked Richard, as they sat beneath a tree enjoying the spectacle of their beloved friends having fun. Pearl and Aunt Emma were doing the twist. Paul and Fiona twirled around as if on a ballroom floor, not a leafy glade.

He nodded, and Louise tore open the envelope to reveal a fat wad of papers. She frowned at Richard, wondering what on earth it could be?

'Let me see,' he said, taking the papers from Louise. His draw dropped. 'Did you know about this?'

'What?' Louise saw her mum and Aunt Emma watching them with broad grins as they failed to conceal their spying.

Richard handed her the papers. 'Your mum's the buyer of our land.'

'She said it was her present to us.' Louise tried to make sense of this sudden jar to her reality. 'Mum has bought the land for us?'

Pearl and Aunt Emma gave up pretending not to watch and joined them. Richard jumped up and hugged Pearl. 'Thank you, mother-in-law. You have no idea what this means to us.'

Pearl hugged him back and then Louise. 'When I joined my brother Geoffrey in Australia, he told me that our dad left half of his estate to me. So, I thought what better way to use it than to buy your land for you. There is one condition.'

'Anything,' Louise said.

'Well, I would like to live in one of the cabins.'

Louise nodded enthusiastically. 'Yes. We'd love that, wouldn't we Richard?'

'Absolutely. I'll start building it tomorrow.'

'And,' her mum continued, 'I would like to care for my grandchild during the day whilst you train as a librarian, Louise.'

'Oh Mum, you are the most amazing wonderful mother I could wish for.'

'There's a gift here from your uncle Geoffrey too.' Pearl handed Louise another envelope. 'I know what's inside. Be prepared for a bit of a shock.'

It was a death certificate for Elizabeth Sommerfeld, born Elizabeth Hardy, dated 1953. Two years after her fake funeral. Cause of death cancer.

42

OCTOBER 1951

'It's going to be cold up there, we could wait until the spring. She's not going anywhere,' Daniel said as they approached the biplane.

Beth hadn't told him that she only had months left to live, maybe a year if she was lucky. 'No. I've waited thirty-six years for this. A bit of weather's not going to hurt me.'

'Then wear my flying jacket.' Daniel removed his jacket and dressed Beth with the love and care he might have shown their daughter, had things been different.

'I'm going to fly this plane.' Beth said this as a statement rather than a question, but looked to Daniel for confirmation.

'You sure are. But don't worry, I've got dual control. I've been teaching men and women to fly for the past two decades.'

'But not me.' It was the life he had once promised her. But Beth didn't regret the life she had lived with John. The precious years she had spent with her granddaughter, Louise, had been the happiest.

'You could have come sooner,' Daniel said. She had told him John died in 1945.

'I'm here now. I only came for a flying lesson. You don't think I came all this way just to see you?' she laughed, then winced at the pain. Fortunately, Daniel did not notice.

'Remember when we first went up in your plane together?' Beth said when she was tucked inside the cockpit.

'One of my treasured memories,' Daniel said. 'I couldn't believe I had this beautiful, vibrant woman alongside me. A woman who shared my passion for flying. I was already in love with you.'

'And I you. I tried not to fall in love but you made it so hard. Why did you let me when you knew how it would end?' Beth couldn't forgive him. It was the reason she'd kept away after her darling John passed.

'I didn't want to fall in love, either. I think we both believed ourselves immune. I pleaded with my superiors to find another way. If I'd known you was pregnant, I would have refused and taken the consequences.'

'Firing squad?' Beth said wryly. 'I don't think that would have helped.'

'No.' Daniel sighed. 'We can't change the past but we can make the most of the present. Ready to take her up?'

As Daniel took the plane up, high above the sprawling terrain of farmland, Beth felt as though she were ascending to heaven. On the other side of the world, loved ones would be saying goodbye, believing her to be dead, and soon she would be. But not yet.

They passed over wooded mountains. Daniel pointed out places of interest, but Beth wasn't listening; she was replaying her life. It was right that it should end here, with Daniel, the love of her life. He grinned.

'Are you ready to take control?'

'Yes.' She had survived two wars, been thrown off course

by life events, and had unexpected joys. Now, she was flying as free as a bird. Later she would tell Daniel it was her turn to leave him. But not yet.

Before you leave

I hope you enjoyed reading, *The Canary Girl's Secret*. If you could find time to leave a review, even if it is just a star rating on Amazon, I would be grateful as it helps other readers discover this book.

Please sign up for my newsletter to receive giveaways, information about future publications, and behind-the-scenes information, as I love connecting with readers.

www.deborahklee.com

AUTHOR'S NOTE

The inspiration for Secrets of a Sunken Village came from the real village, West End which was flooded to create Thruscross Reservoir in 1966. Whilst actual events informed some of the story, the events and people described are fictitious. The Thruscross Church graveyard was relocated to a cemetery above the valley.

When I visited the area to research this series, I spoke to a few local people who lived through the creation of the reservoir. One of them informed me that one or two of the graves were found to be empty during the exhumation process. It was this gem that sparked the idea for Ma Beck's story.

The Barnbow Munitions Factory explosion was a true event. It happened just after 10 in the evening on Tuesday 5th December 1916, when several hundred women and girls had just begun their night shift. Thirty-five women were killed and dozens more injured. News of the explosion was not made public at the time due to censorship. This must have made the trauma harder to bear for the survivors.

In researching the background for, *The Canary Girl's Secret*,

Author's Note

I discovered the true story of a Grizzly bear and a Russian bear escaping from Halifax Zoo in 1913. The Russian Bear was captured immediately, but the Grizzly bear made its way to the canal before being found and returned to the zoo. I love finding these little gems in my research as they help shape the story.

ACKNOWLEDGMENTS

The most important people to acknowledge are the loyal readers who support me. Through my newsletter and your replies, we have become friends. When I write, I imagine you reading the story. So, you are the reason I write. My inspiration. So, thank you.

As always, a team has worked with me to prepare this book for publication, including: beta readers, Janet Bridger, Anita Belli, and Elizabeth Holland, and proofreaders, Sherman Klée and Elizabeth Holland.

Asya Blue Designs created the beautiful cover, and Gerald Hornsby formatted the book for publication.

Finally, I must acknowledge Vivienne, Annette Holbrook, and Joanne Hughes, who responded to a newsletter inviting readers to name characters in *The Canary Girl's Secret*. Iris was named after Joanne's mother, Connie after Annette's mother-in-law, and Hannah after Vivienne's granddaughter.

If you have not yet signed up to my newsletter, I would love to include you in this valued readers' circle. See: www.deborahklee.com

Printed in Dunstable, United Kingdom